The st[...]
drew them together...

Would love itself tear
them apart?

STILLPOINT

Portraits

Blind Faith
Masquerade
Stillpoint

STILLPOINT

MARILYN KOK

BETHANY HOUSE PUBLISHERS
MINNEAPOLIS, MINNESOTA 55438

Published by Bethany House Publishers
A Ministry of Bethany Fellowship, Inc.
11300 Hampshire Avenue South
Minneapolis, Minnesota 55438

Printed in the United States of America.

Library of Congress Cataloging-in-Publication Data

Kok, Marilyn, 1955–
    Stillpoint / Marilyn Kok.
    p.   cm. — (Portraits)
    ISBN 1–55661–821–2
    I. Title.   II. Series: Portraits (Minneapolis, Minn.)
PS3561.O378S75   1996
813'.54—dc20   96–25294
                                                     CIP

For Randy, always,

and for Julie Pangrac, who said,

"Why not Hong Kong, with a typhoon?"

The longer I live in the kingdom of God

the more convinced I become that

nothing of value is ever accomplished alone.

Thank you.

Soli Deo gloria.

"Though the fig tree does not bud and there are no grapes on the vines, though the olive crop fails and the fields produce no food, though there are no sheep in the pen and no cattle in the stalls, yet I will rejoice in the LORD, I will be joyful in God my Savior. The Sovereign LORD is my strength; he makes my feet like the feet of a deer, he enables me to go on the heights."

Habakkuk 3:17–19

MARILYN KOK is the daughter of missionary parents who served in both India and China. Schooled in Taiwan, she is also a graduate of Texas A & M University and Wheaton College. Marilyn has recently retired from her teaching position at Millikin University to concentrate on writing. The parents of six children, she and her husband make their home in Illinois.

One

Kylie Austin arrived at Kai Tak Airport anxious and uneasy.

Hoping to catch her breath, she stayed on the upper level for a few minutes, looking out at the view before her. The water of Hong Kong Harbor, ruffled by a slight breeze and the gently swaying boats, caught the brilliant June sunshine and transformed the bay into a treasure chest of glittering gemstones. Colorful and vigorous, Hong Kong was always moving, always intriguing.

But even sunlight on the water couldn't distract Kylie this day.

Besides, if the forecast was correct, the sky would soon be clouding over, wind ripping through the water.

How appropriate—an impending storm just as Jack Sullivan arrived in Hong Kong.

Kylie glanced at her watch. Ten-thirty. In a few minutes, Jack's plane would be arriving.

Was it any wonder she was tense?

Three years earlier, twenty-seven-year-old Kylie had applied for a position in the Hong Kong branch of Reaves Imports and Exports. She wanted to handle the movement of porcelain from China and Hong Kong into Reaves' international markets. Having lived in Hong Kong on and off since she was fourteen, Kylie was more familiar with the strange and fascinating culture than most *gweilo*, or "foreign devils." Add to that her year studying in China, a master's degree in business, and two years' experience with a rival company, and she had easily convinced company president Harry Reaves that what she lacked in age, she made up for in savvy.

She had not convinced Jack Sullivan.

When Kylie had walked into Harry's Chicago office for that first interview, there was Jack, lounging on the office couch, long legs stretched lazily out before him. He was in his early thirties and tall, judging from the length of him, with a lithe, athletic body and fair hair. He looked relaxed, but his strong, dynamic face had a touch of arrogance, and his blue eyes didn't miss much. Taking in his chinos and casual shirt, Kylie couldn't understand at first why he was in the room, yet there he remained.

Harry had risen immediately, come forward, and shaken Kylie's hand, his friendliness putting her at ease. He introduced Jack as a vice-president in the company, his right-hand man and faithful troubleshooter. Jack had returned that morning from a trip through Eastern European countries, checking on Reaves' newly established branches in Warsaw, Budapest, and Kiev—hence his casual traveling clothes.

Jack Sullivan had stood and shaken Kylie's hand as well, but without Harry's easy acceptance. His continued scrutiny throughout the interview kept Kylie tuned to his presence. An hour later, Harry apologized for an unexpected commitment and sent her to lunch with Jack.

When Jack made it clear that he doubted Kylie's ability to handle the job in Hong Kong—too young, too naive, too inexperienced—Kylie metaphorically stared him down, projecting an image of professional self-assurance. With typical cynicism, her diplomat father once told her, *"If people doubt you, never defend yourself. Show contempt for that doubt, and they'll revise their opinion. If they don't—let them go hang."*

Yet even as she appeared to treat Jack with disdain, Kylie felt drawn to the man. Something about him captured her interest—the brooding thoughtfulness of his gaze, the occasional glitter of humor in those mesmerizing blue eyes. She found herself watching for his smile—aware not only of him but of herself as well.

As a woman who could attract the attention of a man like Jack Sullivan.

As a woman who might want to.

Her reaction startled her, and now this very disturbing man was coming to Hong Kong. Kylie would be working with him, she having uncovered the trouble that Jack would have to shoot down. Who could blame her for seeing the days ahead as a challenge?

Kylie sighed and then took a deep breath. Time to go downstairs.

Jack would be making his way through immigration, baggage claim, and finally customs. Because Hong Kong was a duty-free port, customs was rarely a problem for passengers. A ramp led down from there into a large waiting area. She had arranged to meet Jack outside the McDonald's to the left of the ramp.

In the evenings, when 748s arrived at ten or fifteen minute intervals, the place was always packed. Even now, there was enough of a crowd. She didn't see Jack.

"Kylie?"

His voice startled her. It was deep and warm, and when Kylie turned, she thought wildly that it just wasn't fair. He was too handsome—a man any woman would notice even in an airport crowded with designer suits. He had the same lean body and muscular shoulders that she remembered, the same eyes and charm and unforgettable smile. Nothing had changed, especially not her instinctive response to him.

"Kylie," he said again. He smiled and held out his hand in greeting. "Thank you for meeting me."

Chin up, she told herself. *Stand tall even if you don't feel it.* "No problem. I'm glad that you're here, although I'm hoping your trip will be wasted."

He nodded ruefully. "I understand entirely. A common enough feeling, since I usually show up when problems occur. I also hope your concerns will prove groundless—though it's still nice to see you, Kylie."

A pause, during which he smiled again and Kylie felt the

absurd desire to lower her lashes. Would she have to fight a blush every time he smiled?

She lifted her chin a little higher. "I'm worried about Murray Russell. That's why I called Harry. If I had known he would send you out here so promptly, I might have waited awhile to see if anything else developed. However, since you're here, let's get started. We'll get you registered at your hotel and eat there. I'm sure you want a full report."

She began walking across the waiting area toward the queue for hotel limos and private cars, her heels clicking out a determined beat. He had to hurry to keep up with her.

"If you didn't want back-up, why did you call in the reserves?"

Kylie stiffened. Was he questioning her decision to alert the main office? She stopped and looked sideways at him, causing the crowd to flow around them. "I did not ask for help. I called Harry simply to inform him that something strange was going on. I could have handled this end just fine without you!"

"We've never doubted your ability, Kylie," he said mildly.

"I'm glad to hear it, though I'm not sure I believe you. What interests me now is how we are going to explain your sudden appearance in Hong Kong. If something is going on, your presence is sure to alert . . . well, whoever." What could she say—enemy, culprit, perpetrator? It all sounded so ludicrous, and now Harry had overreacted by sending Jack Sullivan to her aid.

"Harry's taken care of that."

"And how has Harry taken care of it?"

"He suggested to Carson Grey that I was coming here to visit you."

Kylie snapped around to face him. "Say that again."

He grinned a bit sheepishly and shrugged. "Here's the story that Harry suggested: We've seen each other over the years. When you came stateside last month, something clicked between us. I'm here to see if we have a future."

With difficulty, Kylie closed her mouth. If Harry had told

this story to Carson Grey, the head of the Hong Kong operation, then everyone in the office would know by now. She could just imagine their reaction. "When did Harry tell Carson?"

"He let it slip last night."

Fortunately she had come straight to the airport this morning.

"This is preposterous, Jack. We hardly saw each other last month."

"Ah, but the fireworks were instantaneous." He smiled slowly down at her, blue eyes disturbingly intent, and Kylie suddenly found it hard to breathe. How ironic, after all this time of dealing with a coolly analytical Jack, to finally receive this tender gaze, this slow blink over blue charm, and have it all an act!

He must have seen her uneasiness. "Kylie," he said, purely pragmatic again, "no one here knows what happened between us in the States last month. We can easily convince them that we're attracted to each other. We'll exchange some private smiles across a crowded room, and maybe a touch here and there. Nothing else. Can't we manage that?"

"All in the line of duty?"

"We're the right ages, and both of us free—aren't we? Or was Harry wrong? Are you involved in a relationship right now?"

"No," Kylie admitted. "Harry himself checked that out last week. If I had known why he was asking, I would have invented someone."

"Well, Harry invented someone for you. Don't worry. *I* know why I'm here."

Jack adjusted his luggage, causing Kylie to notice the two bags. "How long are you planning to stay?" she asked, a frown furrowing her brow.

"At least until this thing gets cleared up."

"Great," Kylie muttered.

Jack laughed outright. "Try to moderate the charm, Kylie. I might be tempted to make this grand passion real."

As she glared at him, his expression slowly became more serious, and he motioned toward a quiet spot near the exit. "Look, Kylie," he said softly but urgently, "I'm not sure what's going on here and neither is Harry. But we're both concerned, not just about the business but about your safety. If it's something illegal, my sudden appearance will certainly set off alarm bells. It's vital that we pull off this little deception."

The dark warehouse came to Kylie's mind, the furtive, frightening sounds around her, her own footsteps as she ran toward the exit and the tightness in her chest as she tried to catch her breath. She had probably been stupid, spooked by too many late-night movies and the cavernous room, but when Murray later turned up missing, she had panicked and called Harry.

"I never thought he would react by sending you," she said, her voice small and unsure.

Jack nodded sympathetically. "Harry's been having his own doubts about Hong Kong. Your call just speeded up my visit. If it's nothing, we can all give a big sigh of relief. If not, you'll have the satisfaction of knowing you were right."

Thinking of Murray, Kylie found that a small comfort. Where had he gone? Why did he vanish like that?

The retired couple sharing their limousine to the hotel was, of course, swept away by Jack's charming smile.

"Are you on your honeymoon, dear?" the woman asked Kylie, her voice a little wistful.

Kylie had a sudden fit of coughing, but Jack gazed soulfully at Kylie and said with a sigh, "Not yet, but perhaps soon."

"You don't have to overdo it," Kylie hissed as they emerged from the limousine at the Mandarin.

His eyes gleamed with humor. "Just getting into practice." He became suddenly serious. "Hold my hand," he demanded. "No, I mean it. Hold my hand."

Reluctantly, she slipped her hand into his, the strength of his grip coursing through her fingers and up her arm. She was turned toward him, her back to the entrance of the hotel, so when Carson Grey's voice boomed from behind her she almost jerked her hand out of Jack's.

Jack wouldn't let go. "Relax," he whispered close to her ear, sending a shiver pulsing through her body. She wasn't sure whether it was Carson's sudden appearance or her own response to Jack's whisper that made the color rise in her cheeks. She did know she was angry.

Carson's corpulent body was only a few feet away from them, his short stature compensated for by the step on which he stood above them. In his early sixties, Carson was the grand old man of the branch, the only employee who had worked with Harry himself when Harry had opened the first Reaves office here in Hong Kong thirty years earlier. Still sharp and vigorous, Carson Grey let very little get past him. Born of British civil servants, he had married into the Chinese culture. His wife, Mei-lin, was the daughter of a powerful Hong Kong banking official.

"Well, well, well!" Carson said, holding out his hand. "Jack Sullivan himself. Welcome to Hong Kong."

"Carson, nice to see you again."

"So," Carson said, his beady eyes taking in the handclasp. "Harry Reaves was right about you two."

With sudden strength, Kylie pulled her hand away from Jack's. "Nothing's settled," she exploded.

Carson laughed. "So our little Kylie's proving a hard fish to net!"

Jack smiled affectionately down at Kylie. "The best ones always give the most trouble."

By sheer force of will, Kylie kept from stomping her high heel on his foot.

"Don't I know it!" Carson responded. In his usual custom, he reached out and patted Kylie's arm, letting his palm linger a moment at her elbow before withdrawing it.

Feeling Jack stiffen, Kylie jumped into the conversation

before he could say anything. "Carson, it's nice of you to come by and welcome Jack. Will you be having lunch with us?"

"No, no," Carson said, all business again. "I have another appointment and have to hurry now, or I'll be late." He glanced up at the clouding sky. "Storm's coming. Hope no one has trouble getting back here tonight." Seeing Jack's blank expression, he said, "Tell him, Kylie. I'll see you later."

Following the patient bellhop to the registration desk, Kylie explained: "Carson's arranged a get-together tonight. Most of us from the main office will be here at the Mandarin to greet you."

"Good. That will give me a chance to catch up on who's who."

Registration complete, Jack led Kylie into the restaurant and they ordered. "Now," Jack said, leaning forward slightly, "we can talk."

Kylie regarded him thoughtfully. Jack Sullivan had that rare combination of intellect and common sense that almost always guaranteed success, and in Jack's case, that success generated an unassailable confidence in himself. Kylie could see why Harry relied on him so much, but the threat of his dominance frightened her. Hadn't she learned long ago how dangerous it was to trust anyone but herself?

"Tell me what happened with Murray Russell," he urged.

"Harry must have explained."

"I want to hear about it from you."

Kylie swallowed. It all seemed so ridiculous now. If only Harry had let her work it out by herself!

"Kylie," Jack prompted, and she began.

Murray Russell was a young Australian expatriate. For the last eighteen months, he had worked in the Reaves warehouse, packing artifacts for shipment out of Hong Kong. Less than a week ago, late on a Friday night, Kylie got home to discover a message from Murray on her answering machine. Something strange had happened. He wanted to meet her in the morning, early. He would be at the warehouse at six o'clock. She should come alone.

In his mid-twenties, Murray was a lackadaisical worker, more interested in fun than promotion, but though he lacked ambition, he certainly didn't lack a sharp and observant mind. If something didn't seem right to him, Kylie was prone to believe him.

She called him that same Friday night, but his roommates said he was out. No idea where.

So she went the next morning to the warehouse, alone as requested. The security guard waved her past the main entrance. The packing room where Murray said he would be was large, lined with supplies and set up with tables in the middle for the delicate work of packing the company's artifacts. Kylie walked down the length of the room toward the shelves at the far end, her footsteps echoing eerily around her. Murray wasn't there. She was alone, uncomfortably so. She waited, but he never came.

"The room began to seem too large and much too empty," Kylie admitted to Jack. "I began imagining noises and footsteps. The shadows around me seemed to move. It was when I realized that I was deliberately hiding behind a stack of packing crates that I decided to clear out. That's what spooked me, I suppose, and caused me to call Harry."

"And Murray?"

"I called his flat several times over the weekend. His roommates finally got annoyed. When he didn't come to work on Monday, I went by his flat that night and quizzed his roommates again. They were amused. Murray often stayed out overnight, they said. I should be able to guess why." Kylie shrugged. "His friends in packing weren't any help either. I finally called the police on Tuesday afternoon. They brushed it off. Hong Kong is full of transients. A man like Murray Russell, in his twenties and unmarried, with a no-future job in a warehouse? They figured he lost interest and moved on."

"What do you think?"

"They're probably right."

"Did you consider hiring a detective?"

"Yes," Kylie admitted slowly, "but I couldn't justify the expense to Reaves, and by then I was beginning to feel a little foolish."

"Harry called a friend from back in his days of living in Hong Kong, starting up the business."

"A friend?"

"Sanford Chang. A detective."

Kylie became still. "What did he find out?"

"According to Murray's roommates, Murray didn't return home on Saturday or Sunday; you knew that. On Monday, even they began to wonder—in spite of what they said to you. I suspect they didn't want to get Murray in trouble if he really was cutting work. On Tuesday, a packing company came in, gathered up Murray's belongings, and shipped them back to his family in Australia."

"Back home?"

"His family said he's gone 'walkabout.' He'll show up for his things sooner or later."

"He's traveling light."

"Exactly. Until he uses a credit card or leaves some other paper trail, there's no way to follow up on him."

Kylie pushed the remnants of her salad around on her plate. It didn't add up, somehow. She looked across at him, letting her gaze wander over Jack's face. "If you know all this," she finally asked, "why are you here?"

"Harry's worried."

"About me? Good grief! I can take care of myself."

"No doubt, but there's Reaves to think about, too." Seeing the hardness in her jaw, Jack sighed. "We'll get further if we work on this together, Kylie. I need your knowledge of the Hong Kong operation and of the people working at Reaves. I need your experience of Hong Kong, too, and your facility with the language and insight into the culture."

"And what do I need from you?"

He grinned. "Muscle power, of course! You be the brains; I'll be the brawn."

She gazed at him suspiciously, convinced he was patronizing her. "So what's the plan of action?" she finally asked.

His lips relaxed into a lazy smile and he sat back, satisfied.

She spoke again, her voice sounding a little harsh. "Jack? What do we do next?"

He straightened and flexed his shoulders. "Right," he said. "Next I get some sleep. Jet lag, you know. We'll meet here tonight and see what develops with everyone else. I'm hoping that my arrival will shake things up."

"Okay. Then I'll go back to the office. Should we meet early?"

"Sure. I'll meet you in the bar at 5:30." He lifted mocking eyebrows and grinned. "After all, Kylie, if you show up with everyone else, I'll have to give you a greeting designed to convince them of my sudden interest in you—and you're making it abundantly clear that you wouldn't like that!" Seeing her expression, his eyes grew more serious. "It's their reaction that's bothering you, isn't it? Is it so unusual for you to show up with someone?"

She thought of her customarily harmless dates: the five-star gourmet dinners with a French cardiologist; the occasional lunch with a lonely German businessman still mourning the death of his wife; the refined meals with an English professor who nurtured a hopeless passion for a Chinese actress. All these men Kylie saw on a semi-regular basis, but always as a companion, never as a romantic interest. As for the group of young expatriates that she sometimes joined for an outing on the weekend, that was purely for fun.

"I keep my private life private," she said.

"And Carson Grey?"

Kylie waved off Jack's concern. "He's harmless. He likes to see himself as a dirty old man, but in spite of his weight he'd run a record-breaking 100-meter dash getting away from me if I ever took him seriously. He's really very fond of his wife."

"Even so, you shouldn't have to put up with that."

She made another dismissive gesture with her hand. "What's important is that he takes me seriously on a professional basis. I'm good at what I do, and he knows it. His occasional leers and bawdy comments are his way of asserting his superiority. I can deal with it."

"Okay," Jack said, though he still sounded doubtful.

He stood up and they walked to the lift. Before letting the doors close behind him, he paused. "I have to say this, Kylie. In spite of my doubts three years ago, you're absolutely right. You are good at what you do. Reaves is fortunate to have you."

The lift doors closed between them, and for the second time in three hours Kylie found herself having to consciously close her astonished mouth.

This man never failed to throw her off guard.

Fortunately, in the past three years their paths had crossed infrequently. He came twice to Hong Kong, once for a general inspection soon after she joined the firm, and once later to meet privately with Carson Grey.

The last time Kylie had seen Jack was a month earlier on a trip to Chicago. Jack happened to be there himself and took Kylie to dinner—more to please Joy Reaves, Kylie thought, than from a desire to spend time with Kylie.

Harry Reaves and his wife, Joy, had practically adopted her, sharing their home on her occasional trips stateside. Joy was in her mid-sixties, a plump, warmhearted woman whose own children were already married and raising families. She apparently needed a new target for her matchmaking instincts.

"He's got more than those blue eyes to offer a woman," Joy said as they were walking in the garden after a dinner with Harry and Jack.

"Really?"

"Don't sound so skeptical, honey. He's a strong Christian. Did you know that?"

Which made him a possibility, but was it supposed to make a difference in the way she reacted to him, woman to man? Jack Sullivan didn't seem interested in anything beyond a business relationship—and neither was Kylie.

She reminded herself of that again as she stepped out of the hotel toward the taxi queue.

Neither was she.

Two

K ylie gave the driver her office address, but moments after she got into the taxi her cellular phone rang. The message from Lily Fong, her assistant at Reaves, sent a chill through her.

She leaned forward. "I need to return to the Mandarin."

Back in the lobby, she paused for a moment. Was she over-reacting? Perhaps it was all coincidental, two misfortunes following each other only by happenstance.

If so, thank goodness. If not . . . she felt the uneasiness return and picked up the hotel phone decisively.

"Jack Sullivan's room, please." And then a moment later, "Jack. This is Kylie. Something's happened."

"Where are you?"

"Downstairs in the lobby."

"I'll be right there."

From his appearance, he hadn't progressed very far toward getting the rest he needed. He was wearing the same clothes and looked as alert as ever.

"Can you come with me to the warehouse?" Kylie asked. "I'll fill you in on the way."

"I'm ready."

The same taxi was waiting for Kylie. Once underway, Jack turned to Kylie. "All right. What's up?"

"Robert Xin, the warehouse manager, has been in an accident. He was coming back from lunch, crossing a street, when a car hit him."

"How badly hurt?"

"He's in the hospital, unconscious. They're operating. They won't say anything about his chances."

"And the driver of the car?"

"Hit and run. The police are tracing the license plate but they told my assistant that with very little effort the car could stay hidden forever."

Jack studied her face, noting the tension around her eyes and the grim set of her mouth. "Do they believe it was intentional?"

"Hit and run accidents occur everyday, but the cars usually turn up. If not, then they start treating it as intentional."

"You think it was?"

Kylie looked out the window at the passing streets, feeling the tilt and turn of the taxi as the driver negotiated the traffic in typical breakneck fashion. She sighed and turned back to Jack. "We'll find out soon enough."

"What do you expect to discover at the warehouse?"

"Again, I don't know. Lily says a shipment of porcelain came in this morning. I want to look it over."

Jack nodded.

The taxi drew to a sudden halt. They were near one of Hong Kong's many piers, the location of the warehouse chosen for proximity to the airport and the shipping lines. The Reaves warehouse was wedged between two other buildings down a side street. A back entrance allowed access for trucks.

"Have you been to our warehouse before?" Kylie asked Jack.

"A few years ago. With Harry and Carson."

Kylie suddenly realized how little she knew about Jack, not even how long he had been working for Reaves or how he had joined the company. Things she probably should know. Apparently while Jack had maintained his distance, she also had been holding back from him, not even expressing useful professional curiosity. Had she let her personal reactions to this man hinder her ability to do her job?

A security guard stood just inside the building. Stairs at the end of this anteroom led to office and storage space above them. Reaves rented only the ground floor.

The guard nodded to Kylie as she added her name and Jack's to the roster. An electronic lock barred the inner entrance to the Reaves warehouse. "The other buyers and I have magnetic keys, and Carson as well, of course," Kylie explained as she used hers to gain entrance. "I can get you one tomorrow if you'd like. Everyone else has to be given access by the security guard. There's one on duty at all times. Once inside, the workers have their own keys to the central packing room, where most of our inventory gets repackaged for shipping."

Jack nodded. "It's always been the same with Harry. Lots of security up front as discouragement."

"In actual fact," Kylie said, "few of our individual pieces are particularly precious. We deal almost exclusively with reproductions rather than collectibles. The inventory has value, but mainly in bulk. That's why it's hard to imagine exactly what Murray was so worried about."

Before going in, Jack paused. "You do find some collectibles. I've seen one or two myself."

"Of course. Pieces that belong in museums turn up occasionally. We come across them unexpectedly. As you pass Hong Kong's tenements or walk along the waterfront, remember that somewhere in those high-rises or run-down little *sampans*, there's more than one priceless vase or jade treasure. Refugees smuggle them out of China, hidden among their meager possessions, and they hang on to them as long as they can, hoping to keep them in the family if possible. Dealers like Reaves are always happy to stumble upon those rare pieces."

Jack nodded and motioned her forward. "Okay, then let's see what we've got, Kylie."

They made their way into the front office, with desks and phones for the occasional work that buyers did on the spot. Kylie greeted Tiffany Lin, the warehouse secretary. Tiffany was in her early thirties, attractive and ambitious, but with a hard edge that Kylie found unpleasant. Fortunately Kylie rarely had to work with her.

After introducing Jack to Tiffany, Kylie headed through the small hallway past the rest rooms, tearoom, and cloakroom toward the double doors that led into the large central room. "All of our inventory goes through this warehouse," Kylie reminded Jack as she slid her electronic key through a second lock, "except our few authentic antique pieces, which we tend to keep closer at hand."

Inside, expecting a bustle of activity, Kylie stopped abruptly. Empty packing crates sat on the central worktables with open crates on the floor beside them. All the workers were in the back of the room, sitting around one of the tables.

At their entrance, a young Chinese woman advanced toward them. With a university degree from the States, Kylie's assistant, Lily Fong, was a rising star in the Reaves establishment. She had come to the company inexperienced but was almost ready to move on, perhaps to take a position like Kylie's in a rival firm.

"Lily, what's the holdup?" Kylie asked as she drew near.

"We had shipments come in from three kilns this morning. Unfortunately, Robert kept the manifests with him when he went to lunch. The office is faxing copies to us."

"Couldn't you get the manifests from the accident site?"

Lily made a face. "Oooo, Kylie, don't ask."

"Never mind then," Kylie said, waving off the thought. "But why would he have it with him at lunch?"

Lily shrugged. "You know Robert. He thinks the place would fall apart without him. Usually he just oversees the work, but every now and then he takes over a shipment completely, not only with porcelain but the other divisions as well. This was one of those times. He probably took the manifests with him to make sure no one did anything over lunch without him on hand."

At Kylie's entrance, the other workers had scattered, finding busywork to do. Lily walked off to check on them, and Kylie smiled ruefully at Jack.

He said, "I suppose without the manifests the workers don't know how to repackage the crates?"

"Exactly. The kilns in China ship their goods to us, and we check for quality and then sort out the orders for shipment to retail outlets throughout the world."

Kylie pulled a crate closer and pulled out a vase, running her fingers gently over the smooth, classically proportioned surface, covered with an almost luminous ivory color.

"Beautiful," Jack said.

"Isn't it? A reproduction, of course, from the Sung period, but a very good one. They say that the true collector of porcelain should have only one piece at his death—a white Sung bowl without any decorations."

Jack took the piece from Kylie. "It's hard to imagine the original piece being more perfect than this. How much would an original cost?"

"An avid collector of Sung porcelain would pay a lot— five figures, maybe even six. The problem for the collector is not deciding how much to pay, but finding Sung porcelain to pay for."

"Were these Sung reproductions a special order?"

"You mean did we request this particular reproduction? No, not this time. We do occasionally, but in general the kilns make their own choices about what to produce. We're interested in the quality of the pieces, not so much the exact design. This kiln is particularly adept at Sung reproductions."

Jack lifted another piece out of the crate.

"That's a blossom vase," Kylie informed him. "Reproduction again, of course, from the fourteenth century. This has a characteristic copper-red glaze. This underglaze process, in which colors are applied before the glaze is added and fired, requires very high temperatures. Only cobalt blue or copper red can withstand the heat, and the red is particularly hard to get right. It can easily drift into brown. So you can see why, even in reproduction, the workmanship of this piece makes it valuable."

"These crates are from several different kilns? Perhaps you

should trace for me the route that any one piece would travel. It would start in one of these family kilns?"

"Village kilns, actually. Very small, but worked by more than one family. In some regions almost the entire village contributes in one way or another to the industry. Some of these village kilns probably go back through the generations to the emperors of the Sung and Ming and Tang dynasties."

"You set up contacts with these kilns?"

Kylie smiled. "Yes. Things have opened up tremendously on the mainland, but even now, everything's a question of contacts. Who we know, what relationships we can use to our advantage."

Jack nodded. Too late Kylie realized that he probably knew all this. "Sorry. I don't mean to sound patronizing."

"No, no. This is how I do my job, never working alone, always in tandem with someone on location. I'm curious about how the kilns decide where to send their products. They could choose another company to work with."

"As I said, in China, it's who we know that really matters. Other than that, public relations and price, not necessarily in that order. Reaves has a good name, and because of the quality of the stores we ship to, we can afford to pay the kilns well. Harry has never been out for a quick buck, you know."

"Yes, I know. Quality workmanship brings a quality price. It's a maxim that's worked well for him all over the world."

As they were speaking, Kylie unwrapped a few more pieces and then moved on to another crate.

Jack held up another piece, a soup tureen and cover, about fourteen inches across, with blue decoration on a white background. "How much would a piece like this sell for in Chicago?"

"That's a reproduction of the kind of pottery China made for export in the eighteenth century, during the Qing dynasty. With the matching undertray, it would sell for at least five hundred, probably more. Ours are not authentic antiques, but quality is quality. The pieces are beautiful and well worth the prices they command."

She had reached again into the crate and stood studying two plates. Something in the design caught her attention.

Jack came closer. "What is it?"

Kylie didn't hear him at first, just stood turning the pieces in her hands. "This is strange," she finally said. She put one dish down and turned the other over carefully, running her thumbs over the design. The dish was blue and white, with a pattern of leaves around the edge and a carp in the middle. Kylie frowned.

Lily, like a few of the other workers, had noticed Kylie's silence. "What's up, Kylie?"

Too late Kylie realized her mistake. She laid the dishes gently back into their crate and covered her reaction with a smile.

"What is it?" Jack asked again.

Speaking a little loudly so that the workers could hear, Kylie said, "These weren't the plates I was expecting, that's all. I thought they would be reproductions of pieces from the sixteenth century."

"They're not?"

"These are from a much earlier period, the fourteenth century, perhaps. But never mind; I must have been mistaken."

Lily stepped closer. "We'll know if the shipment's correct as soon as the manifests come through. I think I'll go down to the office and see if they're here yet."

Kylie checked her watch and then spoke to the workers. "It's almost three. Why don't all of you go down the hall for an early tea? Lily can come get you when there's some work to do."

Within moments the room had emptied.

"Okay," Jack said, "give me the real story. What was so surprising about those dishes?"

Kylie picked them up again, studying them carefully. "I think I know what was bothering Murray," she said slowly. "Do you notice any differences between these two plates?"

Jack took them from Kylie and inspected them himself.

"Yes," he said slowly. "I guess I do. This one is smoother. On this plate, the little blackish spots aren't quite as bumpy."

"Exactly. Look. This pattern of spiky leaves around the edge is very characteristic of the early Ming, but on reproductions these black spots should be raised, giving this piled texture. They *are* on this dish, as they should be, but not on this one. I suspect that someone was lazy in applying them."

"And so?"

"Perhaps someone within the kilns is passing seconds to us and charging us at the higher prices. On the original Ming pieces these black spots appeared accidentally, but since that time, people have been applying them deliberately to reproductions, so that they have this raised texture."

Jack held up the dish with the smoother finish. "So wouldn't the smooth dishes be the better production?"

Kylie smiled. "No, no. Remember, they're supposed to be *reproductions* of the authentic pieces. I know it sounds odd, but with as much history as these pieces have, even reproductions have standards they have to meet." Kylie held up the smoother piece. "These need those piled spots. The kiln hasn't gone to the trouble of putting them on."

"And you think Murray might have noticed this? Did he really know enough about porcelain to pick up on it?"

"No, probably not this. It's a little obscure. But if other, more obvious seconds were coming through, maybe. I can't believe they've been doing this. It could ruin Reaves' reputation if enough of this slipshod merchandise got through to our retail customers."

"You never saw any problems?"

"No, and apparently neither did Lily. I do check through shipments as often as I can, but I suppose whoever's doing this could have scheduled the bad shipments during my trips into the mainland or stateside." She bit her lower lip, struggling to control the anger that rose instinctively within her. Reaves prided itself on reliability and quality. This felt like a personal betrayal.

"Which means someone around here was working with

the people in China," Jack said. "A warning, Kylie: We should keep this to ourselves for now."

She became still, weighing his words. "You think someone here might be getting a kickback. Maybe even one of the buyers."

"As I said, a warning."

And a timely one, as it turned out. Behind them, the door to the hall opened. Expecting Lily, Kylie turned to discover Winston Lu, another of the buyers at Reaves.

Winston was in his mid-thirties and tall for a Chinese man. Though the men in the Far East were supposedly known for their Oriental inscrutability, Winston showed his feelings freely. Kylie had seen his eyes soften with sensitivity and flame with passion—especially when he was angry. Early on he had made a play for Kylie but had been quickly repelled. In truth, Kylie's religious scruples would not have fit Winston's lifestyle, but even so, she knew as only a woman could why Winston was rarely without a date.

He came rapidly toward them now, taking in the man standing beside her, the frown on Kylie's face, and then the plates that Jack was holding. "Kylie? What's happening?"

"You heard about Robert, I suppose?"

"Yes, too bad," Winston said, but he was obviously more interested in Jack. Winston had worked at Reaves for almost four years before being promoted. During those years he would have known who Jack was but wouldn't have had much chance to talk to him. Now he wanted to meet Jack as a buyer, establishing his new, more responsible position.

Kylie introduced him and Winston laughed, winking elaborately. "I heard all about you and our friend Jack Sullivan, Kylie. Or should I say *your* friend, Kylie?"

"Thanks for stopping by, Winston. We'll see you tonight."

"Oh, come on, Kylie. I obviously interrupted something when I came in!" He leaned over to take a closer look at the plates. "Nice, nice, but I doubt Jack came all this way to

Hong Kong to review our shipments. You should have taken the afternoon off, Kylie!"

Kylie refused to respond, except to say again, "We'll see you tonight, Winston. Go take care of your own business."

"As you wish, lady. Just wanted to meet the big guy!"

As soon as the door closed behind him, Kylie began wrapping paper around the two plates, then added straw and another layer of wrapping, this time of bubble-wrap. Strapping tape around the packages, she put them into the leather carry-all bag that she habitually carried as an alternative to a briefcase.

"What are you doing?" Jack asked.

"I'm going to take these two pieces to a friend at the History Museum. The Fung Ping Shan Museum has a better porcelain collection, but I know a man at the History, Charles Wu, whom I've worked with before. He can confirm this for me."

"Right now?"

"I'll call to see if he's free," Kylie said. After a brief discussion, she put away her cellular phone. "It's three now. He can see me at four-thirty. We have a little time. The museum is on the Kowloon side. Before we cross we could stop at your hotel, or we could go on over and tour the museum, if you'd prefer."

"Let's go straight over. I'd prefer not to carry these things around too long."

Somewhat surprised, Kylie nodded. So he must be taking the situation seriously. Perhaps, in fact, he always had. Tucking her purse into the carry-all, she took a deep breath. "Okay then; let's go. I'll stop by the office downstairs to let Lily know so she can sign out these pieces for me."

"You can't just take them?"

"Another of Harry's little security measures: track every piece all the time. It's part of his business genius to be so meticulously careful about the details. He doesn't leave anything to chance."

In the office, Lily had already collected the new manifests

and gone to round up the workers.

"Mr. Hughes brought the manifests over personally," Tiffany informed Kylie. "He's with Lily. Would you like me to page him?"

Kylie glanced at Jack, her eyes communicating her surprise. First Winston and now Phillip?

Phillip Hughes managed the jewelry division of Reaves, Hong Kong. But as far as Kylie knew, the company wasn't expecting any shipments in that division today. So why had Phillip hand-carried the manifests instead of allowing them to be faxed as Lily had almost certainly requested? Perhaps he also wanted an advance meeting with Jack.

"Did he ask to see us?" Kylie said.

"No."

"Then don't bother paging him. We'll be seeing him in a few hours, anyway, at the Mandarin."

She scribbled a note for Lily, identifying the two pieces she was taking. "Have Lily sign these out for me," she told the secretary, leaving the note on her desk. "She has my cellular number if she needs to reach me."

In the taxi, Jack seemed worried. "I wish you could have just taken the plates, without leaving notice."

Kylie turned in surprise. "Why?"

"If your suspicions are correct, Murray's gotten into a lot of trouble for the information you now have, and we can only wonder if Robert, too, has suffered for the knowledge."

"But don't you see?" Kylie exclaimed. "If I'm right, then Murray really did go walkabout, just as everyone thinks. We may not like it, but sending inferior merchandise is everyday business practice for some people. We blow the whistle on them—very diplomatically, of course, so that they don't lose face, and then, because they know we're watching, they'll maintain standards. Business as usual. No big deal."

"You really are relieved."

"Of course I am! Though if Murray were here, I'd give him some grief for all the worry he's caused by disappearing like that. But at least he's okay."

"I hope so, Kylie. I hope so." He sounded far from convinced.

"Spoilsport!" Kylie sat back comfortably, feeling better than she had in a week. If this worked out, she and Jack could end their charade—theirs would be the shortest romance in history!

Three

As Jack rode with Kylie toward the Cross-Harbour Tunnel, Kylie suddenly turned toward him, the barest hint of a smile in her eyes.

"Would you like to cross on the ferry?" she asked. "It looks threatening but still hasn't started raining, and we're early enough to miss the major crowds at rush hour."

"Fine with me," Jack answered, hiding his surprise. "What would a visit to Hong Kong be without a romantic trip across the harbor?"

He had to stifle a grin as he watched the play of emotions cross Kylie's face. She was wondering about him, trying to decide if he was teasing her. *Absolutely, Kylie Austin. You're far too serious. It's time someone brought a little humor into your life.*

"If that's what you want, you'll have to go at night," she finally responded. "All I can promise now is a good view."

"Will you come with me, Kylie? Will you be there in the moonlight?"

She shook her head in mock despair. "No one's watching now, Jack Sullivan—or are you so clumsy at romance that you still need to practice?"

He laughed. "Whoa. You got me that time! Lead on. Moonlight or not, let's take the ferry."

The taxi let them off at the Star Ferry Pier and within moments they were on the upper deck of the green and white ferryboat.

Jack followed Kylie as she went toward the stern and

leaned against one of the supporting posts, looking back toward Hong Kong Island. The gray sky was darkening, with blacker clouds on the southeast horizon. Here and there shadows darkened the spaces between the buildings, the darkness lengthening, deepening. The air was heavy with humidity, the rain imminent.

Jack had heard on the plane of the typhoon approaching the Chinese mainland. It was expected to hit land farther north along the coast, so Hong Kong would get plenty of rain but miss the full force of its winds. But it wasn't only the storm he felt now; a sense of foreboding seemed to be emanating from Kylie.

He had found her sudden decision to ride the ferry interesting. It proved she did have an impulse now and then to do something spontaneous, perhaps even a little frivolous. He would mark this down as another insight into the elusive Kylie Austin. He'd had few enough up to this point.

When his old friend Harry Reaves had first mentioned three years ago that he was interviewing a young expatriate not yet through her twenties for the porcelain buyership in Hong Kong, Jack had been instantly intrigued. In spite of Harry's legendary affability, the CEO of Reaves Imports was not given to sentimentality. Why had this woman so impressed Harry?

Jack knew the answer the moment Kylie Austin walked into Harry's office that first morning so long ago. Even now, as they stood on the upper deck of the ferry, this composed, almost austere woman carried with her an aura of formidable discipline, as if she were moving to a carefully measured beat that only she could hear. More than once Jack had wondered where God fit into the music of her life.

As attractive as she was physically—rich brown hair pulled neatly back to reveal flawless bones and coloring that rivaled her most priceless porcelain—it wasn't her looks that had sustained Jack's interest in Kylie Austin. Something in her chocolate brown eyes made him suspect that under the cold persona she presented to the world was a vibrant, passionate woman, with feelings as deep as a man could ever hope to plumb. But if the gold was there, the path to it was fraught with pitfalls. Only a careful, steady approach would ever win this woman's trust and then her friendship. As for the passion, that would require a patience Jack wasn't sure he had.

Whatever emotions she normally hid, her face was now suffused with very visible regret.

"What's the matter, Kylie?" he asked.

She didn't respond, merely looked back at the cluster of buildings on the island they had left behind, took a deep breath, and drew her purse and carry-all more closely against her.

"Kylie?"

"Oh. Sorry. What did you say?"

"You look almost sad. What is it?"

"Nothing really." She seemed ready to leave it at that, but when he said her name again she shrugged apologetically and gave a small, deprecating laugh. "Really—nothing. It's just that they used to call that section of the city Victoria. Did you know that? Now they call it Central. I think it's kind of sad."

"Sad?"

She shrugged again and sighed. "It's all changing so fast. They used to talk about the battle between the Lion and the Dragon—Great Britain and China. That was so much of the essence of Hong Kong. Now, they're chasing away the Lion, shedding all those years of British influence. I can't blame them, not really. But Communist China as an alternative? In hardly more than a year Britain will pull out completely, and then where will we be? What will happen to this wonderful city then?"

He shook his head. "Life's full of change, Kylie. You can't fight it. Find the things that last and hold on to those."

"Such as?"

He raised his eyebrows and shrugged, hoping she didn't think him unsympathetic. "You tell me."

She looked away, watching the waves furl away from the

boat and disappear in the water. "Harry, I suppose," she said, sighing.

"That's a start. Go on."

"Harry will find a way to keep this branch going somehow. If not here, then in Taiwan probably. Maybe right in China itself. Now there's a thought."

Jack nodded. "He's a crafty old fox, for sure. He's probably had a contingency plan for years if things go bad."

"But Hong Kong itself will change."

"And you love it."

She turned sharply. "Can you blame me? Oh, I suppose you've seen it all, jetting from one place to another. One city is so much like any other—people, buildings, museums, restaurants. But this is my home! Sometimes I'm so sorry I wasn't born twenty years earlier."

"Hmmm. You'd be . . . what? Fifty? An older woman, still beautiful, even more mysterious." He looked down at her, his eyes glittering with humor. "Yes. Our little deception would still work, I think. Definitely."

"I'm serious!"

"Kylie," he said more gently, "it's already changing, all the time. Listen, can't you hear it? You can't stop it. Take today as it comes, and don't worry about tomorrow."

"You don't understand."

He held up his hands in surrender. "I'm sure you're right. I don't completely understand, but I do sympathize." He took a deep breath. "She is a wonderful old city, and I hope you'll be willing to introduce her to me, roots and all, after we get this thing cleared up. I'd love to have a tour of Kylie's Hong Kong."

"Perhaps."

The careful, measured Kylie was back. Jack sighed. Was he fooling himself about the ardent, impassioned woman he suspected?

"What?" she said, noticing his eyes on her.

"I'm just thinking that you must have someone tucked

away here. Bring him along when you give me the tour. I want to meet him."

He could almost hear the portcullis falling. "We've crossed the harbor," she announced coldly and turned away. "Time to get off."

∾≋∾

Kylie hurried away from Jack through the crowds and alighted down the gangplank. She would love to have a few minutes alone, even five minutes of privacy, to collect herself. Why had she blabbered on with him, divulging feelings that must surely have bored him? To make matters worse, she was angry now, and anger led to mistakes; she had heard that often enough. She took a few deep breaths, slowed down deliberately, and stepped off the ramp. As she started walking down the pier, he was still about ten feet behind her, separated from her by the crowd.

That's when she felt a sudden yank on her purse and carry-all and saw both bags being whisked away.

The question registered: How could someone get them off her arm so easily?

Then she saw the knife.

The sunlight caught the metal, flashing a reflection briefly into her eyes, and then the hand that held the knife vanished into the crowd, her bags with it.

Kylie couldn't move; couldn't even make a sound.

Then out of the corner of her eye she saw a shape gaining on her from behind, passing in a blur, pushing the people aside so that for a brief moment she saw her purse and the big black carry-all. Then her purse was being thrust roughly into Jack's arms, and the crowd cut off her view again.

People crowded in, congratulating Jack and calling for the police. In a daze, Kylie looked up at him. He was holding the purse out to her, amazingly apologizing for losing the carry-all.

"Never mind," she murmured, intending to maintain her

calm. Instead she moved helplessly into his arms.

He seemed surprised for a moment and then held her close, gently stroking her hair. "You're all right," he whispered. "You're okay."

Then he touched her arm. "Kylie!" he exclaimed, drawing back abruptly.

There was blood on his hand. Her blood. She looked down at her arm in amazement. Blood was dripping down her arm, staining her sleeve.

"You're hurt!" he said. "What happened?"

Still dazed, Kylie held the cut straps of her purse out for Jack to see. "He must have cut my arm, too."

Jack pulled out a handkerchief and tied it around her arm, then flung his jacket quickly around her shoulder to cover the wound. "Let's get out of here. You need first aid. We'll go to the Mandarin. They'll have a nurse on call."

Kylie allowed herself to be hustled into a taxi, and Jack directed it back through the Cross-Harbour Tunnel to his hotel on the Hong Kong side.

"I don't understand what happened," she said once the taxi was moving. Her words sounded dull to her, from deep in a well.

Jack studied her with a mixture of concern and dismay. "I'm not sure either. I was walking behind you, trying to catch up, and then I saw your bags disappear from your arm. I saw a baseball cap. It's not much, I know. That's all I can tell you about him."

She began to shake. "A baseball cap," she said. Her voice was high and jittery. "Let's look around for a cap-line, shall we? Excuse me, sir, but do you show evidence of a cap-line on your hair? Oh, then do you have my carry-all?"

Jack put his arms around her. "You okay, Kylie?"

She bit her lip and then took a deep breath. She wanted to stay in his arms, she realized, and let him soothe away all the trauma. She wanted to convince herself somehow that everything would be okay, just because he was there. The stupidity of this desire unnerved her almost as much as the attack. She, with a lifetime of practicing self-sufficiency, was abandoning it because of a little cut on her arm?

She sat up and moved away from him on the seat, smoothing her hair purposefully back into place. Another deep breath, straight back, level shoulders. She took on the posture of intentional poise, just as her father had drilled into her.

He must have realized what she was doing. Mercifully, he sat in silence, letting her gather up the tattered shreds of her poise as the taxi made its way through the tunnel into the streets of the Causeway Bay area, and on toward Hong Kong Central.

Finally he asked again, "Kylie?"

"I'm fine," she said, more calmly. "Thank you. Look, here's the Mandarin. I'll just go on home, okay? I'm really fine. This cut has already stopped bleeding. I'll get it cleaned up, change my clothes, and no one will even know that anything happened. Okay?"

His eyes narrowed resolutely. "No, Kylie. Not okay. Go home if you want, but I'm coming with you."

Showing his true self, Kylie thought, *arrogant to the bone.*

Seeing her resist, he shook his head in warning.

"No options, Kylie. This is the way it's going to be. I'll help you get that cut cleaned up, stick a band-aid on it if that's all it needs, but *I'll* be the one who decides that's enough—not you. Besides, I think we should talk about what happened."

"What do you mean?"

"Relax. Let's get you cleaned up first."

She gave her address and then retreated into her corner of the taxi, turning her face determinedly toward the window. As the driver negotiated the crowded streets and hectic traffic toward the Mid-Levels where her flat was, an unfamiliar sense of unease came over her. In all these years—sixteen since she had first moved to Hong Kong with her father—she had never been robbed in this fashion. Crime existed in Hong Kong, plenty of it, and prudence was always wise. But never, never had she been mugged. Tears filled her eyes. Angered, she brushed them away and told herself to stop being so melodramatic. Life goes on.

Still wearing Jack's coat, Kylie led the way into her building and they rode up in the lift to her twentieth-floor flat. One of the perks of working for Reaves, the one-bedroom flat was luxurious by Hong Kong standards. A wide bank of windows gave the living and dining area a northern exposure, capturing sunlight and warmth by day and the dazzling lights of the city by night. Her furniture, all with the clean, spare lines of contemporary design, was set off by a few modern Chinese paintings and pieces of porcelain that she had acquired. All in all, the room had a deliberately serene and peaceful aura.

"I'm going to change," Kylie said. "Have a seat; there are soft drinks in the fridge."

After stepping into her room and closing the door behind her, Kylie could go no further. She leaned carefully against the back of the door and fought for control, pulling in her feelings closer and tighter until they seemed to form a little ball inside her. In her imagination she put her hand on them and squeezed, draining every ounce of fear or confusion from them. She was okay. She could handle this. Harder; get a grip; tighter. It was all there in her hands, all her worry and concern, and she had it firmly under control.

Only then could she take a deep breath and imagine herself far away, in a place of shelter removed from tempest and storm, where she could see every danger approaching. It was an old mechanism for her, this vision of escape. Isolated, she could close her eyes and forget about who might be watching, what they might see, what they might decide about her. There she could dance in glorious, spacious, prodigal freedom.

No one could reach her, not where she was now, alone in a vast wilderness.

Why then was she finding it so hard to forget the comfort of his arms? And why was the memory of that sensation causing so much regret . . . and longing?

Determinedly she thrust the questions away. Taking a

deep, slow breath, she stepped away from the door and forced herself to relax. She had her refuge within her. She was strong. Nothing could hurt her.

When she came back to the living room, she was in sweat pants and a T-shirt and carried a small basin, hydrogen peroxide, and some bandages. "Here you are, Jack, everything you need. Let's do this in the kitchen."

Jack was standing by a recessed display case. He held up an ivory-colored stem cup. "This isn't Ming, I suppose," he said. "Hardly any decoration. What did you say—Sung, wasn't it?"

"You learn fast," Kylie said. "It's Tingware, actually, named for the place it was first produced. Tingware is some of the first true porcelain made."

"Authentic?"

"No. Maybe someday I'll have a real one. Like everything else in the room, it's a reproduction."

"And all from the same period." He turned to look at her across the room. "It suits you, this Sung or Tingware or whatever you call it. Classic, beautiful, perfectly proportioned."

Feeling none of those, she scowled. "Let's get started on the cut."

"It was a compliment, Kylie." His eyes were gentle.

"Yes, well, I feel more like a lump of clay sitting on a pottery wheel."

"Everything spinning? Out of control?"

She couldn't look at him, the kindness in his voice threatening her defenses. She responded almost harshly, "I suppose you're used to having people feel that way."

He had come across the room to where she had set down the basin of water and was rolling up her sleeve. "Why is that, Kylie?"

"You always show up when people are in trouble. You said so yourself."

"I'm here to help, Kylie; to slow things down a little and get them back under control." His voice was close beside her. He paused in his work. "Will you let me try?" he asked.

She didn't think she could respond without crying. Apparently sensing that, he continued his work silently, running warm water and then peroxide over the cut. He worked carefully and quite impersonally, yet she wanted to yank her arm away from the physical contact. Did he know how hard she had to fight to stay calm, how much she wanted to turn and weep on his shoulders?

Remnants of shock, she told herself sternly, and had to fight the tears anyway.

"You were right," he finally said as he dried his hands. "That wasn't too serious. No stitches, I would think."

"I have some butterfly bandages in the box." She lifted diffident eyes to his.

He responded with a smile. "A regular Girl Scout."

She refused to be drawn. "I've always found that a little planning and forethought makes life much easier."

"Yes, I can believe that. No surprises. That must be your motto." After unrolling her sleeve again, he stepped back. "There you are, Kylie. All patched up. Do you need to get ready for this evening or do we have time to discuss what happened?"

"Tea first," she declared. She missed his assessing eyes as she turned to fill the electric teakettle. "Would you like some?"

"Sure." He stood and walked to the north windows but turned to watch her instead of gazing out at the city before them.

"Earl Grey or Darjeeling?"

"Whatever."

"Cream and sugar?"

He shrugged. "I never drink the stuff, Kylie. Fix it the way you like it; I'm sure it'll be fine."

She glanced across at him, taking in his easy, natural stance and relaxed posture.

That is how life works for him, she thought as she set out two mugs. Let any obstacle come. Whatever happened he could handle it. What would it be like to have that kind of confidence?

Abruptly she put the teakettle down. "I forgot. I have to call Charles at the museum."

"I called already, while you were changing. I left regrets with the receptionist."

How very resourceful! "Did you say what happened?"

"Absolutely not."

She looked across at him. "That reminds me. At the pier, why didn't you wait for the police? They would have been there in a minute."

He shrugged. "Chalk it up to spending so much of my time in foreign countries. Nine times out of ten—no, ninety-nine times out of a hundred, the police cause more problems than they're worth. What could they have done? Whoever stole your bag was long gone. They would have whisked you off to a hospital, and then we would have had to hang around giving statements."

"So, no police," she said.

"Not if I can help it. They ask too many questions. They would have wanted to know, for example, why the guy took your carry-all and threw your purse back."

Her hand arranging the tea bags trembled slightly. "I wondered the same thing myself."

"What did you decide?"

Her answer was slow in coming. Finally: "No common thief would have given up the purse."

"So?"

"They were after the porcelain. That's about all I had of any value in the carry-all."

"No papers from the office?"

"Some correspondence to catch up on; nothing important. A report on porcelain sales from Sotheby's and Christie's, a copy of *Asian Art*, some other reading."

"So it had to be the two plates."

She poured the boiling water and brought the two mugs to the table, sitting down abruptly. "Who could have known we were going to have them appraised?"

"Oh, come on, Kylie," he said, joining her at the table. "Why else would you take them? Lily and the packing crew saw you studying those dishes. Winston did as well. Any number of people could easily have seen the note on the secretary's table. For all we know, even Carson may have gotten wind of your concern about those plates."

She stirred her tea absently and then took a drink of the steaming liquid, lifting regretful eyes to him. "Not very smart, I suppose."

"You were hoping for a simple explanation."

"But why go to all this trouble over a few inferior pieces?" She shook her head in confusion. "It doesn't make sense."

"Think," he demanded, but kindly. "Put the facts back on the table and start again. You have two dishes. One is a good reproduction, exactly what you were expecting, little bumps and all. The other? No trademark little bumps. So you decide it was a bad reproduction. Think again, Kylie."

The room became very quiet as he waited. The steam rising from their cups was the only movement. Kylie sat very still, tracing her assumptions back for a mistake.

Her brown eyes suddenly widened and she gasped. "You think it wasn't a reproduction at all!"

He didn't deny it. "It *must* have been an original, Kylie. Only something of that value would cause this reaction."

"But Jack, that little plate—it's not going to set anyone up for life."

"What about lots of little plates, and blossom vases, and wine jars, and all the rest? What about a steady stream of artifacts, not only porcelain but jade and lacquer and ivory as well, all coming out of China through Reaves? Send enough and they certainly would make a man wealthy."

Kylie rose, crossed her arms, and walked briskly to the

other end of the living room and then back again, several times. "How?" she finally exclaimed, spinning to face Jack from across the room. "Where are they coming from?"

"Somewhere within China, I suppose."

She shook her head in denial. "You *can't* be right. Jack, this isn't possible!"

"You said it yourself, Kylie. Somewhere in the high-rise tenements people have countless hidden treasures. Can't that have happened in China as well? Perhaps someone's hidden away a fortune in artifacts. Or maybe they've come across a hidden tomb. Didn't the Chinese bury porcelain with their dead? Or perhaps someone in one of the museums is squirreling away the treasures, one piece at a time. Actually, the stuff might be coming through Taiwan. When the Nationalists fled the mainland, they took thousands of art pieces with them, didn't they? Why not some individual doing that, unofficially, on the side, using Reaves as their conduit to get the pieces to collectors? Kylie, the possibilities are endless."

Across the room from him, Kylie found it difficult to breathe. "The possibilities may be endless," she said dully, "but not the people who are doing it. Someone at Reaves, someone at the main office, someone I know and work with has to be in on this."

Jack came across the room to stand mere feet from her, capturing her gaze, communicating a world of compassion to her. He put his hands on her shoulders and rubbed his palms slowly over her tense muscles, being careful of her wound. "Yes, I'm afraid you're right. I'm sorry."

"Someone used a knife! They could have really hurt me."

He nodded and then withdrew his hands. Even so, Kylie found his presence comforting. Not for this moment the isolated escape, she admitted weakly. She took a deep breath, acknowledging the goodness of God to send Jack to her aid. Then she took a step back and away from him and walked again to the window. Behind her, he took a seat in the living room.

"What happened to Murray?" she asked doubtfully, gazing out across the harbor.

"We can only guess. Perhaps someone paid him off, and he'll turn up in Brazil or Benin or someplace off the map."

"Or maybe they killed him."

"We have no cause to believe that yet."

"But Robert!"

Jack's face became still, his expression reserved.

"You're not so sure about Robert, are you?"

He came to stand beside her, silent for a minute. When he finally did speak, his expression was void but his voice firm. "It's time for you to get ready, Kylie. We need to be at the Mandarin in half an hour. We'll talk about it later tonight, okay?"

Later tonight. Meaning the swirl of suspicions and doubts was only beginning. The memory of the knife flashed in her mind again, and she caught her breath.

"Let's tell the police—let them take care of it!"

"Tell them what? We have no proof, only suspicions. It's your word that the piece was authentic, and you think so only now because of the mugging. You didn't recognize it at the time."

"But who, Jack? How can I work with these people, knowing one of them may have . . . might have . . . I'm so afraid for Murray!"

His hands again on her shoulders, he turned her partially toward her bedroom. "Get changed, Kylie. Take your time, but when you come out be ready to face this thing like the professional I know you are. We're going to get to the bottom of this, but we have to keep our courage and wits up. Now, go."

We have to keep our courage up? she thought, looking up at his calm and determined expression. As if this guy had ever had a problem he couldn't face! She felt like one of those fragile women in the movies who wrings her hand as the hero fights in front of her.

Shoulders up, back straight. Poise, confidence, even when you don't feel like it. She knew the drill.

"You're right," she said, much more calmly. "You're absolutely right. I'll be out in a minute."

Four

She emerged wearing another classically styled skirt and blouse. Seeing Jack's response, she raised her shoulders slightly. "What?"

"I would think you'd be glad to get into something more comfortable."

"Everyone else is going to the hotel straight from work. I'd prefer no one know that we're coming from my flat."

"Hmmm. Well, let's go then."

In the taxi, Jack suggested that she list the people who would be at the Mandarin.

"You know Carson, of course, and his wife, Mei-lin," Kylie said. "Phillip Hughes handles our jewelry division; jade is his specialty, of course. His wife's name is Sylvie."

"Hughes is the man Harry added to the branch since I was here last."

"Phillip's export business folded a year ago. Harry's always admired his work, though; Phillip has an almost unequaled knowledge of jade."

"His business folded?"

Kylie nodded. "I'm not sure why, but he had to declare bankruptcy."

"I'll check with Harry," Jack said. "Go on."

"Winston Lu handles everything else: ivory, wood, silk, and so forth. He's still young, in his thirties, but very ambitious."

"Has he married?"

"Not a chance. He likes his freedom."

"No comment from me," Jack said, grinning. "Okay. That's enough to go on. Tell me again about names in Hong Kong. Do all the Chinese have Western names?"

"Actually, most have both Western and Chinese names. Traditionally, Chinese people have been somewhat fluid with their names. The old custom was to give newborns temporary names, designed to drive away the evil spirits who were thought to be the cause of infant mortality. Names like 'ugly,' or 'stupid,' or 'here's one even the dogs wouldn't want.' That's the child's 'milk' name. Around four or five they get a nicer nickname and then eventually their adult names. The teachers who taught in British schools were so confused by all these names, not only with the changes but with how to pronounce the names, that they arbitrarily assigned the children Western names for use in school. From that came the custom of most people in Hong Kong having both Chinese and Western names. Last names aren't so much of a problem for Westerners. Apparently there are only about twenty different Chinese last names."

"Interesting."

"Oh yes. For being such a small place, Hong Kong has layers and layers of culture, customs behind customs. I'll certainly never grasp it all, even if I live here all my life."

"But you'd like the opportunity to try."

"Absolutely." She smiled, pleased that he seemed to understand her fascination with Hong Kong. "You explore the world, Jack. I have enough right here to keep me busy!"

⌒⌒⌒

At the Mandarin, Jack went up to his room while Kylie ordered an iced tea and retreated to a quiet corner of the lounge. They had arrived at the hotel late, after five-thirty, and yet it was almost six before Carson Grey and his wife entered the lobby and came across to join her.

Mei-lin Grey was one of the most stylish and sophisticated women Kylie knew—and after years of following her father around Kylie knew a few. She had never seen Mei-lin in anything except designer clothing. Tonight she wore a smart two-piece suit, and as usual everything else about her appearance was perfect, enhanced by Carson's short, rounded body.

Perfect, except that Mei-lin was definitely upset about something. As she came across the lobby, she left her husband to hurry along behind her, barely achieving the illusion of walking with her.

Because they were late? Kylie wondered.

Upon reaching Kylie, however, Mei-lin's customarily chilly smile appeared, and she briefly shook the younger woman's hand. "Kylie, my dear, what's this I hear about you and Jack Sullivan?"

Kylie winced. "Please, Mei-lin, nothing's settled. He had some vacation time; he's spending it here. Don't make too much of it."

Carson put a hand on his wife's arm. "Don't press her, Mei-lin. Kylie's our shy little butterfly, didn't you know? She'll flutter away if we take too much notice of her."

Kylie scowled. "Thank you, Carson . . . I think."

"Then tell me, dear, what have you heard from your father lately?" Mei-lin said.

Kylie smiled politely in response to Mei-lin's question. Always one to take note of power and position, Mei-lin had a proprietary interest in George Austin, who had recently been named to a position on the National Security Council.

"He's fine, Mei-lin, thank you. I spoke to him a little over a week ago."

"And he's married again, I understand?"

"No, Mei-lin. He hasn't married again."

"Imagine, a handsome man like your father? What must the ladies be thinking?"

If the ladies in her father's world knew anything, Kylie decided, they would understand George Austin to be a lost cause. Discreet he would always be, affectionate to a point, but never tied down. Not again. As far as Kylie knew, her father wasn't even divorced from her mother. Too handy an excuse not to remarry, she supposed.

Mei-lin rose to welcome Phillip and Sylvie Hughes, while Carson leaned toward Kylie and murmured, "So what were you two up to all afternoon?"

Kylie caught her breath. Perhaps Jack was wrong, and Carson didn't know about the trip to the warehouse or the two missing plates.

"Lily called me about Robert," Kylie answered. "How is he?"

Carson shook his head. "Looks bad, Kylie. But don't you worry." And as if unable to contain himself, he patted Kylie's hand.

"Oh, here's Jack," Kylie said, and jumped up to meet him walking across the lobby.

As much for Carson's benefit as anything, Kylie tucked her hand through Jack's elbow and smiled up at him.

"Hello, Kylie," he said, drawing her closer against him. He smiled down at her, and for an abrupt moment time stood still. His eyes said it all—*you're a beautiful and desirable woman, Kylie Austin, and I'd like nothing more than to spend an evening with you.*

In a panic, Kylie swallowed painfully and forced herself to smile in return, reminding herself this was one of those bogus "private" glances he had spoken about.

He leaned toward her and whispered into her ear, sending another shiver through her: "Good job; very convincing!"

Kylie continued smiling, struggling to keep a grip on her reactions. All an act, she kept telling herself. Jack Sullivan knew how to play on a woman's feelings. Of course he did. What did Kylie expect?

Fortunately Phillip Hughes came forward then, introducing himself to Jack. In his mid-fifties, Phillip Hughes still had a full head of hair and just enough weight to give the appearance of a comfortably wealthy businessman, and so he should have been. He was one of the best men in the jade business; he had a singular sense for the stone, finding the best pieces in the most unexpected places, able to name the origin of a stone almost instantly, and always choosing the best quality for purchase. Yet everything about him, his posture, his demeanor, the slant of his head, spelled failure. If Kylie felt sorry for him, however, it was more because of Sylvie than because of the bankruptcy.

French in her background, Sylvie Hughes was of medium height but very thin so that her cheeks and nose usually looked pinched. Her eyes, however, were her worst feature, and then only because she tended to focus too resolutely on one person with an intrusive, discomforting stare. Kylie knew she must have suffered in the past year and that her husband's fall from grace must seem like a constant cross to bear, but really, did she have to put on her pain every morning like makeup? Kylie had yet to see anyone break through Sylvie's bitterness.

While Jack and Phillip talked, Kylie turned to Sylvie. "Hello, Sylvie. How are you?"

Sylvie didn't answer at first, but looked Kylie over carefully as if searching out some evidence of duplicity in her question.

"How are your boys, Sylvie? I understand Francis is working in Tokyo?"

"The 'boys' as you call them are both older than you are, Kylie Austin, and I'm sorry, I can't tell you how they are. We rarely hear from them."

Phillip abandoned his conversation with Jack and leaned closer to answer Kylie's question. "They're fine, Kylie. Our boys are just fine."

Kylie drew back slightly, instinctively repulsed by the overpowering smell of alcohol on his breath.

Seeing her response, Phillip frowned and took his wife's arm. "Come on now, Sylvie," he said. "Let's go get a drink. This is supposed to be a cocktail party."

"You shouldn't be drinking any more; you've already had enough," Sylvie hissed. "Besides, if you'll just wait a minute, they'll come over here and get your order anyway."

"Then let's go sit down, Sylvie. Shall we?"

Poor Phillip, Kylie thought. And poor Sylvie. She looked up at Jack and shook her head slightly, knowing she shouldn't pity Phillip and yet feeling helpless to stop. Hearing Winston, Kylie turned to greet him and his date. What a welcome relief from Sylvie and Phillip!

"Ah-ha-ha," Winston said, holding his hands up as if to frame Jack and Kylie in a picture, "the happy couple."

"Give it up, Winston," Kylie shot back.

"Why must you be so unfriendly, Kylie? We've just gotten here."

Kylie held out a hand to introduce herself to Winston's date. As usual, she was beautiful and blond.

"I'm Camilla Svenson," the woman said, her Swedish accent caressing the syllables.

"What brings you to Hong Kong?" Kylie asked.

"I am a flight attendant. I am flying on SAS."

Like a cat after catnip Carson came rushing over to meet Camilla and lead her to the bar. Kylie exchanged glances with Winston, she rolling her eyes and he shrugging not at all sheepishly.

"What can I say?" he whispered. "They flock to me! But I'll always have time for you, Kylie. Just say the word. I'm still waiting to give you a ride in my new Mustang."

"A Mustang? Now if it were a *Mercedes*, maybe."

"Give a man a break," Winston retorted, a shade bitterly. "It's only been in the last year that Reaves has provided a fancy flat in the Mid-Levels for me, you know. I'll need a little time to catch up."

It was an old complaint among the local staff. The custom was to provide expatriates with housing and let the locals fend for themselves. Only with his promotion to buyer did Winston qualify for the housing allowance that his expatriate counterparts enjoyed.

Kylie nodded sympathetically. "I know, Winston. I'm sorry. I'd love to ride in your Mustang, really. Let's do it next week sometime, please."

STILLPOINT

"Yeah, okay."

"Hey, Winston," Jack said, "you better go rescue poor Camilla. Carson's looking pretty determined."

When he left, Jack leaned closer. "What was all that about?"

"I'll explain later," Kylie said. She stood watching Winston and his beautiful date a moment longer. "You know," she murmured thoughtfully, "he really does live extravagantly. He's got a fancy American sports car—around here Mustangs are pretty highly valued, you know. His flat's becoming a showcase. And Camilla's in a long line of lovely ladies who get the very best treatment Hong Kong can provide."

"A motive?"

"Maybe. He must be doing *something* on the side. Anyway, we can talk about it later."

"At dinner? Will you stay and eat with me?"

"If we can get away from Carson and Mei-lin. They'll want to take us somewhere—at your expense, of course."

"Don't worry," he whispered into her ear. "I'll have the perfect excuse ready when the time comes."

Then Jack went into action. As the couples settled into couches and armchairs and began to nibble on the egg rolls and wontons and other appetizers provided by the hotel, Jack turned on the charm and began to subtly but inexorably extract information from each of Kylie's colleagues. By the end of the next hour, he had pulled out of Carson a description of his courtship with Mei-lin, and from Mei-lin a description of her early childhood in Shanghai before World War II, during the years when the nationalist Kuomintang controlled the mainland government, and of her family's escape to Hong Kong.

Then, lavish in his praise of some jade pieces that Phillip had recently sent to Harry for his collection, Jack also managed to loosen Sylvie up enough to talk about her prize collection of antique jade buckles. It was the one possession that Phillip had managed to save from the bankruptcy proceed-

· 55 ·

ings, though Kylie wasn't sure exactly how.

As for Winston, no charm was needed to get him to talk. The trick with him was to somehow shut him up. Jack even managed that.

The rain had started by the time the group split up, winds gusting the moisture around the panoramic windows of the hotel. *And so the storm comes*, Kylie thought as she and Jack stood near the hotel entrance. She tried to shake off the feeling of dread that haunted the edges of her thoughts, but each time the door opened to release someone else from their group, Kylie had the sensation of danger swirling around her.

Pushing the sensation away, she turned to Jack and whispered, "I'm impressed. You could have been a diplomat."

"Faint praise, I think," Jack responded, grinning ironically, "but I'll take what I can get from you, lady."

"Now, now, you two, break it up," Carson said, coming up behind them. Everyone else had left, leaving only Carson and Mei-lin behind. "Where shall we take you two for dinner?"

Kylie raised knowing eyes to Jack, which he met by putting his arm around her shoulders. "We'll beg off," he answered Carson firmly, then motioned out the windows and added "or perhaps I should say, 'we'll take a rain check!' "

Jack grinned only briefly, however. Looking down at Kylie, his warm eyes searched her face for a long, eloquent moment, and then he turned to the other couple. "With so little time available to us, we better not waste any. You understand, don't you, Carson, Mei-lin?"

Mei-lin certainly did. Putting a firm hand through Carson's arm, she began to push him toward the door.

Carson looked back over his shoulder. "You take tomorrow off, Kylie. Show Jack around. Have some fun!"

"There you have it." Jack grinned as the doors swung shut behind Carson and Mei-lin. "I got rid of them and managed to get you a day off as well."

"You're incorrigible!" Kylie declared, lifting his hand purposefully off her shoulder and ducking out from under his arm. "And I already told Lily I wasn't coming in tomorrow."

"This is all in the name of our mission, Kylie. Don't you believe me?"

Kylie pursed her lips and glared at him. "Look, I'll go along with this charade. I've certainly become convinced that something's going on, and I recognize the need for precautions. But please, Jack, don't get any ideas about anything serious—no, and nothing frivolous either. I have my own life here, and I like it a lot, just the way it is."

He held up his hands to fend off her insinuations. "Me, too, Kylie," he said. He looked away for a moment, and when he spoke again he chose his words carefully. "I've seen how Carson treats you. I appreciate how difficult it is to be taken seriously as a professional under those circumstances. And I'm sorry that Harry chose this deception as a reason for my being here. Unfortunately, he and Joy . . . Well, again, I'm sorry. I should never have agreed to this arrangement, but you can be sure I'll respect your desire to be treated as a business colleague when we're alone."

Kylie stared at him hard. Could he really be that rarest of rare things, an honorable man? Kylie certainly knew Harry Reaves had made it a practice to deal with honor. Harry set the highest possible ethical standards for his business. Was Jack Sullivan another like him, a truly trustworthy man?

If anything, his words troubled rather than comforted her. It would be so much easier to snub him if he were more like poor old Carson Grey.

"You sure you don't have someone waiting for you back in Chicago?" she asked.

He smiled, apparently satisfied. "I'll tell you anything you want to know about me at dinner. Where shall we eat?"

"Actually . . ." She frowned. "Perhaps we should go back to the warehouse?"

"With the idea that there might be other . . . anomalies somewhere in the shipment?"

"I can go myself if you're too tired. It's seven-thirty. You could get an early night."

"Harry didn't send me over here so I could catch up on my sleep," he said drily. "Let's go."

꩜

Again Kylie was surprised when she entered the warehouse. Expecting the room to be empty, she found the crew still there, still working. Kylie looked around in dismay. A neat row of freshly packed crates and boxes was lined up beside the back wall, near the loading dock.

Dumbfounded, Kylie called over the temporary crew chief, Samuel Huang. "Why are you still here?" she asked sternly, speaking in English for Jack's sake.

"Why, Miss Austin, you the one tell Lily we finish!"

"What!" Kylie drew back in surprise.

Samuel nodded. "Lily, she come in with note. She say you want us finish packing tonight. We finish. See?"

"Yes, I see," Kylie said, defeated. "Okay, Samuel, keep on working. I'll get this cleared up with Lily."

Kylie stepped back from the table, frowned briefly at Jack, and then called her assistant on her phone.

"It was on your note, Kylie. Don't you remember? It listed the two plates that you had taken and a request at the bottom that the crew keep working overtime until the entire shipment was ready. They should be almost done by now."

"Yes, actually, they are," Kylie said, not even trying to hide her frustration.

"Did I do something wrong?" Lily asked, a little resentfully. Kylie had to bite back her frustration; Lily was making it more and more obvious that she considered herself overqualified to be a mere assistant.

"No, no," Kylie said, suddenly very tired. There was no need to take this out on Lily—or the crew, for that matter. "I'll talk to you tomorrow."

She pushed the phone's antenna in and put the unit back into her purse. Only then did she repeat for Jack what Lily had said, bracing herself for what she would see in his eyes.

She knew it already. Someone had added the instruction to her note, someone who didn't want them examining the other pieces.

The same someone who had been willing to slice Kylie's arm in order to steal the two plates. Who might have done more than that to Robert and Murray.

☙

Seeing Kylie's thoughts disintegrate, Jack took her arm gently and led her out of the workroom into the warehouse office. "We'll go get dinner," he said decisively. "There's no way we can unpack everything tonight without going public with our suspicions, so we'll relax a little back at the hotel, and then try to decide what we're going to do next."

Kylie didn't move, so Jack put his hand on her back and pushed her gently toward the door. "Let's get out of here, Kylie," he said softly. "People are beginning to wonder what's the matter."

"All right, all right. But aren't you too tired? Jet lag must be catching up with you."

A surge of compassion swept over him. Did she think he could really leave her feeling so worried? Apparently others had done so often enough. Careful not to reveal what he was feeling, he settled back beside her in the taxi. "This is the time to talk about what's happened, while everything is still fresh in our minds."

"Fine. Then let's go back to the Mandarin. The Grill there is world-class."

☙

He was way ahead of her, Kylie realized. After a silent taxi ride to the Mandarin, during which Kylie's thoughts blew around in her mind like the gathering storm, and a quick dash through the rain, Jack led them toward the restaurant, announced his name, and let the *maitre d'* lead them to a reserved table by the window.

He was, however, very tired. Kylie could see weariness in the set of his shoulders and the way he rubbed his eyes. He was paying her quite a compliment by revealing his exhaustion. He'd certainly given no hint of it to anyone else during the evening.

"Let's get started," she said, as soon as their meals were ordered. "What did you think of them—Carson and the rest, I mean?"

"Human, which is to say complex, multi-faceted, impossible to peg into neat little holes. They all have motives, obviously, but that's hardly surprising. Tell me one person in all the world who wouldn't like a little extra money."

"Even you, Jack?"

"Even Harry, and he's loaded."

"Fair enough," Kylie agreed, "but not many of us are willing to commit a crime for it."

"Tell me about Winston."

"He's in his mid-thirties, has come up in the business the hard way. His father is an artisan, originally from the Zhejiang province, who carves beautiful wooden pieces. Unfortunately, Winston's father spends most of his time on second-class tourist fare—nativities, chess pieces, statuettes, anything that will sell. Even so, I guess Winston learned the difference between knickknacks and the real stuff. He spent his teen years doing odd jobs for showrooms here in Hong Kong, then got a job at the Hong Kong Museum for next to nothing and worked there for five years. Whenever he could he wandered around the Orient—Japan, Taiwan, Singapore, Bangkok, checking out local craftsmen and museums. He told me once those years were his college, but he also took conventional business courses on the side. He's no slouch. He joined Reaves five years ago working for Nat Rawlings, the man he eventually replaced. His training has been unconventional, but he's as sharp as they come and has a great future with the company."

"And the apartment?"

Kylie explained and then frowned briefly. "I can't blame him for indulging in a few creature comforts, I suppose. I just wonder sometimes how he does it. Hong Kong's horribly expensive."

"And Phillip Hughes?"

Kylie shook her head ruefully, saw Jack's reaction, and then shrugged apologetically. "I know, but I can't help feeling sorry for him, even though that's absolutely the last thing the man needs. Anyway, Phillip is as good as they come with jade, and he's not far behind with cloisonné. Reaves is making buckets off the jade he's channeling through our company to the States and to Europe. He's a wizard. I can't figure out what happened with his business. He should be at the top of the heap, but a year ago he lost everything."

"I know," Jack said, pausing and then coming to a decision. "I called Harry this afternoon while you were downstairs in the lobby. Phillip gambles. Carson knows about it, keeps a sharp eye on Phillip, and Harry insists that Phillip stay in therapy as long as he's with Reaves."

"And that's why he went bankrupt? Poor Sylvie!"

"Through the years, he's squandered almost everything he earned. His two sons won't even speak to him. It was the day he packed up Sylvie's collection of jade buckles that he realized he needed help. He actually took the collection to a dealer, set the price and everything, and then realized he couldn't commit that final offense to Sylvie. That's when he admitted defeat and let his company go."

"And Harry bailed him out."

"For which Phillip, by the way, has mixed feelings."

"Not Sylvie. She hates Harry. Don't ever get her started."

"Harry owns the buckle collection, you know."

Kylie's jaw dropped. "I've always wondered how Phillip managed to keep it."

"Harry bought it and leases it to Phillip, all unknown to Sylvie, of course. That way Phillip can't ever sell it. It was his idea—Phillip's, I mean. I don't think he's a bad man; he just has a very destructive addiction.''

"Poor Sylvie," Kylie said again.

"Care for a word of advice? Keep your pity to yourself, Kylie. Grace is always hard to accept. It would be like salt on a wound for Sylvie to discover you knew about all this.''

Kylie sighed, pushing her plate of food away. "Life can be pretty awful.''

"Sin, Kylie. It's a fallen world and only by God's grace is redemption even possible—for *any* of us.''

Hearing the compassion, she lifted her eyes slowly to his. She wondered how many people saw the side of Jack he was showing her now. Harry could afford to be magnanimous, but someone had to wield the hatchet in a corporation like Reaves. That would be Jack. Perhaps because of his tiredness, his eyes were softer, revealing what was probably a habitual kindness that he usually kept hidden on the job.

She wished she could open up to him in return and explain her cynicism. She was becoming more and more certain that Jack Sullivan would keep her small secret wounds and bruises to himself. And perhaps in the telling she would find some relief from the old aches.

But she couldn't do it. She cared too much about maintaining her facade with this man.

She sat up straighter. "What did you think of Carson?''

Jack leaned back in his chair again. "Same old Carson. Likes to be in charge, likes his creature comforts, likes to keep Mei-lin happy—not necessarily in that order.''

"Her father is an old-time banker. That's why the family came here when the Communists took over. Capitalists to their teeth.''

"I've heard that compared to the old money the Chinese have in Hong Kong, even Harry's borderline destitute.''

Kylie nodded her agreement. "Though most of that money's leaving these days. Mei-lin must have really loved Carson—even through all these years. She married way beneath herself financially.''

"I imagine he cut quite a romantic figure back in those

days. When Harry was first establishing Reaves, here in Hong Kong, Carson was his right-hand man, and he's now been director of one of Hong Kong's most reputable wholesale art firms for over thirty years. We can't know, but perhaps at a time when she felt trapped, Carson offered Mei-lin independence, adventure, as well as a chance to domineer. For whatever reason, don't worry about Mei-lin. She'll not have let him forget her sacrifice."

"And love? Surely a little?"

"Of course love. A little. We're not binary creatures, with simple yes/no choices. Our motives are always mixed, and the consequences impossible to accurately predict."

Kylie drummed her fingers briefly against the tablecloth. "This is awful, dissecting people this way. I hate it."

"You like these people, don't you?"

"Yes, I do! I don't think I realized quite how much until today. I don't want any of them to be involved. Couldn't it be someone outside the firm, someone in the packing plant, some lowly employee that I don't even know? Hong Kong is full of deception, you know. The *dai pai dong* merchant, selling his food from a street stall, could be ten times richer than either you or I will ever be. Maybe that's true here, and it's really the janitor at the warehouse who's behind it all."

Jack didn't even try to dissuade her, merely shook his head regretfully.

Kylie let out a long sigh and defiantly crossed her arms.

"Hey," Jack said, grinning slowly. "Let's talk about something else—you, for example."

Kylie glared across at him. "Because I'm the next suspect?"

Fortunately Jack laughed, the most reassuring response he could have made. "Or me, if you'd like. You wanted to know who I have waiting for me back in Chicago, didn't you?"

Kylie leaned forward. "Yes. Tell me."

Jack laughed again. "A sister named Elizabeth who is, coincidentally, married to a nice college professor. Two nephews and four nieces, children of said sister. Two brothers, one in Indiana, one in Colorado. Parents in Florida, nice people. You'd like them. Friends, acquaintances, all very—"

"I know," Kylie interrupted. " 'Very nice.' But no 'nice' friend of another nature, the kind you marry and settle down with?"

"Well, that's the rub—that 'settling down' part. Joy and Harry think it's long past time that I stopped traveling so much. Harry wants me in the main office—so he can think about retiring—but I'm not ready yet. Since I first realized there was a great big world out there, I've wanted to be in it, see it, experience all the incredible varieties of life that God has allowed to develop on His good earth."

Kylie nodded slowly. She was charmed by his easy reference to God but—Harry retiring? Kylie pushed the thought aside. "What's your favorite place?"

"I have lots of favorites."

"Impossible. Favorite means the one favorite, better than all the rest."

Jack rubbed his chin momentarily, considering, and then smiled at Kylie. "You'll be surprised, I think. It would have to be Botswana. I visited a friend there; she was doing some animal research near the Okavango Delta. I loved the place. The air, the sunlight, the people, the wildlife; everything pulsed with energy and life. I'll never forget Easter morning near the Kalahari Desert. We sat outside in the dawning sunlight, listening to the people sing, watching them dance. The rhythm, the light, the smells, the breeze—incredible! I'd settle down there if anywhere."

"Botswana," Kylie repeated blankly. She was surprised. "No restaurants, no skyline, no business or industry?"

"Clear night skies where you can see the stars, and air so fresh that you genuinely feel lighter after breathing it. Quiet, so quiet you can hear the wind rustling the acacia trees, and no traffic! Can you imagine it, Kylie?"

She nodded halfheartedly. "Yes, barely, but I wouldn't want to live there. It's been cities from the word 'Go!' for me. Who needs diplomats out in the wild?"

"I've met your father, you know."

"My father?" She became suddenly still.

"Harry took me by one day when your father was at the consulate in Warsaw. It was just after you joined the firm. We were beginning our eastern European branches."

Kylie swallowed painfully. How . . . pleasant. Like being told that someone had seen a picture of her as a baby lying naked on a sheepskin. "He's quite remarkable, isn't he?" she said carefully.

"Yes, quite."

"We lived in Hong Kong, did you know, during my high school years."

"Yes, I knew." He waited, but she was obviously unwilling to say more.

She took a last swallow of iced tea and pushed her chair back. "Well, enough for tonight, surely? I'll come by in the morning. We can eat breakfast here if you like, or I could come later."

"Breakfast is fine. Eight o'clock."

Kylie managed, "Then I'll see you tomorrow. Goodbye," and hurried through the lobby and out the front of the hotel.

Once on the steps, pausing before she stepped toward the taxi queue, she took a deep breath and forced herself to relax, wishing she could swear. No other response seemed quite appropriate for what had happened back there.

So did he already know, this strangely disconcerting man, about her lingering bruises, her hidden fears?

Why else had he brought up her father?

It was much later, as she was crawling wearily into bed and trying impossibly to relax that the thought occurred to her: All she needed now was for him to tell her he had also run across her mother somewhere—but then what would he have been doing in such a scuzzy section of San José?

As she did every time she thought of her mother, almost against her will, Kylie murmured a plea for her mother's protection.

You can still save her, can't You? she begged. *Can't You?*

Five

ylie slept poorly, disturbed by the storm outside and by sounds she must have dreamed, wishing for the first time in her life that she had a dog. Between fitful dozing, she pored over her knowledge of the firm—reviewing standard procedures, the other divisions, her memories of personal encounters with each of the executive staff. It wasn't until four o'clock in the morning that she finally thought of something she could do. She got up immediately.

It was Friday. If she wanted to do any research at the office before people started arriving for work, she had to leave immediately.

The main offices of Reaves, Hong Kong, were housed on the thirty-second floor of one of Hong Kong's older skyscrapers—though no building in Hong Kong was very old. Building and rebuilding was constant—the jackhammer Hong Kong's perennial percussion accompaniment. Compared to newer ones, however, the building that housed Reaves was short on glass and chrome and profligate on space, with relatively high ceilings and spacious rooms. The definitely uptown address must have seemed like a gamble when Harry first leased the space, but the quality accommodations had gone a long way toward maintaining Reaves' reputation.

The central lobby of their suite proved Reaves' wealth by leaving large areas open. Here and there in recessed display cases the company's choicest wares were displayed: a gorgeous jade statuette of the goddess Kuan Yin, an ivory tusk of intricately carved elephants, a lacquer box that had belonged to a fourteenth-century emperor, and other treasures. Of lesser value, but nevertheless revealing outstanding craftsmanship, larger porcelain and teak artworks were given floor space around the lobby.

Off this main lobby, one set of doors led into a conference/showroom and another set of doors discreetly led toward the office space. No less luxurious, these were nevertheless more utilitarian. Kylie slipped hurriedly down the hallway and into her own office, refusing awareness of the shadows and silence.

Her office featured a fine teak desk and Oriental carpet, with a display case of some of the finest ceramic reproductions that had come through Hong Kong since she had arrived at Reaves three years earlier. A comfortable sofa and chairs were positioned to catch the morning sun.

The sky outside was dark, and rain battered her windows, the sound too close to Kylie's own emotions. Ignoring the very real possibility of panic, Kylie went straight to her desk and clicked on her computer. It took only a minute to call up the company's personnel files, but what she saw on the screen caused her to freeze momentarily. She must be on the right track. Someone had erased the files she wanted.

The silence in the room, broken only by the quiet hum of the computer, suddenly sent a chill through her. When had solitude, her old friend, become sinister? She quickly turned her computer off, vaguely aware that someone with enough knowledge could be following her progress on the computer, looking at the very screen she had been viewing, waiting.

She forced herself to go into the next office, where Lily kept backups of company files. The sooner Kylie found the right ones, the sooner she could get out of there.

Working as quickly as her tightened nerves would allow, it took Kylie almost half an hour to locate the disk that had Mary Chiu's file on it, and then a little longer to find Terry Wong's.

She called for a taxi to take her back home, gave it a few

minutes to arrive, and then escaped down the hallway to the lift. As she settled into the automobile, she smiled weakly into her compact mirror. How foolish to be so paranoid! At least she now had something to show Jack.

A cold shower and fresh makeup served to revive her spirit, and in her business clothes and severe hairstyle she felt like she had her armor back on.

Kylie called Jack from the Mandarin lobby at 7:45, to let him know she was there, then took a seat near the lifts to wait for him.

"Good morning."

He was standing above her, crisp and clean in gray slacks and a blue striped shirt.

"Ah," he said, taking in her outfit as Kylie stood up. "Still the professional woman. I thought we'd be moving around a little, doing some checking around town. Are you sure you'll be comfortable in those clothes?"

"We won't be crawling through rafters, will we?" Kylie walked toward the restaurant without waiting for a reply.

Jack looked after her, wondering what she would look like with her face smudged and her hair a mess. A tantalizing thought: pushing a curl back from her face and wiping the smudge away, waiting for the inevitable blush.

"Are you coming?" she asked. "Or aren't you hungry?"

Allowing himself no comment, Jack followed silently. She was so sweetly serious about everything; he was finding it very hard not to tease her.

"Any new thoughts?" Jack asked as soon as they had ordered.

"Actually, yes," Kylie said. "It occurred to me during the night that we've seen some strange turnover in the warehouse. I mean, we always have people coming and going, but during the past six months two of our steadiest workers have been laid off. Robert said their performance wasn't up to par, and I suppose Carson had no reason to doubt him. Now I'm beginning to wonder."

"Tell me about the workers."

"One is an older woman, Mary Chiu. Chinese, probably close to fifty. She's worked in the packing house for almost fifteen years. She always had a deft touch with our most fragile pieces; rarely any breakage. I wonder what happened to her."

"The other?"

"Oh, that's Terry Wong, one of the most fun-loving guys I've ever met—even beats Winston Lu. Terry likes to party and to drink, but he came in to work regularly and worked hard. Said he knew a green pasture when he saw one. He'd been with us for almost six years."

"Any idea where they are now?"

"Well, yes, actually. I went by the office on the way here to check out their files."

"This morning? Was anyone there?"

Kylie sighed. "Security in the building, of course, but no one in our offices. Don't worry; nothing happened. Anyway, I have Mary's address; I can't imagine she's moved. And I have Terry's parents' number. We can look them both up today. Mary first, I would think. She worked for Reaves longer. She might have some vague trace of loyalty to the old place."

"More likely the opposite," Jack said drily, "but we can try. How many people do you normally have working in the warehouse?"

"Usually around twenty to thirty, all told. They unload the trucks, repack the merchandise, get them ready for shipping. The place keeps pretty busy."

"Then let's get going."

"Should we call Mary? I have her number."

"No. Let's surprise her. On the way to her place, let's stop by the hospital to check on Robert."

"He'll be at the Queen Mary Hospital on Pokfulam Road. It's one of the nearest public hospitals to the warehouse where the accident occurred."

In the gleaming corridors of the hospital, Jack insisted on talking to a doctor. The news was grim. Robert was in a coma; recovery seemed unlikely. His relatives were with him, but he would probably never regain consciousness.

Kylie was silent in the taxi, then turned abruptly to Jack. "Was it deliberate? Tell me what you really think. Did someone try to kill Robert?"

"The police have yet to find the vehicle. You said yourself that probably meant it was intentional."

"But why? Don't you think Robert must have been in on this thing? If so, why would he be killed? Now they'll have to find someone else."

"It's happened countless times, Kylie. Someone gets greedy. Or maybe Robert got cold feet about being involved. Perhaps he wanted to pull out, and they wouldn't let him."

A sick feeling was developing in Kylie's stomach and she thought she might throw up. She raised agonized eyes to Jack.

"Yes," Jack said reluctantly. "Maybe it was what happened to Murray that made Robert want to pull out. I'm sorry, Kylie."

She wrapped her arms tightly around her chest but couldn't stop trembling. "Let's tell the police."

"Not yet."

"But Murray—he could be in danger."

"We still don't have anything to go on."

She retreated to her far corner and pulled in her feelings again, knowing hopelessly that no visualization technique would ever get her through this time. Surely even her father had never been involved in something like this.

If only it would stop raining!

"Kylie," Jack said gently, "let's pray. Come on, I'll do it. You listen."

Deep inside Kylie, some inner sense trembled. This man was so strong and decisive, so much in command, and he was going to pray? Kylie's heart tightened. When, in the four years that she had been a Christian, had any man suggested prayer? Yet Jack did it so naturally. She bit her lip, unnerved and confused.

His quiet words broke through her panic as he prayed for protection, courage, and the strength to face battles and know that God was with them. He spoke with such intimate confidence that almost against her will Kylie was comforted. The One to whom Jack spoke with such familiarity—calling Him Father—was the King of all ages.

The old niggling doubt resurfaced. Nowhere was it written that the King of all ages guaranteed anyone's physical safety. No reason to think He would come through for them in the way they wanted. Or in any way they would even recognize.

⁂

Mary Chiu lived on the seventeenth floor of a resettlement estate in Kowloon, built in the late 1950s on the site of squalid slums. The buildings rose like untidy stacks of little boxes, the window openings barred with iron even on the highest floors. Today, with the rain beating against the building, the TV antennas and laundry that habitually hung like untucked shirts from windows and balconies had been taken inside, but Kylie found that even more disheartening: the building pulled in upon itself, defenses raised as if under attack, and the rain falling down the sides of the building looked too much like tears.

The government provided these low-rent apartments in which thousands and thousands of Chinese people lived. Kylie knew that inside the apartments, tiny as they were, the space was probably nevertheless filled with modern possessions. The combined incomes of the many family members allowed people in Hong Kong to purchase televisions, stereos, clothes, electric cookers, air conditioners, and sewing machines—almost everything, in fact, except more space.

With so many people living in the apartment, someone was sure to be in at Mary's flat.

Not Mary, announced Mary's mother after Kylie knocked on the door. From what Kylie could see through the narrow crack allowed by the chain on the door, Mary's mother was tiny and old, both her hair and skin taut against her bones. Like many of the older generation in Hong Kong, she was wearing what Kylie called Chinese pajamas, with a standup collar on the top and baggy pants cut off at mid calf. She looked so unfriendly that Kylie was just as happy that she didn't open the door wider and invite them in.

Her bad humor mushroomed further when Kylie announced she was from Reaves. A torrent of sharp Cantonese poured from the woman, the many tones of this southern dialect making her words sound even harsher. Fluent in both Mandarin and Cantonese, Kylie had no trouble understanding the woman's message, the gist of it being that her daughter had received nothing but trouble from Reaves, that Reaves deserved nothing but curses from the Chiu family, that if Kylie would wait just a minute she would go and get a knife and show Kylie exactly what the Chiu family thought of Reaves.

The thought of the frail Chinese grandmother attacking the strong and capable Jack Sullivan was so comical that Kylie had to struggle for a suitably chastened expression. She truly was sorry for the obvious distress Mary had experienced.

"Where is Mary working now?" Kylie asked.

The woman spat, her aim through the crack mercifully off. If Kylie wanted to see what Reaves had done to her daughter, Kylie could go down to a Kowloon toy factory, where Mary now worked as just another member on a manufacturing line. Discovering another sullied source for ire, she began again to berate Reaves. The idea that a woman who had worked so hard for so many years would have to start again at Mary's age . . . Reaves had a well-defined system of bonuses for long-term employees, and losing this seniority was causing the old woman's latest spate. She concluded her tirade by spitting out the words, "*Che, chuan, dian, jiao, ya . . .*" and leaving Kylie to finish off the old Chinese rhyme.

Seeing Kylie's grimace, the old woman laughed bitterly, knowing she was understood.

Jack took Kylie's arm and pulled her away down the hall. "We'll catch up with Mary later, Kylie. What did she say there at the end that made you frown?"

"A poem, one that my old teacher, Mr. Hu, taught me. Mary's mother must have come originally from the same region as Mr. Hu. She definitely used his dialect."

"What does it mean—the poem?"

"It lists the most reprehensible people in old China, people who enjoyed taking advantage of anyone in adversity: cart drivers, boat owners, innkeepers, chair bearers, and the officials who brutalized people in the old magistrate's courts. The poem goes on: *Wu zui ye gai sha*, which means 'all of them should be slaughtered.' It's bad company that she's put Reaves and Robert in, and I'm not sure I blame her. If Mary was fired unjustly," Kylie said grimly, "I'm going to see that she gets her job back."

"Mary's not dead," Jack said blandly, and when Kylie raised astounded eyes to his, he merely shrugged. "If we're right about Robert, I suspect Mary will consider herself fortunate to be away from Reaves."

Standing inside the high-rise, Kylie drew her jacket more tightly around her, fighting the urge to shudder. How quickly things in life could change! Two weeks ago, she had felt so much in control of her life. Now here she was, waiting for a taxi with Jack Sullivan, worrying that Murray Russell might be dead.

There. She had put words to her worst fear.

It didn't help.

Jack also seemed lost in thought. Determined not to let him see the extent of her fears, Kylie made the call on her cellular phone to Terry Wong's parents. Terry was working in a fast food restaurant near the Repulse Bay beach, on the other side of Hong Kong Island.

Flags near the Cross-Harbour Tunnel were now at Typhoon Signal 3. "That means the storm is somewhere near
Hong Kong," Kylie explained, "within four or five hundred
miles, I think."

"They told me at the hotel this morning," Jack said. "It
was at Signal 1 late last night."

"It might never get higher than three, though it certainly
is raining harder."

"Will the restaurant where Terry works still be open?"

"Probably. No one goes home at Signal 1. A few businesses start closing down at Signal 3, but most let people go
only at Signal 8. They used to have flags for every number
from one to ten, but it was too much. Now they jump from
one to three and then up to eight. Nine and ten are the
worst."

The water was sloshing down on the taxi's windshield,
making it difficult to see until they entered the respite of the
tunnel. Before 1973, when the tunnel was completed, people
on either side of the bay had to watch carefully during typhoon weather, lest they miss the last ferry. At Signal 8, the
ferries tied up for safety in the typhoon shelters; in those days
many residents were stranded on the wrong side of the bay.

Even so, Kylie was glad that Repulse Bay was on Hong
Kong Island, and she wondered briefly if she and Jack should
abandon their investigation until after the storm abated. "We
need to be careful to get back in plenty of time," she said. "I
have a lot to do if a typhoon actually heads this way."

"Such as?"

"Fill the bathtub. The water often stops. Try to water-
proof the air-conditioning vent. Check on candles."

"Because the electricity goes out," Jack provided.

"On lower buildings, people put up shutters to protect
themselves from flying debris, but they rarely do on high-rises
like mine."

"You sound very calm."

Kylie smiled deprecatingly. "Perhaps because I've never
been in a bad typhoon. They don't come around that often.

Only a few times have I seen Signal 10, and then only briefly. I understand the worst danger—'' she shuddered—''the worst danger in the Mid-Levels where I live is from mudslides, or 'landslips' as people here call them. In the most recent Signal 8 typhoon, three people were killed in landslips, probably because of all the rain we'd had before the typhoon. The ground was already saturated. The roads on the Peak and over to Repulse Bay were the hardest hit.''

Knowing that Jack was watching her, Kylie shrugged off her concerns and managed a smile. ''Anyway, you'll be safe. The hotels are well-equipped to handle the storm. In fact, many expatriates have typhoon parties. They gather in the big hotel lobbies, eat, drink, talk, dance, and then go home when it's all over.''

''You'll be okay?''

''Of course,'' she said dismissively. Did he imagine because she needed help in clearing up this problem at work that she couldn't handle a little bad weather?

They rode in silence then until they had skirted around the island, past the Aberdeen Harbour with its typhoon shelter for boats, and passing close to the entrance of Ocean Park. The complex included the world's largest oceanarium, a huge amusement park, a swimming area, and much more. Among its bragging points were the world's longest outdoor escalator and the world's longest roller coaster.

The Repulse Bay beach, always popular, was abandoned today, due to the gathering storm. With any luck, Terry would be free to talk to them.

The rain was falling in torrents now, with the wind blowing so hard that the water came down at a sharp angle, almost sideways. Instinctively, as they drew up at the Western-style carryout where Terry worked, Kylie reached for her umbrella.

Jack, seeing her frustration, raised questioning eyes.

''My umbrella,'' she explained. ''In my carry-all.''

And he nodded, understanding completely.

His immediate comprehension halted her momentarily, as she counted out payment for the taxi, for it signaled an intimacy she hadn't counted on. Inevitably, given the circum-stances, Jack Sullivan was gaining a knowledge of Kylie that she wouldn't have granted in any other circumstance.

"Lady. You gonna pay?" The taxi driver's words broke into Kylie's reverie, and she held out her hand with the money.

Inside, she looked helplessly down at her sodden clothes. The rain had drenched her skirt and blouse, plastering the material against her body and curling wisps of hair against her face. Catching Jack's amused expression, Kylie shook her head ruefully, knowing that her carefully groomed appear-ance was only a memory. She withdrew a few paper napkins from a dispenser on the table to wipe moisture from her face.

The restaurant was almost empty.

"Well," she said resignedly, "let's get this over with. Terry will be easier to talk to, I suspect, than Mary Chiu. He's the type to land on his feet and will probably find some ad-vantage to working here instead of a stuffy old warehouse."

The clerks behind the counter were discussing the weather, wondering when the next signal would go up. They knew that at Signal 8, the restaurant would close and they could go home.

"Is Terry Wong around?" Kylie asked.

A shout toward the back, and within moments, Terry ap-peared.

~~~

"Sure," he said, "I can talk. Why don't you go ahead and order, and I'll come around in a few minutes? I have a few things to finish up in the back to get ready if the restaurant closes."

While they waited, they ordered one of the "lunchboxes" full of Chinese food that the restaurant served. At first, both Kylie and Jack were silent. Outside the wind was picking up; the rain pounded against the glass at the front of the restau-rant. At their table, Kylie carefully unwrapped her food, but

Jack left his unopened. He was obviously more interested in Kylie than in the food.

"What's the matter?" she finally asked.

He grinned slowly, lifting his eyebrows provocatively. "I was wondering what you would look like with your hair down."

Kylie wrinkled her nose in disgust. "A gentleman would never comment on the appearance of a woman who had just run through a windstorm!"

"I, however, don't feel much like a gentleman at the moment. If I had a camera, I'd save your picture for posterity. Definitely a collector's item: Kylie Austin, windblown, typhoon-drenched . . . and still beautiful!"

She looked down, terribly flustered, and he gave a soft chuckle. She tried to force her features into a cool expression but the color in her cheeks betrayed her, and every time she looked up her eyelashes fluttered down again to hide her confusion. The silence between them lengthened, exaggerated by the sounds of the workers behind the counter and the wind and rain outside.

Finally he spoke. "So tell me about yourself, Ms. Kylie Austin. Maybe with your hair at least a little looser, you'll let yourself relax in other ways. I'd like to know you better."

She cast another astonished glance across the table at him, but he appeared unfazed, his eyes filled with challenge. He obviously realized how closely she guarded her privacy, and yet what he said was true. They had been together only one day—one day?—and yet in that time he had more than earned the right to at least a few of her secrets.

For a moment, she let her chopsticks explore the rice and vegetables and tiny pieces of meat in her lunch container. She finally put them down and took a deep breath. "What do you want to know?"

"My dear Miss Austin!" he began loftily, and then leaned forward, eyes intent. "If you don't realize yet, Kylie, that almost everything about you intrigues me, you do yourself a disservice! For starters, where did all your knowledge of Asia come from?"

"Asia?"

"Yes. How do you know so instinctively how to bridge the two worlds in your life, switching so fluidly from language to language, culture to culture?"

She sat back more comfortably in her chair. At least this question she could answer freely.

"My father and I came to Hong Kong when I was fourteen, at the end of my eighth grade. He enrolled me in the International School here in Hong Kong, but the school I had just come from was awful. Junior high! The social games the kids played bored me. Classes bored me. I felt like I was dying. So here in Hong Kong, all summer, I begged my father to let me stay home from school.

"Even now, I'm amazed that he agreed," she said, "though not right away, of course. First he tested me. One morning at breakfast he picked up a plate and said, 'Let's see how well you can learn on your own. Search out the provenance of this dish.' I didn't even know what *provenance* meant, but I found out. For days he kept me working on that dish. Once I'd located the factory it came from, I had to find out the process of making it, and determine why that particular brand carried the value it did, and on and on. Almost three weeks on that one plate, and then one day he announced that he had hired a tutor for me, and I didn't need to go to school again until college."

"A Chinese tutor, I presume."

"Yes, Mr. Hu. In the afternoon, working on my own, my father made me study Western authors." Kylie gazed pensively out at the pounding rain, blind to the rivulets of water pouring down the window panes. The memories of her father's demands deflated her even now. She had gone from minimal challenges in her junior high school to unmeetable ones with her father. Even a full scholarship to Yale had not seemed to please him.

Kylie mentally shrugged away old disappointments and

smiled across at Jack. "The work in the afternoon was a regular college prep program. It was Mr. Hu, in the mornings, who gave me Hong Kong. He was a real Chinese scholar, so old that he just missed earning his scholarly status under the old Confucian system of testing."

Jack shook his head, unsure of what she meant.

"Under the Emperor," Kylie explained, "before the revolution in 1912, a man went through a rigorous series of tests to earn scholarly status. He sat for several weeks in a tiny hut, under the most rigorous conditions, writing essays on topics chosen by the Emperor himself. The successful graduate was designated a scholar, a *xiu cai*. Poor Mr. Hu; I think he always regretted not earning that status."

"And what did Mr. Hu teach you?"

"He taught me the language—Mandarin in my formal classes, and how to read and write Chinese characters. Those are skills, by the way, that I've been almost daily thankful for. China has so many dialects that from town to town it's often hard to communicate. Fortunately the written language spans the country. Being able to read and write Chinese characters truly opens the country to a visitor."

"That must have taken hours."

She smiled. "I'm no calligrapher! Sometimes my spoken language is almost too perfect—it upsets Chinese people to hear such a pure form of Chinese from a foreigner. But when they see my pathetic attempt to write Chinese characters, they regain all their face and more!"

"What else did Mr. Hu teach you?"

"What I know and understand of Chinese culture came from him. Museums, folk medicine, temples, soothsayers— he took me to them all. In the morning, I spent the early hours sitting with him in Chinese teahouses. Do you know what I'm referring to? In Hong Kong people carry little cages with finches through the park, giving the bird some fresh air and sunshine, and then retire to a teahouse, where they hang the cage from hooks in the ceiling, and sit and chat for hours.

"At first he made me angry. He gave me a stool and told

me to sit against a wall near his little table, while he gossiped with his old cronies. When he wanted anything he would flick up his hand like this . . ." Kylie demonstrated for Jack. "And then I'd have to get up from my stool and get whatever he needed. 'Beck and call' says it all, believe me. Very old world, Mr. Hu was. Then gradually I realized what a privilege he was granting me, sharing his world with me, and as I learned the language I realized he and his friends weren't gossiping at all. They were having some pretty serious discussions about politics and philosophy and religion and history. I found it all utterly fascinating. In the process I picked up the Cantonese dialect, which by the way I speak with the slang of a native. No one's threatened when I slip into that language."

"You didn't miss all the fun of high school?" Her look made him laugh. "No, I suppose you didn't. Well, very interesting, just as I expected."

Aware of his regard, Kylie found herself blushing—like the schoolgirls she had sought to escape, she thought with chagrin. To cover her confusion, Kylie rose quickly to throw away the cold remains of their lunch. Jack hadn't even opened his, and Kylie had barely touched hers.

Soon after she returned to the table, Terry joined them. "So what you want know of my dismal conclusion at Reaves?" he asked them in English for Jack's sake. "Not much help now, I think! But better late than never."

Kylie responded, "Just tell me what happened, please, Terry."

Terry grinned again, no less ironically, and then shrugged. "I like better here anyway. More babes! The beach—is close, you know? Okay, so Reaves. Here is what happen. Things go on like normal, you know? Shipments come in, packing, whole routine. Then one day, I notice old Robert—what a mother chicken—he acts strange. We come in and shipment already unpacked. He come in during night, I think, and unpack them. But certain shipment only, you know? Not all shipment. So I start watching, but I can't tell why."

"And that's when you were released?" Kylie asked.

"You mean *fired*? No, not right then. One day, I think maybe I look at invoices. Maybe Robert steal pieces." He shrugged and then grinned again. "Yeah, okay, I think maybe I get his job, you know? But I no spy, right? I get caught very first time. Tiffany come in, she see me going through files, she tell Robert. So now I at beach. No big deal."

"You didn't see the invoices?" Jack asked.

"No. And what can I find, anyway? I think 'promotion!' and don't think very smart, you know? Crazy. If I get invoice before shipment, then check pieces when we repack, then I know if Robert stealing." He shrugged, a true sanguine. "No matter."

"And what happened to Mary Chiu?"

Terry gave a skeptical snort. "Who know? Not me! Mary don't tell anyone anything! One day, she there, the next, gone. Who know why?" He glanced at his watch. "Well, gotta go! You guys get home, too! I just hear on radio. Typhoon headed straight for Hong Kong. Signal 8 up, but they say not for long. Storm getting worse. Ciao!"

It took them a few minutes to find a taxi, and even then Kylie had to offer double the fare to keep from sharing with another couple. As the driver sped around the island, Kylie gazed out at the windy scene, her own thoughts a mirror to the confusion outside.

Where had she been during the time Terry talked about? Taking trips into China, searching out new markets, carrying out the upper end of the business, while all along the process was crumbling beneath her. But shouldn't she have noticed what was going on?

"Kylie?"

She turned to give Jack a wry smile. "Better late than never is small comfort at this point!"

"It's human nature to trust, Kylie, until that trust is violated. Look for a balance, if you want, but don't veer further off into cynicism."

Her eyes narrowed and resentment welled up inside her. "You thought all along I was too naive for this job. I find no

STILLPOINT

satisfaction in discovering you were right!"

"No," he said gently. "I wasn't right. Look, we'll take it
for granted that not all your colleagues are in on this. That
would mean at least one person and possibly two other people
have been duped as well. You were the one Murray called.
You were the one who alerted Harry. Hold onto that, Kylie.
You're the one who is getting to the bottom of this thing."

He lifted his hand to her face, and very carefully, almost
tenderly, as if recording the action in his memory, he freed a
strand of hair that was stuck to her cheek, freshly wet from
the rain. "No apologies, Kylie Austin."

She blinked. Her own father might have said the same
thing, though never so gently. From her father, a demand;
from Jack, reassurance. Her eyes grew wide, and his own
darkened in response, intent and searching, and very gentle.

She lifted her hand slowly to his chest, laying her palm
against it. *His body is warm*, she thought. And then, *I should
push him away.* But when he slipped his hand behind her
neck, threading his fingers into her hair, and then pulled her
closer and kissed her tenderly, her best intentions vanished in
a shock of sensation, sweet and sharp and utterly consuming.

"I go home now!" the taxi driver declared, his loud words
interrupting the kiss.

"What?" Kylie asked dazedly.

"You get out here," the driver said. "I go home now.
Storm much worse."

They were at Kylie's flat.

"But this man has to get to the Mandarin!" Kylie objected.

The driver was determined. "Not in this taxi. Go, now.
Out, out. I go home."

Still in a daze, Kylie paid the fare, and they both got out
into the driving rain.

• 83 •

Six

~~~
≈≈≈≈≈≈≈≈≈≈≈
~~~

"Y ou *can't* stay here!"

Jack stood with Kylie in the lobby of her apartment building, sheltered from the increasingly frenzied storm outside. Around them, residents hurried past, carrying in late purchases of groceries and candles and other supplies. Most of them were cheerful, the typhoon as yet still a source of high drama and excitement.

Kylie didn't seem to notice them. She faced Jack, her eyes a little wild. Now finally, strands of hair hung completely loose over her shoulders. In one hand she held her dripping shoes; in the other she pointed outside toward the storm. "You have to go!" she told him.

Jack wondered what she expected him to do. Walk to the Mandarin?

Her tirade gathered force. "Don't you know what people will say? All the effort I've put into maintaining a witness, all the flak I've taken, and now you're going to stay overnight! I can't believe this is happening. Harry and his schemes! This is ridiculous!"

If Jack wanted her guard down, his wish had been granted, and he couldn't be more dismayed. To have this happen after he himself had so lost his head. He should never have kissed her. Talk about pitfalls! It would take a long time to regain lost ground, and now he was being forced upon her.

He stepped back from her slightly, hoping to diminish whatever threat he posed for her. "Fine. I won't stay here if you don't want me to. Just tell me how to get to the Mandarin."

She glared at him as if it were all his fault. "This is hopeless!"

"Then how about if I stay with a neighbor?"

She became still, the solution a new consideration. As she thought about this possibility, she slowly became more reasonable. Finally, she shook her head. "No. They'd think I was crazy—a real Puritan—to put so much importance on appearances. Or that you really were a threat, and I know you're not." She sighed loudly. "Well, fine then. We better get going, or they'll close down the lifts, and we'll have to walk up twenty flights of stairs."

A woman about Kylie's age emerged from the elevator as they were getting on. "Kylie, you're finally home! We're having a typhoon potluck in my flat later. Come down when you can!"

"Where are you going?" Kylie asked.

"Out to my car. I left something in it. See you later, okay?"

"She lives down the hall from me," Kylie explained as the elevator started rising.

"Australian?"

"Yes. Sonia went out once or twice with Murray, a while back. I haven't said anything to her yet about . . . his leaving."

Sensing a sudden rise in her anxiety again, Jack let the rest of the elevator ride pass in silence, wishing he could put his arm around her and hold her close again. Like so many people who kept a tight rein on their emotions, now that those emotions had broken free, Kylie seemed to be having a hard time reining them back in. If only she felt more comfortable with him. If only he could be more of a comfort to her.

On her floor, it seemed almost like a party. Most apartment doors were open, and neighbors flitted from room to room, exchanging advice and lamenting the sorry state of their groceries. Someone asked if anyone had extra toilet paper. Kylie smiled good-naturedly as a man in his thirties commented on her drenched clothes.

"Do you know all these people?" Jack asked as Kylie unlocked her door.

"Barely—except the lady across the corridor. Everyone knows Nell Finnegan. Everyone knows everything there is to know about Nell Finnegan."

Jack smiled, understanding. A woman who loved being alone across from a woman who couldn't believe anyone could feel that way. It must be a perpetual struggle for Kylie.

"You'll know them all a lot better before this typhoon is over," he said. "I think you'll find your worry about being alone with me wasted."

"I wasn't worried."

"You know what I mean."

"I suppose."

In the apartment, Jack said lightly, "You go change; shower while you have the chance. Just tell me again what you have to do to get ready, and I'll get started."

"First, the water containers. If you want to start on that, you can. Use whatever you find in the kitchen. I'll need to set out candles, and check batteries in my flashlight. I'll get some plastic sheeting and duct tape for the air conditioning vent. Should we pull things away from the windows? I'm not really sure."

"Your neighbors will have suggestions," Jack said calmly, and he was right.

As Jack was filling Kylie's one pitcher and her pots and pans with water, he couldn't help glancing at the windows in Kylie's apartment. The six large windows spanning the living room and part of the dining room seemed incredibly vulnerable to the wind; how could something as fragile as glass withstand the force of a typhoon?

Someone knocked on Kylie's apartment door, still standing open. When Jack went to see who was knocking, he found an older woman there. She was perhaps sixty, plump, with rosy cheeks and fluffy gray hair. Seeing Jack, she looked him over in surprise, eyes agog.

"*Hello!*" she exclaimed, drawing out the word provocatively. "I'm Nell Finnegan!" She stepped purposefully into the room, obviously intending to stay long enough to satisfy her curiosity about Kylie's masculine visitor.

Jack smiled to himself. So this was Kylie's inquisitive neighbor.

"Jack Sullivan," he said, holding out his hand, amused to have her hold his just a little longer than necessary. "I'm a business colleague of Kylie's."

"Is that so, dear? How very *nice* for Kylie! Where is Kylie anyway? I thought I saw her come in a minute ago."

"We got caught in the storm. She's changing. Since you're here, Mrs. Finnegan, perhaps you can tell me—is there something we're supposed to do about the windows?"

"Like what, dear?"

"Kylie mentioned something about shutters? Does the building provide those?"

"No, dear, I'm afraid not. This glass is supposed to be strong enough, don't you know?" And then with a giggle, "But I wouldn't sit too close to it!"

Mrs. Finnegan must have decided that if Jack wasn't going to be more forthcoming about himself, she would tell him all about herself, so as Jack pulled furniture away from the window areas, Mrs. Finnegan talked. She and her husband, Edward, had lived off and on in Hong Kong for "many, many years, dear" working for the British government. "We were here in 1971, the last big typhoon, but the worst weather we've seen wasn't actually a typhoon. It was the monsoons in 1966. Edward and I were *quite* young then, as you can imagine."

Jack carefully kept his face blank to indicate he couldn't calculate ages very well, and Mrs. Finnegan laughed her girlish giggle. "Well, yes, dear, we are a little older now. Edward's retiring next year! Anyway, don't you know, dear, we had so much rain that year, all at once, that buildings here in the

Mid-Levels collapsed, literally collapsed! Even a high-rise like this one—the foundation pillars were knocked out and the entire building crumbled. People lost their lives! And the property damage! The water poured down the streets so fast that cars jammed up at the bottom, like a pile of toys! I can't tell you how awful it was."

Finding Jack close by, Mrs. Finnegan took advantage of the opportunity and patted him on the arm. "That won't happen now, of course, dear. The city's spent a fortune since then on shoring up the Peak where slips are likely to occur."

"I'll have to tell Kylie," Jack said. "She's been worried about that."

"Oh, of course we *worry*. We wouldn't be human, now, would we, if we didn't do that?"

From her bedroom doorway, Kylie spoke, her voice calm and composed. "Mrs. Finnegan, does your husband have some old sweat pants and a sweat shirt that Jack can borrow? Jack was trying to get back to the Mandarin when the storm veered in our direction."

"Yes, dear, I know. Jack has explained everything. I doubt Edward's clothes would be big enough for Jack here, but Callum McGrath, two stories down, is about the same size—those Scots, you know, dear, are a dour lot, but they do grow their men big on the highlands! I'll just tell Edward where I'm going and then toddle down the hall and see what I can find!"

"Better than the BBC," Kylie said after Mrs. Finnegan had left. "Now the whole building will know you're here."

But she seemed resigned to Jack's presence. She was looking out the windows at the sky outside. "I can't believe how dark it is. Usually, even at midnight, the city is bright."

Jack thought she looked smaller somehow and more vulnerable. No shoes, he realized, and no makeup. She was wearing faded jeans and a bulky blue sweater, although it wasn't cold. Was it nerves that were making her chilled? Her hair was still wet but hung neatly now to her shoulders. Incongruously, on her feet she wore wild, jungle-print socks.

She must have seen the direction of his gaze and his consequent smile. "A gift from a college friend," she informed him and then moved toward the kitchen where she filled the teakettle. "I suggest you follow Mrs. Finnegan down to the McGraths'. She'll start talking and never get back to us, and I'm sure you'd like a shower before everything quits."

"On my way!"

The festive atmosphere continued in the hallway, a natural defense against the dreadful power at work outside. If the destruction turned out to be minimal, these high spirits might very well leave most of the people in the high-rise with almost pleasant memories of the storm—though Jack suspected that few people who had lived through the torrential rains of 1966 remembered them with any fondness.

He walked down the two flights of stairs and found Mrs. Finnegan standing at the entrance of an apartment almost directly below Kylie's. By his calculations the floor had four, maybe six, apartments. Kylie's apartment was on the northwest corner, facing the harbor. The McGraths' was on the southwest corner, facing the Peak.

"Oh, Jack, dear," Mrs. Finnegan greeted him. "Fiona is just getting some clothes for you. Poor thing; Callum didn't make it back from Kowloon in time. He'll spend the duration at the Shangri-La."

"How unfortunate."

Mrs. Finnegan chuckled gleefully. "Though not for Callum—don't you know? He'll have the time of his life! But poor Fiona's worried about landslips." She waved a hand through the door toward the windows in the McGraths' apartment. "The mountain does seem very much *there*, doesn't it?"

It definitely was, covered with vegetation, divided periodically by concrete reinforcements designed to halt landslides. But something closer caught Jack's attention.

"What's the scaffolding for?"

"They're doing some work on the west side of the building," Mrs. Finnegan said, sounding disgusted. "Why they choose typhoon season I'll never know."

Jack frowned. He could well imagine the damage if the structure broke loose. "Will it survive the storm?"

"One never knows, dear. Ah, here we are."

Fiona McGrath was only slightly younger than Mrs. Finnegan, but taller and thin, with iron gray hair and sharp, observant eyes. The two friends stood side by side, looking Jack over. It was a head-to-toe assessment, making him feel very much like a small boy dressed up for church, waiting approval. He had to fight the compulsion to stand up straighter and apologize for his damp and rumpled shirt.

"Kylie Austin's friend," Mrs. Finnegan said. She gave the word *friend* just enough emphasis to make Jack wonder how many men Kylie showed up with. Not many, apparently.

As Mrs. McGrath handed the clothes over to Jack, Mrs. Finnegan again reached over and put her hand warmly on Jack's arm. "You *will* come down to Sonia's later, won't you, for our little get-together?"

"If we can, Mrs. Finnegan," Jack answered and left the two women standing there, watching him head back toward the stairway.

"Call me Nell!" Mrs. Finnegan called after him.

⟨∭⟩

Kylie was in the kitchen when he returned to her apartment. She saw the lingering smile in his eyes.

"Enjoy yourself?" she asked drily.

"Yes. A charming woman." Kylie rolled her eyes and Jack laughed.

"I can imagine," she said.

"I take it Nell responds like that to most men, is that what you're saying? Not just me?"

Kylie let her gaze wander over him, taking in the trim body and strong muscles, and then rolled her eyes again. He almost laughed aloud: talk about a backhanded compliment. She couldn't hide her blush.

She turned back to her work without responding to his questions. "I'm going to make some supper while the electricity's still on."

"Okay. I'll take that shower," he told her and then made his way to the windows in her bedroom. He wanted a closer look at that scaffolding. The apparently fragile structure ran up and down the building outside the southwest apartments. While it never actually reached Kylie's windows, if a large enough piece broke off it could swing around toward the large windows in her living area, possibly breaking them under the force of the wind. He wondered if he should mention the possibility to Kylie, and yet, Fiona McGrath, seemingly under far greater threat, had taken no precautions. He decided not to worry her.

Like the rest of her apartment, Kylie's bedroom was spare and plain. A simple bedstead, dresser, and chair, with tans and creams throughout. Along one wall, a computer table, scrupulously tidy. The only decoration was a sprig of silk mimosa in a bud vase on her dresser. The bathroom, likewise, had no flowery shower curtain, no little bowl of soaps like Jack's mother liked, nothing extra anywhere. In fact, Kylie's entire apartment was almost Japanese in its simplicity. Perhaps Japan had been another stop on her father's diplomatic journey.

If not for the jungle-print socks, Jack would have wondered if Kylie's life held any whimsy at all. Why had she worn them tonight?

When he came out from the shower, she had shut the apartment door, cutting them off from the camaraderie outside in the hallway. Propriety at war with privacy, Jack decided, and her instinct to withdraw had won out.

She was standing at one of the windows, holding back the drape so she could look outside.

"What do you see?" he asked, coming to stand beside her. She lifted the drape a little more to reveal the city. Lights still shone dimly through the pounding rain, but the view was far shortened because of the storm.

"The rain seems to be coming from every direction," she

said, "and every now and then—there, did you see it?—a leaf hits the pane. From the trees on the peaks behind us, I suppose, which means the wind is circling all the way around to this side of the building. Listen! The wind is all around us."

Sounding very much like an express train, the wind rushed past the building, battering the rain against the windowpanes, driving it relentlessly toward where Kylie and Jack stood behind their fragile glass barrier.

"I wish it weren't so dark," she said, her voice troubled. "I wish I could see what's happening. There's such massive power out there, and I can only see the rain that's two feet from me. I hate it, being so cut off. Oh! Did you see that?"

And of course he had. Even as they watched, building by building, block by block, Hong Kong lost its lights. In mere moments, the city was plunged into nearly total darkness, and the room behind them as well. Kylie hugged herself, drawing back sharply against Jack's chest. Instinctively he put his arms around her, and she let herself lean against him for a moment, savoring the cocoon of security he wrapped around her, his torso strong and solid against her back. His breath on her cheek was a gentle contrast to the unruly wind, the muscles of his arms safe and sure.

Shouts from the hallway ended the moment; footsteps and laughter as people tried to get back to their own flats. Kylie pulled abruptly away from Jack and turned back toward the room, groping toward the table.

"Where are those candles you mentioned?" he asked.

"Here." Kylie lit a match. In a second, a candle was burning. "I have flashlights, too. Let me get you one. Did you fill the bathtub?"

"All done."

"Then let's eat while the food's still hot. Without the electric stove or microwave, everything's going to be cold from now on."

By candlelight, she set out dishes for the meal. "I didn't have much on hand," she said apologetically. "I rarely eat in, I'm afraid. I have some canned goods from who knows when, and a few things in the refrigerator. Sorry."

The fare included Ramen noodle soup, English wheat-meal biscuits, oranges, and some black olives. "You see what I keep in my kitchen," she said with a small laugh. "I have some breakfast items, too, but I thought we'd save the corn flakes and bagels for the morning."

As Jack said a prayer, Kylie had her own thoughts to bring before God. Why had He brought *this* man to help her through the storm? She readily conceded Jack's strengths. He was patient, confident, godly, and courageous, but even so—why this man, whose kiss had touched her deeply, sending a pulse of longing through her that was at once shattering and exciting? Whose arms around her felt so good and whose touch made her fingertips tingle?

Interesting choice, God.

Kylie had a brief sensation of Him smiling, and she let out a slow breath. She was grateful, really, in spite of her confusion. With the loss of electricity, the storm had invaded the room now, the darkness foreboding, unknown dangers seeming to lurk in the shadowed corners of the room. Outside the wind whistled and moaned, heaving rain against the windows and walls, heightening her sensation of being under attack.

Without Jack there, she would be in bed now, her body curled up as small as it would go, the covers pulled up almost over her head and a pillow hiding the rest of her.

She heard Jack finish his prayer and opened her eyes, clasping her trembling hands beneath the table. Her eyes widened in horror. Ever so slowly, from side to side, the soup was sloshing, back and forth, back and forth, in dreadful time with the building itself. Kylie gripped the edge of the table in a woeful effort to stop the movement.

Even by candlelight Jack's vision still proved sharp. He stood, poured her soup back into the pot, and began piling up bowls and spoons and glasses.

"What are you doing?" she exclaimed.

"We can't stay here by ourselves. We're going to pack all this onto a tray and take it down to . . . Sonia's, wasn't it?"

"Oh, Jack, I'd rather not, really."

"Yes, you really would, Kylie Austin. In a situation like this we need encouragement. Take my word for it."

"Misery loves company?"

"How about 'we're all in this together'? We don't have to stay long, but I think we should go." Even as he spoke he was piling dishes and a flashlight into her hands and picking up the pot of soup. "Come on, Kylie. Let's not let it get cold. I'll come back and get the rest."

Later, as she sat beside Jack on Sonia's couch laughing at one of Mrs. Finnegan's stories, she happened to catch Jack watching her and smiled. Leaning toward him she whispered, "You were right. Thank you. This is a lot better than staying in the flat."

He pulled a face. "I'm hurt that you would prefer their company to mine."

"This way I have both," she shot back and blinked her eyelashes at him.

Then she had to wonder—was the way he looked at her part of the old "charade" or did he really enjoy being with her? Either way, the effect of his smile was the same.

Besides Sonia, Fiona McGrath, and the Finnegans, the group included Gunter and Elsa Vogl—a German business-man and his wife, and two single brothers from England, Malcolm and Nigel Hopkins. After dinner, eaten quickly while everyone's offerings were still hot, the group sat around the living room swapping stories. During this time, Kylie learned that Jack had grown up in Harry Reaves' hometown, had first met Harry through church, and had worked at Reaves during summer vacations in high school and college. After graduating from Harvard Business School, he had been ready to rise in the ranks to vice-president.

"I suppose Harry Reaves has no sons," Gunter drawled.

"He did, but none who wanted to go into business."

"So you're the heir apparent."

Jack nodded briefly. "Only for the position of CEO, not for the riches, I'm afraid."

"Riches enough, I would think," Sonia said quietly to Kylie in the kitchen. "You should keep your eye on that one!"

They were spooning up ice cream from the Hopkins' freezer. When Kylie didn't respond to Sonia's teasing, Sonia went on to ask, "How's Murray doing?" And then, with no premonition, "We're taking our holiday together this year in Japan, you know."

It was a moment before Sonia noticed Kylie's slack jaw.

"Why are you looking like that? We're not all nuns, you know. Murray and I are all right together."

"When did you arrange this vacation?" Kylie asked, trying to keep her voice steady.

"Oh, a few weeks ago. I've been in Sydney on business this week. I have two more weeks of work scheduled here and then my holiday starts. Is there a problem? Murray said he could get off. Has something happened?"

Sonia must have finally noticed Kylie's expression because she stopped serving ice cream and was staring at Kylie.

"Something has happened, hasn't it?"

"Murray's disappeared," Kylie said. "His parents think he's gone 'walkabout.'"

"No!" Sonia said. "Murray wouldn't do that! We're all set!"

Jack must have heard Murray's name; he came over to hear the conversation.

Kylie explained what Murray's roommates had said. "If I hear anything, I'll be sure and pass it on to you. Will you tell me if you hear from him?"

Sonia wasn't fooled. "You think something's happened to him, don't you? Why?"

"Were you close?" Jack asked.

"No, not really. Chums, you know. Did some things together. Nice to hear Australian once in a while, let the old twang come out." She made a face. "You're not going to tell me why you're worried, are you?"

"We don't know much more than you do, Sonia, but I'll tell you as soon as we do."

"Well, thanks, Kylie, I suppose."

Shortly after this, Kylie and Jack went back to her flat, the old worries crowding in again and ruining the party for Kylie.

She immediately began to put away the remnants of their contributions to the typhoon potluck, standing at the kitchen sink washing dishes in cold water, being careful to use as little as possible. *He probably thinks I'm compulsive*, she thought as he came to take a towel and dry the few things for her. *How can I explain how good it feels to do at least this one familiar thing?* She gave a sour little smile. *How bad can things be, really, if I can still clean my kitchen?*

"I'm so sorry this happened—your having to be here, I mean," she said as he moved around her, putting things away. "I'm sure you'd be much more comfortable at the Mandarin. I should have paid closer attention and gotten you back in time."

"I don't mind, Kylie."

"No, really. And I'm not even prepared to feed you."

"It's okay."

When the dishes were done, she turned from the sink, wondering what to do with him now. "Music?" she asked. "I have batteries and a CD player. Would you like to listen to some music?"

"Sure. Put in a CD and then come sit down. Let's take the chance while we have it to put Reaves and porcelain and questions about smuggling aside and just relax."

"What kind of music?"

"You choose."

Her taste ran mostly to Baroque, but with the storm so wild outside, she felt a sudden craving for Tchaikovsky. For a few minutes as the music swelled through the darkened room they sat silently together on the couch, neither speaking, merely listening, breathing in the music.

Kylie thought afterward that if they hadn't been sitting

side by side on the couch she never would have said so much about herself. Face-to-face she would have worried too much about how he was responding to her, especially because of the kiss. It already seemed a long time ago, that kiss, with the violence of the storm and the darkness making a barrier between her and the sensation of his lips against hers. Here in the semidarkness, their legs stretched out onto the coffee table, she felt none of the panic that kiss might have caused under other circumstances. They were merely spectators together, watching the drama that the storm had served up for them.

He asked her first about inconsequential things, like how she survived with so little in her kitchen.

"I eat breakfast here," she said, "but never cook anything else. Lunch at my desk or with a client; dinner often the same. On the rare nights I come home early, I get carryout. Why cook for just me when I can buy such good food ready-made? What about you?"

"When I'm home, I cook."

"It's a hobby," she said, accusingly.

"I admit it. What do you do for fun?"

She couldn't think of an answer immediately. So much of her time was consumed by work. "I take classes. Ceramics right now, with a private instructor."

"To help in your work."

"Yes. But I enjoy it."

"Harry said you haven't been a Christian for very long."

"Four years this last spring."

"Tell me how it happened."

She took a deep breath. It hadn't taken him long to get to the most serious topic of all. She stalled for a moment, and the sounds outside intensified. Would she really rather be thinking about the storm? Surely anything was better.

"I was working for a rival company," she finally began, "as an assistant much like Lily. I don't make close friends easily, but one of the other assistants took an interest in me. Justine Leung. She was sweet, outgoing, friendly—well, I suppose the only kind of person who would stick with me until I opened up a little. I know I'm a private person. And she was a Christian. I knew she had strong ethical standards. It was more than just not drinking or swearing. It was her attitude about life, somehow, that was different. She didn't put down the other workers, even though our business is pretty competitive. We were all hoping to rise through the ranks, but Justine actually helped the very people who were in competition for her job and for the jobs she probably hoped to get. All my life, I've been taught to watch my back. My father taught me skepticism above all else. Believe the worst about people, expect the worst. Everyone looks out for his own interests; it's our natural condition and it's sentimental to believe otherwise. Until I met Justine, I never had reason to question that teaching. Even now it's so practical. I can't ever quite discount it."

Jack grunted softly. "Sad, but I can believe it."

"One day, Justine was accused of stealing a very expensive jade pendant. All evidence pointed to her. She was in exactly the wrong place at the wrong time, and it was only her word that she didn't take it. They didn't have proof, of course, because she hadn't actually taken it, but her future in the company was ruined and she was told quite explicitly to begin looking for another position. Within a week, however, I found out who had actually taken the pendant. I was sitting in a restaurant with a friend, and this guy was in the next booth. He was bragging to someone about pinning the crime on Justine. I couldn't believe it. I went to Justine and told her to confront the guy, to fight her dismissal, that I would help her. She wouldn't do it. She said the damage had been done; we had no proof; things would work out in the end. Justice would be served eventually, she said. I couldn't believe it! How stupid she seemed to me.

"But day after day she continued working, knowing that no one trusted her. One day her time ended and she was out of work. She found a job in a factory, still looking for work with jade somewhere, but through it all so much at peace. I couldn't get that out of my mind. Where was her source of peace? I would have been ruthless in clearing my name. Or at the very least bitterly angry. But not Justine.

"I finally went and found her, and that's when she told me about Jesus. She told me real peace was being right with God, knowing that Jesus' death had removed God's anger from us. We are afraid because we are under the righteous judgment of God. We fear His wrath and transfer that fear to everything else in our lives, constantly watching our backs, always looking out for ourselves. Only when we know His forgiveness, when we know He's on our side, can we learn to rest easy.

"She said something like, 'All my life is in His hands, Kylie, my days, my time, even the breath I breathe. He has promised never to forsake me, and His wisdom is perfect. I can't tell you why this dreadful thing has happened. I may never know. But I will trust Him anyway. If He gave up His Son for me, why would He withhold this job unless it were for my own good?' And she showed me a passage from the Old Testament about fig trees not budding and olive crops failing that ended with something about rejoicing in God anyway."

Jack held up his hand briefly to halt Kylie. He looked up, as if searching his memory, and then recited, " 'Though the fig tree does not bud and there are no grapes on the vines, though the olive crop fails and the fields produce no food, though there are no sheep in the pen and no cattle in the stalls, yet I will rejoice in the Lord, I will be joyful in God my Savior. The Sovereign Lord is my strength; He makes my feet like the feet of deer. He enables me to go on the heights.' "

Kylie had turned slightly to watch Jack reciting the passage, amazed to hear the words come so fluently from memory. "Yes. That's the passage."

"So go on. What happened next?"

"Nothing. Not for a while. It didn't make any sense to me. She was Don Quixote wrapped in a foolish dream."

"And yet?"

"I kept going back to her, finding reason again and again to talk to her about God. I'd tell myself, *absolutely not*, and then find myself sitting in a teahouse somewhere talking about the Cross and sin and forgiveness. The best verse was from Isaiah about His punishment bringing us peace. One day, she leaned toward me as if she were looking straight into my heart and said, 'Kylie, you know you belong to Him. Why do you keep delaying?' And she was right! I did. I knew it. I believed what she said about needing a Savior, about sin and the terrible penalty that I couldn't pay. It was all there. I could no longer call my life my own."

The storm continued unabated outside, the strains of music continued inside, but Kylie sat silently beside Jack, still stunned remembering that moment, the sensation of letting go and falling back and finding Him there—true, strong, real.

She released a quick hard breath and shrugged. "So that's how I became a Christian. I'm not always sure that I want to be one. Life hasn't really gotten any easier for me; I have yet to feel the peace Justine knows. I may have a clearer vision of what life's supposed to be like, but realizing that vision is still just as remote as ever."

He grunted sympathetically but didn't speak.

"You know," she continued, "I look back at my life and see so many ways God was preparing me for His salvation. The books I read—C. S. Lewis and Flannery O'Connor and John Donne's poetry and so much more. And Mr. Hu! There's a sense of divine rightness that I should have first acknowledged Christ in a teahouse. So many of those mornings when Mr. Hu sat in his teahouses after giving his little finch a walk, it was Christianity that he discussed with his old friends. He taught me Mandarin in my tutoring sessions and spoke Cantonese in the teahouse with his friends. The word for *cross* was one of the first words I learned in Cantonese."

"Mr. Hu was a Christian?"

"Led to Jesus by missionaries on the mainland before the revolution."

"Did your father know this?"

Kylie laughed. "Absolutely not! I can't imagine what he would say even now if he knew! But God did. The hand of Providence has left fingerprints all over my life. Mr. Hu was one of the most obvious." She paused again, remembering so many small memories that had taken on eternal significance to her in the last four years. Then she asked, "Was it like that for you? Did you suddenly realize that you were His?"

"I grew up in the faith. I can't remember a time when I wasn't aware of Christ being part of my life."

"To the church pew manner born."

"Well, yes. I went through a time in college when I had to reevaluate my relationship with Christ. Kids go through that stage with everything, deciding what from their parents they'll keep and what they'll change. Diet, clothes, lifestyle, everything. At that time, I had to decide what in my practice of Christianity I would retain. But Jesus Christ was never under review. It's not so much that He belongs to me—"

"I know," Kylie said. "You belong to Him."

"Exactly. Do you still see Justine?"

"Oh, of course. We go to church together. She still teaches me. We talk about God."

"Still in teahouses?"

Kylie smiled. "Not often. She's too busy! She has a good job now representing a consortium of jade carvers. She did come through that trial, just as she said she would."

"Maybe it was for your benefit."

Kylie grunted. "Justine suggested that herself one day before I knew Jesus. I wanted to hit her, I was so angry, but she just laughed. She's very outspoken, as you can probably tell. She said that if Jesus was willing to die for my salvation, what right would she have to regret some little career inconvenience? It was God who gave her the first job and God who would give her another one. The whole experience was awful, but she said she would go through it all again knowing that I would come to know Christ through it."

"She sounds like an amazing woman."

At his words Kylie instinctively wanted to inform Jack that

Justine was married. She bit her lip, both surprised and shamed by her thoughts. She jumped up from the couch to go in search of something to drink.

What was she thinking? To resent even such a small word of praise to another woman? A wave of panic swamped her, more devastating than the howling winds outside. *He's not yours,* she told herself. *He won't ever be yours. Put that thought out of your mind.*

Seven

*J*ey, where'd you go?" Jack called from the living room. "Want something to drink?"

"What have you got?"

"Diet soda and fruit juice, still slightly cold from the fridge, and water—lots of water."

He laughed. "Diet soda will be fine."

When Kylie came back, she gave a rueful smile. "You can probably tell that I'm nowhere near having the kind of faith Justine has."

"How would I know that?"

Kylie turned in surprise. "Because . . . because of everything. I'm a control freak, can't you see that? Everything in order. Everything predictable. You said it yourself—a regular Girl Scout."

"How do you think that happened?"

Kylie didn't answer for a few minutes as she considered how much she wanted to tell him.

"So many surprises," she finally said, "and so few of them good."

He sat beside her patiently, not pressing for more of an answer, willing to wait while she gathered her thoughts.

She took a long, slow breath and gave herself up to her revelations. "We always moved around a lot, as you can imagine, and my father was extremely busy. My mother was like me, I suppose, only more so. She liked her privacy. My father's job put a lot of pressure on her. The social functions were so much more than just social. Each statement, each handshake and greeting and smile was so fraught with meaning and significance. I got a fair sampling of that as I got older. My poor mother couldn't handle it. Being with other people made her nervous and excited. It took her a long time to relax after one of those functions."

Images floated through Kylie's mind: people, smiles, fancy clothes, movement through rooms, music, comments with double and triple meanings, and through it all her mother's face, frozen with tension.

"And?" Jack finally prompted.

"She began to drink. In earnest, I mean. From what I can guess and what I saw it must have been very appealing because it really worked. She relaxed enough to say the right things, smile at the right times. She wasn't so cold and unfriendly anymore. I bet my father was pleased, thinking that she was finally learning to cope."

"But it didn't last."

"Of course not. There's a fine line between being relaxed enough to function and being so relaxed that you can't."

"I'm sorry." After a moment, Jack asked, "How old were you through all this?"

"She started drinking soon after I was born. From the time I can remember, my father was pretty much in denial. I'm sure like most spouses he went through stages—trying to control it and cure it—but looking back it seems like most of the time he just wanted to pretend none of it was happening.

"One of my earliest memories was a house in Washington, D.C. We had a foyer with a coat closet. One afternoon I came in after school—I must have been six or seven—and I closed the door very quietly. I had learned to come in slowly to find out how she was doing on any particular day. Most days a few drinks mellowed her out. My dad could live with that, I think. But some days it affected her differently. That particular day she was throwing books off the shelves, book after book, onto the floor, muttering about trying to find something and smashing figurines and vases down as she cleared the shelves. I was afraid. I crawled into the coat closet and hid until my father came home. He found me there. I guess at that point he couldn't ignore it anymore. Within a week my mother went into a hospital. After that I never let my father know when my mother scared me. I did what I could to get her through those times without my father knowing."

She sighed and leaned her head back, shutting her eyes and shaking her head slightly.

Jack said gently, "All because she was sent away when he found you in the closet? Yet you seem very calm about it now."

Her head came back up, and she looked at him in surprise. "Oh, Jack, I was probably denying the problem too. It's all such an old story and so familiar. Almost any child of an alcoholic can tell you the same one. We go on, becoming more and more focused on everyone else, trying our best to control everything. We spend a lot of time trying to guess what normal life is like, doing our best to create that life for ourselves—and we're just children. How can we possibly handle everything? It's all so predictable. We even have our own acronym: ACOA. Adult Children of Alcoholics."

"And your father?"

"I think, looking back on it, he wanted the half measure—my beautiful mother, warm and gracious. That was what the alcohol usually achieved. I don't think he really wanted her to change. Every time she came out of a rehab program he seemed to sabotage things. I don't really know, of course, but at least when she was drinking he knew what to expect."

"And into all of that came God."

"Yes, I suppose He did. But after so many years of expecting the worst, finding the faith Justine has seems almost impossible. I know He exists. I know He loves me. I know He can help me if He wants to. I just don't *feel* like He will."

"Where's your mother now?"

"When I was twelve my father sent her to another detox program and told her not to come back. I guess he'd had enough. What she made of her life after that was her own choice."

A deep-throated groan came from Jack, an instinctive sound of sympathy. "But that's just what you were trying to prevent."

"That's not the worst of it. Bad enough to feel responsible for her banishment; even worse to find myself being grateful for it. Things did improve after she left. My father, well, he's not a particularly warm and affectionate man, but he did take care of me and give me opportunities for which I am grateful. Life became so much more manageable without her, even if at the time I . . ." She couldn't finish, the agonies for her lost mother too close to the surface.

"You didn't tell me where she is now."

"In San José. As soon as I had a little money, I hired a detective agency to find her. She was there, teaching at a community college, still in a bad way."

"How do you know? Did you get in contact with her?"

"On my way out to Hong Kong the next time, I stopped in California to see her. I went to her flat but couldn't go up. She was leaving for work. She looked so old. Her face was haggard, her hair gray, stuck up in a haphazard bun. She looked awful, and I was so ashamed for her. I just couldn't face her when she looked like that. I couldn't put her through that kind of humiliation."

"Perhaps she's no longer drinking."

"I wouldn't know. I walked away and haven't seen her since." Her voice was a mixture of bitterness and shame. She bit her lip, the tears close, but was afraid she detected something in his posture, some measure of criticism. "You think I should have talked to her, don't you? You think I should have helped her?"

"No, Kylie! I'm not judging you."

She straightened up slightly, lifted her chin, and gave a short, sharp sigh. "Then you feel sorry for me. Forget it! You don't have to pity me. She makes her own choices, and she doesn't affect who I am."

"No pity," he said earnestly. "That's *not* what I'm feeling. Respect. For strength in the face of adversity. For what you've done with your life. For the suffering you've come through." He took her hand and gently opened her fist, smoothing away the tension. "You're well named, Kylie." He drew out the name, giving each syllable the same emphasis.

She made a small questioning sound, and he laughed.

"I asked Winston yesterday about your name. It sounds so Chinese. I figured it must have some meaning. He said *kai* means good, true, loyal, and *li* means elegant. So there you are. *Kai li*—truly elegant. You carry with you an unmistakable impression of strength and discipline. No one would *ever* pity you, Kylie."

As she sat beside him on the couch, utterly and wonderfully charmed by his words, a loud knock came to their door.

Someone was shouting: "Kylie! Kylie! Open the door!"

It was Edward Finnegan.

When Jack opened the door, Mr. Finnegan pulled him and Kylie out into the hall, as if an enemy were in the flat behind them.

"Fiona McGrath's been hurt!" he exclaimed. "Scaffolding pierced one of her windows, blowing pieces of glass through her living room. She ran out of her bedroom to see what had happened and a piece flying through the air cut her cheek quite badly. She's lucky it didn't blind her! A doctor down on the twelfth story is stitching her up right now."

"What's she doing with the furniture in her living room?" Kylie asked. "It must be getting drenched."

"We're moving it into the hallway and her bedroom and trying to board up the opening."

"I'll go help," Jack said, taking the flashlight and disappearing down the hallway.

Edward Finnegan held Kylie back when she would have followed. "You must move your things further away from the windows," he said. "There's always a chance that the scaffolding at the end of the building could swing back around toward you. Put your best things in the bedroom and even into the closet if you can. Nothing's safe if a window breaks!"

Kylie nodded anxiously and went back into her flat to begin. With shaking hands she wrapped up her pieces of porcelain, wishing she had been wise enough to do this before the electricity went out. These she put into the heavy teak chest in her bedroom and then decided she had better put a blanket over the chest to protect it from glass as well. It all seemed overwhelming.

When Jack returned, Kylie was pushing her couch closer to the inner wall of her living room.

He shook his head. "Judging from Mrs. McGrath's experience, nothing's going to help if one of your windows breaks. Put everything you can in the bedroom, and we'll use the bifold doors from your closet to board up the windows in there. That will stop the glass flying at least."

"I wish it weren't so dark," Kylie moaned. She began carrying books into her bedroom, stumbling over obstacles as she went. Jack positioned the flashlight to illuminate her path and then went into the bedroom to pry the bifolds lose from her closet.

"How will you attach them at the windows?" Kylie asked, and when Jack asked for some nails, she added, "Won't that ruin the walls and the closet doors? Are you sure we should be doing this?"

"Mrs. McGrath's wasn't the first window in the building to go, Kylie. You'll be fortunate to get through this with only a few nail holes."

"Okay," she said reluctantly and went back to moving books. She had to admit she felt better about the things in the bedroom when Jack had covered over the windows. She only wished she had enough wood lying around the flat to cover the bigger windows in the living room.

When they had moved all they could into the bedroom, leaving the floor and bed covered with furniture, books, and other items, Jack helped Kylie move all the remaining furniture in the living room toward the interior wall. Then Jack turned off the flashlight and set up candles on the coffee table. "We'll have to sit in here—no room in the bedroom. We'll save the flashlight in case a window breaks."

The candles on the table seemed so hopelessly outclassed by the typhoon swirling around the high-rise outside. Their little flames were preternaturally still, shining with barely a flicker, exaggerating for Kylie the tenuous hold she and Jack had on safety. If the wind broke through the windows, the flames wouldn't last a second, and then the darkness would press in on them again, darkness mixed with rain and flying glass and wind that could move mountains.

Wasn't Kylie herself just as vulnerable?

Perhaps Jack sensed this as well. The couch was at the far end of the living room, pressed up against the coffee table, which formed a bridge to the bookshelves lining the interior wall. Jack had set Kylie's dining room table on its side at the back of the couch, providing an extra barrier between them and the windows so that Kylie felt hidden in a haven of furniture, the windows a good fifteen feet distant from them.

Even so, she hunkered down as low as she could; if she were alone she would have put one of her cooking pans over her head, Johnny Appleseed style. The thought made her smile briefly, but then the words echoed in her mind . . . if she were alone.

Jack was leaning back on the couch, his eyes closed. Kylie thought he must be very tired. She was sorry for his weariness, but not at all sorry for his presence.

What would the night have been like without him? He had been steadfast and sure, unfaltering through it all. That she, so independent, so unwilling to trust anyone, should have been leaning so heavily on him was surprising enough. That he had proved so kind surprised her even more.

How, if not Providence, had it come about that on this night he had been here to help her?

He opened his eyes to find her watching him and for a sensitive moment their eyes held, his a deep pool that she couldn't completely fathom. Then his eyes changed slightly, growing more intense until something she saw in them made her blush. She bit her lip, dismayed by her response.

"You okay?" he asked gently.

"I'm . . . glad that you're here."

He took her hand and held it between his, the warmth and strength calming the tremors that she barely managed to hold back. No words, just the touch of skin to skin, and she felt her heart contract inside her with a longing that she wouldn't allow herself to define. He must have felt her tremble, but in response he merely rubbed his palm against her own and then threaded their fingers together, holding tightly for a moment.

"I'm glad too, Kylie."

Then Jack released her hand and sat forward. "Let's see what else you have to eat around here. Besides black olives, I mean."

He took one of the candles and began rummaging through her cabinets. He tossed aside a half-eaten bag of puffed rice cakes—"I know why you never finished those!"—but pounced on a jar of peanut butter and some chocolate biscuits from England. "Instant Reese's!" He seemed equally pleased to find a jar of kimchi in her refrigerator, glancing at Kylie as he took out the spicy Korean dish as if reassessing her. "Hot, no less? How intemperate, Kylie!"

He carried the snacks and some soft drinks to the coffee table, sat down on the couch, and used a chocolate cookie to dig into the peanut butter. "Come on, Kylie. While the windows hold, let's party!"

She shook her head. "I couldn't possibly eat."

He paused, a cookie halfway to his mouth, and then stuck it back into the peanut butter and put the jar on the table. This time he took both her hands in his and held them to his cheeks. "Kylie, it's all right. Everything'll turn out fine."

The candlelight was dim, but definitely bright enough to reveal the confidence in his eyes. She pulled her hands from his. "You're like Justine," she said despairingly, "both of you laughing at the storm. That's fine for you, but don't expect me to. Everything's crashing down around me. Can't you see it? Not just the storm, but what's happening at work and what's happening in Hong Kong. And now you tell me Harry wants to retire. I feel sick. You can talk all you want about a Sovereign Lord and having feet like deer, but I feel more like an elephant, and one caught in quicksand, no less. You and Justine don't make any sense."

He let go of her hands and picked up the peanut butter jar again, not wanting her to feel trapped. "You said when you were six you came home from school wondering what you would find inside. Maybe you're still doing that. It must be hard to change such an early habit."

"Of course I am. 'All past is prologue,' right? I'm not a fool! I know the effect a parent's alcoholism has on children. I've even been in counseling; my father saw to it. Always willing to provide the best, just never provide it himself." She heard the words, recognized the bitterness, and winced slightly, wishing she could go away and hide. *Maybe I should try the coat closet*, she thought, sickened further by her bleak humor.

"I should go to bed," she said.

"You wouldn't sleep. There's no room on the bed to lay down, anyway. It's covered with books."

"Oh, give me the kimchi, then. If I'm going to have an upset stomach, I might as well enjoy the reason!"

Jack laughed and then grew serious again. If she had looked at him, she would have seen eyes as gentle as the eyes of Jesus when he saw Peter sinking in the water.

"Life is a little like this storm," Jack said. "The circumstances of our lives whip around us like the wind in a typhoon. No matter how much we try to get a handle on things, they're always changing, swirling around, out of control. Soon Hong Kong might very well be closed to the outside world, another Tiananmen Square, with broken promises and a way of life ending. Harry will inevitably move on. You might have to leave Hong Kong, might even have to use your knowledge of business to work in another field besides porcelain. Life changing, and you having to constantly adjust in a world gone crazy. It's like I said earlier, you have to find the things that last and hold on to those."

She had turned toward him, watching him speak. There was something in this man that compelled belief, making it seem more probable that he was right than wrong. What had happened to her skepticism? She said, "And those things worth holding onto are. . . ?"

"Really only one thing, Kylie—one person."

"Jesus Christ."

"He was what Justine held on to during her storm, wasn't He? He is the stillpoint in a turning world. He's the eye in every hurricane that life throws at us, the source of peace in every trial and change. That's our faith. However vaguely we sometimes see Him, Jesus is right there working with us. The moment you became His, He gave you this promise: He will take you through every trial."

"Even before," she said. "He was there even before; I know that. But it frightens me a little."

"Frightens you?"

She swallowed painfully. "If He was there while I was hiding in that closet—you know, the time I came home and my mother was so violent and the other times, too, when things fell apart—if He was there, can there ever be a guarantee that He wouldn't let that happen again?"

"What do you think?"

She laughed, without humor. "Now you're sounding like a psychiatrist!"

"I'm serious. What do you think about that? You must have come to some kind of conclusion."

She shook her head. "Not really. I just keep coming back to the idea that even if He can help me, I have no reason to believe He will. I only have to look back at my own life to see the astonishingly painful things that He allows to happen in people's lives—even people He calls His own."

"It's a dilemma, isn't it?"

"What?"

"I'm here. I think we both know that God arranged for me to help you tonight." He waited for her to agree, and she nodded. "He brought Mr. Hu into your life and Justine. In spite of your mother's alcoholism, you're functioning as a re-sponsible, disciplined, and very successful adult. Surely He played a role in that. You called it the fingerprints of Provi-dence." Again she nodded. "All of *that* is secondary to what He did for you on the Cross, through the blood of His own Son. God brought you into His family. It's in Romans: If He didn't spare His own Son, won't He give you everything else as well? God loves you; He wants what is best for you. Noth-ing will separate you from that love. And yet . . . somehow you have to reconcile all that care and concern with a little six-year-old girl hiding in the coat closet."

"Why isn't it enough?" she asked, truly on the edge of despair now. "All of that and it can't make up for what hap-pened to me as a child!"

Jack took her hand again and kissed it, then still holding her hand leaned back and took a deep, slow breath. When he spoke again, he was praying, although he slipped so naturally into it that Kylie needed a moment to realize what he was doing: "It's all pretty hard to understand, Father, and yet You have the power to change our hearts. Through Your Spirit, please bring us back to Your stillpoint, where we can see things through Your eyes, as they really are, from the vantage point of Your wisdom and Your promises."

They were silent for a few moments. Then Jack stretched his legs out more comfortably and settled Kylie's head against his shoulder. When he spoke, she felt his breath on her hair, as gentle as a blessing. "He is God, and He is good, and no matter what He has allowed in your life, He is able to redeem it and use it for your benefit. For His glory and your good. Now, try to relax; get some sleep if you can. I'll be here."

And in spite of a lifetime of treating such simple state-ments with extreme skepticism, Kylie believed him, and felt herself slip into sleep.

❧

She woke to silence. She was stretched out on the couch.

At some point, Jack must have brought a pillow and a blanket for her. She wondered where he was. The room was dark, and although a small candle still burned on the coffee table before her, she couldn't see Jack nearby.

Silence had settled where once the wind blew. She couldn't hear traffic or birds or people below. Just silence. She wondered if these were the only times in the history of the city when silence found a place to reside.

She became aware of fresh air and realized that Jack must have opened a window. She got up and lifted the candle to see further into the room. Jack was standing at the bank of windows, staring out into the night.

"So this is the eye," she said, getting up to stand next to him.

"Hard to believe, isn't it? When do you think the electricity will come back on?"

"The rest of the storm's coming, you know. It's not over yet."

"If the typhoon is heading inland, the second half won't be as bad, I think. Hurricanes dissipate pretty quickly over land."

"It's a nice thought."

"The worst is over, Kylie. Trust me."

She laughed. "You've had a little talk with the storm, I suppose. I hope you're right." She became aware of moisture beneath her. "Oooh, the rug's wet."

"The windows leaked. They're not airtight after all."

"I'm opening all the windows then, while we have the chance, to air out some of the humidity." As she did so, she asked, "Where did you sleep anyway, since you gave me the couch?"

"On the floor. I was okay."

"Is this how it always is on your troubleshooting jaunts? When do you ever sleep?"

"No, this *isn't* how it usually is. Typhoons and Kylie Austin—quite a combination. Harry should have warned me."

She came back to him and lifted the candle so that she

could see his face a little better. He was teasing her, his eyes full of humor and warmth, and what his smile did to her heart superseded the momentary respite from the storm.

"I'm going back to sleep," she announced and scurried back to the couch before he could say anything else.

⟋⟍⟋⟍

The next time she woke, light had crept into the room like a timid cat, curling itself into the corners and around the furniture. It was 8:30 and raining again, but the storm seemed to have dispelled just as Jack said it would. The wind was much quieter now, and she thought the building had surely stopped swaying.

She became aware of a slight smoky smell, and she sat up abruptly searching for Jack. He was in the kitchen, still in Mr. McGrath's sweats, but needing a shave now. His scruffy beard made him even more handsome: Jack Sullivan, dashing rake, bold scoundrel.

Appearances lied, Kylie decided. Jack Sullivan was as true as they came. His life was filled with commitments: to his job, to his family, most especially to God. A man couldn't give such ready counsel from the Bible without having spent hours in study arming himself with the knowledge and wisdom that came from the Word.

Even so, for her own sake, she would have to ignore that stubbled jaw.

In front of Jack on the counter were a group of four or five candles close together; he was holding a small pan of water over them.

"What in the world are you doing?"

"Coffee," he said, as if that explained everything.

"Don't tell me you're that dependent!"

"Go ahead and laugh! How else am I going to get a cup?"

"Well, when you're done maybe we can toast some bagels over your little campfire!"

"I'd tread carefully if I were you," he growled, "until I have my cup of coffee."

Kylie rolled her eyes and went into her bathroom, shutting the door behind her. She felt vaguely troubled by all that had happened between them during the night and wondered when she could reasonably get rid of him. How soon would taxis be running again?

In the meantime, she intended to get cleaned up. Unlike Jack, she at least had clothes to change into. Shorts and a shirt; perfect for a day cleaning up her flat. Catching sight of herself in the mirror, she didn't know whether to laugh or cry. Her hair, normally pulled back into a tightly restrained braid or French twist, had gone wild with freedom last night, curling wantonly around her shoulders and making her look much younger. Smudges of makeup lined her eyes, making them look large and almost frightened, a waif at the mercy of the elements. With fierce determination, she scrubbed her face clean and pulled her hair into a clasp at the back of her neck. No makeup—she refused to grant that much importance to Jack Sullivan—but at least she looked like a grown-up now.

He was still holding the pan of water when she came out, but seeing her he said, "Come here."

"You want me to take a turn?" She came closer, unaware of what he intended.

"No. I want to do this." He reached behind her and slipped the clasp out, fluffing her hair around her shoulders again.

"Jack!"

"Kylie!" he said, mimicking her objection. He rubbed his thumb lightly across her lips. "I should be glad you didn't come out in one of your little business suits! I refuse to let you revert to your old defenses."

"And leaving my hair down accomplishes that?"

"You know it does, Kylie Austin. We're not exactly 'behind closed doors'—at least not the way the song says—but we've battered down some major barriers between us during the last two days, and I don't intend to let them go up again." He put his palm under her chin and lifted it slightly so that she had to look up at him. His eyes glowed with humor but they held a hint of steel as well. No arguments this time!

She glared back at him. As if she had a choice! Never again could she pretend with Jack that she was the Kylie she presented to the world. Now he knew her problems, knew her fears. Feeling so exposed made her want to grit her teeth.

"This would all be a lot easier to accept if you'd done a little barrier breaking yourself!" she exclaimed.

He put the pan down and took her into his arms, his touch this time almost impersonal, offering comfort but nothing else. He cupped his hand behind her head, threading his fingers through her hair, and held her face against his shoulder. When she finally sighed and relaxed against him, he let his fingers drift through her hair to her neck, the contact of hand against skin warm and soothing.

"It won't take you long to find my weaknesses, Kylie," he said softly. "They're right there, just under the surface, the same as yours were, and God in His mercy will not allow me to keep them hidden forever."

She lifted big eyes to him, wondering what he could possibly reveal to her.

"We're all living on the edge of faith," Jack assured her, stepping away from her. "I have my anxieties, too; they just don't have quite so reasonable a basis. Most people would say I've had the perfect, all-American upbringing, and I have. And yet . . ."

"What?"

"Well, we'll see. For now, if I don't keep this water over my little flame here, we'll never have coffee. Did you say you had some cereal? Let's have that instead of bagels. No cooking. What happens now in the aftermath of a typhoon?"

"You watch the amazing stamina and drive of the Chinese people. It will take far less time than you imagine for them to clean everything up."

"Could I get a taxi?"

"Maybe. It will depend on the streets. I imagine a lot of signs have fallen down. You know how they hang out over the road. And there's sure to be debris."

"So the driver would have to circle around looking for clear streets to drive through. Never mind. I'll stay here until it seems likely that the main roads are cleared. Let's have breakfast—my water's finally hot. And then we'll put your apartment back in shape. What happened to your porcelain pieces, anyway?"

He was very good-natured, Kylie decided during the course of that morning. As awkward as she felt around him, he still managed to make her laugh.

Nell Finnegan stopped by around eleven-thirty, just as Kylie and Jack were shelving the last books from the bedroom.

"Well, dears, how did you survive the storm?" she asked.

"Just fine, Mrs. Finnegan. And you? Any more problems after Mrs. McGrath's window broke?"

"No. Things settled down then." Mrs. Finnegan drifted over toward Jack and patted his arm. "I was so glad to know you were here taking care of Kylie, Jack. How fortunate for her!"

Kylie sputtered, managing to end up with a cough, and then had to hide her smile at Jack's gallant response to Mrs. Finnegan. He first apologized for not being able to offer her a hot cup of tea and then asked if there was anything he could do for her and "Edward." Mrs. Finnegan literally preened under his attention.

Clearing her throat, Kylie asked about the roads. "Do you think Jack could get a taxi back to the Mandarin?"

"Why, yes, dear, I suppose he *could*." Her expression finished the sentence loudly enough: why Kylie would want him to leave Mrs. Finnegan couldn't imagine!

Jack escorted Mrs. Finnegan gently but firmly toward the door. "Thank you again, Mrs. Finnegan, for your help last night. I will return Mr. McGrath's clothes as soon as I have a chance to have them laundered."

"I could do that for you. . . ."

"Thank you, but no," he said. "It's the least I can do."

After closing the door he leaned back against it and, catching Kylie's raised eyebrows, grinned sheepishly. "Now, Kylie, she's—"

"Smitten?"

"I was going to say *sweet*."

"Smitten," Kylie repeated, and then grinned.

"Go get changed," Jack said, at his most dictatorial. "We'll have a real lunch at the Mandarin and then check by the warehouse to see what's happening. If no one's there, maybe we'll get a chance to go through Robert's desk."

Kylie didn't move for a moment, torn between a desire to go with him and a feeling that for her own protection she should let him go on alone. How long could she spend in this man's company and still remain immune to his appeal?

He was still standing against the door, arms crossed, watching her, a slight smile on his face as if he knew what she were thinking. His stance was both relaxed and confident, the perfect combination of strength and calm, and she found herself drowning in the depths of his blue eyes, hit by an incredible sense of self-awareness, her breath short, her heartbeat fast. This man. All these years she had been so much on guard and in barely two short days, he was already breaking down her defenses. Remain immune? She *already* needed an antidote.

She turned abruptly away. She would go with him. He was not a man to make up his mind and then change it easily, and in the process of convincing him to go on alone, she might very easily reveal more than she could bear him to know.

She was *not* in love, she told herself sternly, as she changed into business slacks and blouse. What she felt was that fabled desire that all the love songs spoke about. Attraction. Fascination. Plain old sex appeal. There. She had said it.

And what would she do about it? Absolutely nothing.

Eight

When she came out, Jack immediately recognized that she had changed more than her clothes. The Kylie who had shared secrets in the night had turned back into the impassive businesswoman. He was astute enough to recognize her growing response to him. That it would cause her such alarm saddened him. Did Carson Grey's less-than-honorable behavior represent the norm for Kylie?

In the taxi, he caught her watching him rub his chin. "It'll be nice to get this off," he told her.

"I could have given you a razor."

"No problem."

Kylie blushed, the small intimacies of the morning apparently rushing in on her, and Jack had to look away so that she couldn't see his rueful smile.

The lobby of the Mandarin was crowded with people, all deciding to get a hot meal after the storm.

"Looks like you can take your time," Kylie said. "It's going to be hours before we get a table."

Jack shook his head. "Give me about forty-five minutes. I made reservations for 1:30 while you were changing."

He spent the last fifteen minutes in his room talking to Harry Reaves, catching him up on what was happening.

"A typhoon?" Harry exclaimed. "You don't do things halfheartedly, do you, Buddy? How's Kylie surviving?"

"Okay."

"Well . . ." Harry was silent for a few minutes, and Jack could almost see him pulling in the resources of his prodigious mind and applying them to what Jack had told him about the porcelain. "I think I'll come out there on Monday," he finally said. "Hong Kong's a volatile place these days. Companies moving, people emigrating. I want to see for myself what's happening in the branch and talk to Carson and Phillip and the rest. Don't say anything, though, not even to Kylie. I'll be at the airport Tuesday morning at the latest. Keep me posted, okay?"

Jack hung up and then sat on the bed for a moment longer, thinking. Then he made a second phone call.

Their meal was silent, Jack too intent on his own thoughts to press Kylie to speak. As he signed the check, he said, "I called the hospital from my room."

She became immediately still, waiting.

"Robert died during the night. He never regained consciousness. I'm sorry."

She nodded. "I figured he wouldn't. I'm sorry, too."

"So let's go to the warehouse, try to get a look at his desk, and then head back over to Mary Chiu's flat. Ready?"

The wind was still blustery outside, the remnants of the typhoon. Evidence of the storm was everywhere. Many of the ubiquitous signs that usually stretched across narrow side streets advertising stores' names and wares had been torn down, giving the streets a strangely open and exposed feel. The buildings themselves looked violated. Shutters hung askew, tiles were missing, and here and there window spaces had been boarded up. But what she had told Jack was true: if Hong Kong could boast of anything, it could boast of the industry of its people. The city would soon be cleaned up.

At the warehouse, two extra guards had been posted. Jack knew this was standard procedure for any upheaval. They commanded a steep price for standing guard through celebrations, riots, or the occasional typhoon, but Reaves considered the expense well spent. Kylie greeted the regular guard at the entrance, receiving assurance that there had been no unexpected surprises during the storm.

Inside, all was quiet and secure. Kylie went immediately to Robert's desk. "It's locked," she said.

"Let me try," Jack suggested, and within moments he had neatly picked the lock open. He laughed at Kylie's expression. "Don't look so surprised! In my job, I often have to function as a detective. Didn't you know that?"

He was certainly very good at uncovering *her* secrets! "Do you also carry a gun?"

"No. No guns." He grinned, slanting a look down at her. "You've been close enough to me in the last two days, haven't you, Kylie Austin, to have discovered that fact on your own? Isn't that true?" He paused, waiting for her blush, and then grinned again, satisfied. He worked a moment longer and then held out his hands toward the open drawer. "Here you are. I'll work on his file drawers too."

She sat down at the desk and began rummaging through Robert's papers. "I only wish I knew what I was looking for. Do you get the feeling that we're always about three days too late? Worse yet, that someone's watching us all the time, making sure we don't catch up?"

"We'll get there, Kylie. Don't lose heart. Did you find anything in Robert's drawer?"

"Invoices waiting to be filed. A few pieces of correspondence. It looks straightforward. Here's a few keys, but I have no idea what they're for. Menus, of course. Nothing incriminating."

"Try the files."

She began leafing through the invoices and correspondence, but it all seemed completely predictable. Perhaps somewhere in the back he had kept a special file, but then how could anyone have been fool enough to kill him and leave the very evidence that had cost him his life? It all seemed utterly hopeless.

The door to the office opened, and before she could stop

herself, Kylie swung guiltily around, shutting Robert's file drawer in a hurry.

"What are you doing?" Phillip Hughes asked, his accusing tone absolutely understandable given Kylie's guilty reaction.

Jack obviously had more practice at deception. He answered for Kylie, achieving just the right touch of boredom: "Looking for something in Robert's file. If she'd only hurry up, I've been wondering what it's like out on the harbor this afternoon. I've been hoping one of Kylie's friends—you never have told me his name—might agree to take us out on his yacht to see the damage from the typhoon."

Phillip stood looking from Kylie to Jack, confused by the conflicting messages of anxiety and boredom, and Kylie hurriedly pulled herself together.

"I'm *sorry*," she said, trying to shift the cause of her anxiety from Phillip to Jack. "I said I'd be done in time, and I will be!"

As she turned back to keep looking through the files, she saw Jack roll his eyes and Phillip look sympathetically back at him.

"Maybe you should go on without me," she said.

"You'd have to tell me his name first," Jack said slyly.

"The new boyfriend finding out about the old?" Phillip asked. "Why don't we meet more of these men, Kylie? Winston certainly keeps none of his conquests to himself!"

Kylie turned back around and crossed her arms, glaring first at Phillip and then Jack. Very deliberately, she said, "So, Phillip, how'd you do in the typhoon? Sylvie okay?"

"Fine, thanks. The typhoon was an inconvenience, to be sure, but no real problems."

"And what are you doing here?"

It seemed to Kylie that his face became guarded, almost sly. "Let's just say we both want to cover our bases now that Robert won't be back."

Kylie was left wondering if she had imagined the guile.

"All right. Then let's go, Jack, or we really will be late."

After directing the taxi to Mary's housing estate in Kowloon, Kylie cast a look up at him, caught his grin, and laughed in response. "Friend, indeed. Yacht. Where'd you come up with that?"

Eyebrows went up. "I've spent a fair bit of time since Thursday wondering about the men you keep company with. I can well imagine it's been the same for Phillip. Imagining one with a yacht is not at all difficult."

"Really." She stared at him, wondering . . . yes, this time she was certain. He really was flirting! "I can't believe you!"

Jack laughed. "I can see you now: Hair down, *definitely* down, leaning forward, sun on your face, laughing into the wind. A very pleasant image."

"Well, come back to reality. Instead of all *that*, let's see what poor Mary has to say."

Mary Chiu was home this time. She came into the hallway, away from the curious eyes of her family, but she was not much more forthcoming than her mother. "My days at Reaves are over," she told Kylie in Chinese, not in the least concerned about excluding Jack. "I owe nothing to your company."

"I understand that. Do you owe anything to Murray?"

"Why Murray?"

"He's disappeared. He called me last week, asked to meet me in the warehouse, but when I showed up he wasn't there. No one has seen him since."

For a moment Mary didn't respond and then she frowned. "I still don't owe you anything. Why should I help you?"

"Robert is dead. A car hit him on the way back from lunch on Thursday. He died in the hospital last night."

This time Mary couldn't hide her surprise.

Kylie continued. "If you'd like, you can have your job back at Reaves."

Mary snorted. "Am I stupid? Working at Reaves right

now doesn't seem very healthy, do you think?"

"When this gets cleared up, then. You could still tell me why you were fired."

"Do you think I know? I've thought and thought, but nothing makes sense. The only vaguely strange thing that happened was that I got to work early one day, and rather than sitting around in the tearoom, I began immediately to unpack a shipment from China. The shipment didn't match the manifest. One extra piece of several different kinds. I went to Robert and asked him about it. He reacted so strangely, told me not to work on my own, that I had no business unpacking anything until he told me. As if I haven't done that many times! Three days later, I was fired. Bad attitude, he said."

Kylie stood thinking about Mary's story. After a moment, Mary continued, her words sharply bitter. "And I didn't hear anyone object when it happened." The implication was clear—where was Kylie then?

"You're right. It sounds quite unfair. If you decide you want your job back, please call me. I'll see what I can do. In the meantime, if we figure anything out, I'll be sure and let you know."

For the first time, Mary took a good look at Jack, standing with his back against the wall, obviously waiting for Kylie to finish. Mary stuck her chin toward him. "Who is he, this man?"

"Jack Sullivan, vice-president of Reaves. He's come out from Chicago to see me."

"Ah yah!" Mary exclaimed, looking him over more intimately this time. "Come to see you? Why are you wasting time here?"

Kylie was smiling as she and Jack walked down the hallway toward the stairs. "Something she said?" Jack asked.

"You wouldn't want to know."

"I wouldn't? Or you wouldn't want me to?"

Kylie said nothing else, but she let her enigmatic smile remain, knowing that he could easily interpret Mary's response to him.

At the doorway downstairs, she looked up at him. "Now where?"

"I don't know. I feel like we're at a standstill until Monday. What would you normally be doing?"

Not keeping time with you! Kylie said to herself. "I'd like to run by my church to check on things, see if there's anything I can do to help clean up there."

"Fine."

In the thoroughfare outside Mary's high-rise, the traffic was predictably hectic. Buses lined up for the bus stop, private cars flowed between them, and from everywhere taxis darted in and out unexpectedly. And of course the sidewalks were crowded with people. At the curb, waiting with Jack for a bus to leave before crossing the street, Kylie glanced up, intending to tell him about her church.

She never said the words.

A bump from behind, and she was on the street, her knees crashing into the pavement and her body slumping forward onto her hands. Momentarily stunned, Kylie looked up to see the bus bearing down on her, picking up speed, the sound of gears shifting and rising the only clear sensation she had. She opened her mouth to scream, but the headlights were mere feet away, eye-level and growing bigger and closer; the bus and the scream in a sick contest and the bus winning out. Then she felt Jack's hands gripping her upper arms, pulling her up and back. The bus passed inches from her face and bore the scream away.

Her purse went with it. The bus ripped the bag from her hand. When it had screeched to a halt twenty feet ahead and emitted an irate driver, it was the purse that Kylie and Jack and the rest of the onlookers were staring at. It was smashed flat on the road, crushed by the tire's wheels, its contents beyond recognition.

Kylie let out a small gasp, then turned stunned eyes up to Jack. A few short breaths and she was laughing, short, gaspy giggles, the sound painful to hear. She saw his concern and wanted to reassure him. She was all right, really, all right. But she couldn't stop gasping long enough to tell him.

Jack took her tightly in his arms, holding her face against his shoulder, his arms like steel around her body.

"I'm sorry," she sputtered. "I'm okay. Don't worry. Just—Can you believe that happened? After everything else?"

"Hush," he murmured, looking sharply over her shoulder to study the crowd. She followed his gaze and saw innocent faces full of concern looking back at them. One of the bystanders retrieved Kylie's purse and thrust it into her hands, and a babble of voices rose up around them. Jack turned toward the street and called, "Taxi!"

Inside, he motioned the taxi forward so they could get away from the crowd, then told the driver to stop a few blocks from the scene.

"I don't know where to tell him to go, Kylie. Do you want to go back to your apartment? Stop for some coffee somewhere?"

The laughter had been smothered, and she was staring down with big eyes at the remnants of the purse scattered on her lap. Eyes big, still stunned, she held up her cellular phone for Jack to see. Wires and crushed plastic casing barely hung together, looking too skeletal for comfort. She took a shaky breath and then another and thought she could risk speech.

"Shopping, I think. Do you suppose this is covered by a warranty?" Another giggle bubbled up, still tenuous but slightly more controlled. At his obvious concern, she held up her hand. "No, I'm all right! Please."

She leaned forward and named a big department store on Nathan Road for the driver. "You don't mind, do you?" she asked Jack. "I'll dump the makeup, but I'm not sure I know how to operate anymore without a phone."

Seeing his concern still linger, she gripped his arm briefly and attempted her most cheerful smile. "Hey! I'm *all* right. Don't I sound back to normal? Joke, right? About the phone?"

Obviously he was not to be so easily deceived; her voice still hovered suspiciously above comfort.

"What happened exactly? Did you slip?"

"No! Someone bumped me. And thanks to you, no big deal. We shouldn't have been standing so close to the curb!"

"A bump? Not . . . a push?"

"No!" Kylie shook her head vigorously, back and forth, again and then again. She refused, absolutely *refused*, to believe that anyone meant her harm. She couldn't allow herself even to consider it. "It was an accident! It must have been. How stupid, how utterly senseless—No! I won't believe it!"

Again the pitch in her voice was rising.

"Okay, okay. We'll leave it at that." He studied her face while Kylie desperately tried to maintain her frail composure.

"Kylie." He spoke her name on a sigh of relief so deep she nearly shuddered at the extent of his feeling. "I know you're brave, Kylie. I can see your strength. But for my sake, please, come here and let me hold you. I need it as much as you."

He held her tightly, his compassion gripping her as she trembled, and there in the warmth and closeness of his embrace, her tears finally came.

"You're okay now, Kylie," he murmured into her hair. "You're all right. You're all right."

☾⧜☽

Somehow together they banished the lingering terror of the event. After a few moments Jack pulled out a handkerchief and wiped her tears, abandoning the cloth to her so that she could blow her nose.

Catching his eye over the handkerchief, she smiled. "I do feel better now. Thank you. How melodramatic this all seems. Look, I've gotten your shirt all wet."

The scattered shreds of her purse still haunted him. Glancing down at his shirt, he wouldn't say it, but he couldn't help thinking it: *better tears than blood, better a purse than her body.*

In the department store, Kylie picked out a purse and makeup and other sundries that had been smashed under the bus. As he stood near her at the counter, Jack found himself strangely confused by his response to Kylie. Somehow she had ceased to be an interesting challenge for him; she threatened instead to become a necessary one. Did he want that?

In college he had dated, but never seriously. He'd been far from ready for marriage then. And since college, through business school and during the years working for Reaves, his schedule had been too hectic, his travels too frequent to leave him time or desire to invest in one woman. Friendships, a few dates, but nothing lasting. Even now, he couldn't believe that he was ready for anything permanent.

What a pair he and Kylie made—she hating change and he hating permanence.

Harry wanted him to settle down; Jack knew that Joy's not-so-subtle attempts to help him find a wife had Harry's full approval and sanction. Friends at church seemed increasingly intrigued by Jack's ability to avoid matrimony. Most had already married. And his poor parents! They had long ago despaired of his ever adding to the family's trove of grandchildren. Jack himself suspected that while he might someday marry, he would probably not have children. A wife might put up with his schedule and travels, but how could he do that to children?

Yet here was Kylie. Her effect on him was amazing.

His eyes narrowed as he watched her paying for a new wallet. He would *not* allow this woman to get under his skin. She represented city life, security, roots, the opposite of what he wanted in life. He had a long practice of dissuading women who wanted him. How hard could it be to discourage this one? She wasn't even trying to attract him!

He took a deep breath and shrugged off every shred of emotion he felt for her.

Then she turned and smiled across the corner of the

counter at him and he almost laughed out loud at himself. Brave. Intelligent. And so beautiful. What was that poem? She walks in beauty like the night. Ah, pride. You arrogant fool, Jack Sullivan. Serves you right!

"Okay. All set," she said, coming back to where he was standing. "Now the electronics store."

"Let's get some tea first."

"Tea? I thought you never drank it."

"It worked last time we had one of these little episodes."

Her face fell, and he could have kicked himself. "I'm sorry, Kylie, but we can't avoid the truth."

She lifted worried eyes to his. "You really think it was deliberate, don't you?"

"Yes. An accidental bump and you might have stepped out onto the street. Only a deliberate, forceful push could have brought you to your knees."

"Why? Just tell me why." The fear radiated from her eyes.

"Perhaps you know something that's a threat to whoever's behind all this."

"*What?* I do my job. Travel into China. Set up my contacts. Locate good porcelain. Cajole shipments out of people. Here I do paperwork. Check on things. Work with Chicago on international markets. What can I possibly have come across that would make someone want to kill me?"

"I don't know, Kylie. Perhaps you saw one of the other buyers with someone who could incriminate him. You did move in pretty quickly on those two plates. Perhaps it's what you might find out now because of all your questions. Whoever's behind it must realize by now that you're suspicious."

"No!" Kylie declared. "If it were what I might find out, they'd be trying to kill you, too. I didn't see you in front of that bus this afternoon."

"Maybe he could only push one of us, and you were the greater threat. Or maybe it's something else. Let's take it easy; let things ride for a little while. How about doing something fun tonight to take our minds off all of this?"

She leaned back against the counter and looked up at him, apparently weighing a decision. "Actually," she admitted, "I'm scheduled to meet a few friends for dinner. We're eating Indian tonight. Would you like to come?"

"I'm supposed to be courting you, Kylie," he said, mustering a grin. "Where else would I be on a Saturday night except with you?"

She made a face to counter his teasing and then smiled in turn. "Let's stop by the electronics store—I use a store in Connaught Bay—and then get changed. I'm not going like this to dinner."

"What about the church?"

"Not this afternoon. It's getting late."

꘎꘎꘎

As the taxi took them through the Tunnel and emerged into Connaught Bay, Kylie realized that her quick recovery was an illusion. She kicked off her shoes, pulled her legs up, and wrapped her arms around them, a tightly held mass of tension and anxiety. It was hard to keep from shaking. She suddenly leaned forward and told the driver to go to the Mandarin instead of to the electronics store.

"What's up?" Jack asked, turning from his own thoughts.

Kylie couldn't answer at first.

"Kylie?" Concern filled his face.

"Forget the phone. I'm going home. I'll call you later if I decide to go out tonight. But right now I want to get home."

She stared resolutely forward, unwilling to let him see more of the fear in her eyes, but she knew he had already seen enough. She finally turned to glare at him. "What? I'm not allowed to spend a little time alone?"

He drew back, eyebrows raised, and with great effort she stared him down. Finally he raised hands in resignation. "So be it. Call me. I'd like to go with you tonight."

Before getting out at the Mandarin he turned and suggested one last time that he go with her. She shook her head. "Okay," he said, "but lock your door."

She wanted to snarl in frustration at his retreating back. Didn't he realize she was already a scared rabbit, bolting for her hole? *"Lock your door."* As if she'd do anything else.

In her flat, after changing—and yes, locking her door—she went to the kitchen to heat water for tea, grateful to find the electricity back on. Absurdly, she wondered whether sitting too close to the windows was a good idea. Couldn't someone from a nearby high-rise use a rifle to kill her? She forced herself to laugh down that idea, but nevertheless found herself skirting the interior walls of the flat, and although the electricity had returned she didn't turn on any lights. As the water heated, she moved a heavy chair in front of the flat's main door, wondering what she could say about it if Mrs. Finnegan came to call.

She looked down at her hands. Only with the greatest effort could she keep them from shaking.

And no wonder. Jack had been correct about that "bump" outside Mary's flat building. Kylie could still feel the sudden and sharp pressure on her back—nothing accidental. Someone had meant to push her in front of that bus. Someone that close to her, his hand to her back, wishing her evil.

She made herself say the words in her mind: *Someone wants to kill me.*

She stood with arms wrapped around herself in the small hallway near the door, the space dark and close and far from windows that might expose her, and tried to stop trembling.

Why? Why would anyone want her dead?

And if she couldn't answer that, who?

The questions swirled in an escalating nightmare through her mind until the teakettle's sharp whistle pierced her panic. Instinctively she wanted to bolt to the kitchen and silence the whistle—someone might hear it and know she was inside the flat. Instead, she took a deep breath and opened her eyes, straightening first one arm and then the other. A brief prayer and then she forced herself to walk to the kitchen and slowly and intentionally reach out to remove the kettle from the burner.

Kylie fixed her tea and then pulled out a photograph from a recent company function. There they were: Carson, Phillip, Winston, Lily, and the other assorted assistants and secretaries who worked in the main office.

One of them, somehow, from moment to moment, knew what Kylie was doing, knew where Kylie was going, knew almost before Kylie herself knew.

How could that be?

On the couch in her living room, Kylie scrunched down lower, wishing she could find the courage to close the drapes over her windows. But that would mean showing herself, and someone might be watching.

The telephone shattered the silence. Kylie's hand jerked, spilling scalding tea from her mug down her T-shirt. The phone rang three times before Kylie could answer it, even though it was right beside her on the end table. Her greeting was barely audible.

"Kylie? Are you there? It's Jack. Kylie? I'm coming over there."

Jack continued to speak, apparently trying to convince Kylie to let him come. Kylie didn't listen. She was looking down at the tea stain on her shirt. Who was she kidding?

"So I'll be over there in about fifteen or twenty minutes," Jack concluded and then waited for Kylie's response.

"Okay," she murmured, clamping down on the impulse to laugh at the ridiculous stain spreading over her T-shirt. She would not give way again to hysteria. "I'll be expecting you."

❦

He came with food, a selection of the Mandarin's finest treats for tea. As Jack set out the sandwiches and cakes and biscuits, he explained, "Sugar for shock, I think, and the sandwiches to settle the sweetness."

Kylie stood at the entrance to the living room, watching

as he laid out the feast, replete already with the relief that his presence alone brought to her. "I'm surprised you're not fat," she finally said, "if this is your standard response to trouble! How can we possibly eat all this?"

He laughed. "Mind if I make some more coffee?"

"How? You used up all the candles this morning."

From beside her coffee table, he looked across the room at her, his expression most of all kind but also warm and friendly and full of regard. "I'm glad to see your humor's back. . . ."

He wouldn't be so impressed if he had seen her minutes earlier, she thought. "I'll make the coffee," she announced. "The electricity's back on, so we can use the modern method."

He leaned backward against the counter in the kitchen and watched her work, smiling at her awareness of him. Only when she had poured his mug and they had returned to the living room did he speak again.

Holding out a plate full of food to her, he said, "We can't run away from it, Kylie. We need to think about why someone might want to kill you."

"I know."

"Take the food, Kylie. I know you don't feel like eating, but you need to."

When she still shook her head, he put the food down and reached for her hand, letting it sit lightly upon his own. "Relax," he demanded, and when she finally let her muscles have their own way, inevitably, her hand trembled on his. "Now *eat*," he said again, and this time she did.

"Who do you think it is?" he asked when she had finished a sandwich.

"Phillip," she said without hesitation.

"Why?"

"He was at the warehouse on Thursday when I took the two plates to be assessed. He could have followed us. And he saw me going through Robert's file. He could have followed us then, too."

"That's true, but there's one problem. I saw the person who stole your carry-all, not well and only from the back, but I can tell you it wasn't Phillip. Phillip's a big man, almost as big as Carson, and he has gray hair. The person who stole your bag was smaller and had black hair."

Kylie stared hopelessly at Jack. "Not Winston!" she begged.

"He was at the warehouse that first day."

"But not today!"

"He could have been following us."

Kylie couldn't stop shaking her head. "I don't believe it!"

"Why is it so much easier to believe Phillip did it?"

"He's so new. Winston's been with us five years! And Phillip has this gambling addiction. He can't control himself!"

Jack smiled sadly. "Kylie, he may have an addiction, but I can tell you that from all reports Harry believes Phillip is getting treatment. Don't make gambling the reason to believe him guilty."

"You're saying *Winston* tried to kill me?"

"I'm saying don't jump to conclusions. We don't know who tried to kill you. We need to consider everyone a possibility. Winston, after all, has a lavish lifestyle. That could also be incriminating."

She sat staring across at him. He seemed to be the epitome of cool reason, not at all affected by what had happened to her, ready to approach the problem methodically without any of her desperation or fear.

"How can you be so calm?" she exclaimed.

"Is that what you're thinking? I'm afraid, too, Kylie. Why do you think I'm here? I couldn't go back to my hotel room and pretend nothing had happened! I couldn't let you stay out there on your own without providing backup! I want to settle this thing as much as you do. But we must do it carefully without putting in danger anyone who might be innocent."

She looked away from him, thinking through his statement. He did look concerned, she would have to grant him that. And he was right about jumping to conclusions."

"But Phillip was there both times."

"Possibly someone has been following us all day today, waiting for a chance—" He stopped abruptly.

"To kill me," she provided in a flat voice.

"Well, yes, and still make it look accidental. And whoever is behind this might have accomplices. Lily was at the warehouse—"

"Lily? Oh, Jack!"

"And all the workers and the security guard and the secretary."

"Tiffany."

"Any of those people could have followed us or called the person in charge."

"So Carson is still under suspicion."

"It's rough, isn't it?"

"It's awful! These are my friends, Jack, at least my business colleagues. We've carried on a productive business together, and now one of them has put it all in jeopardy. This is worse than awful. It's a nightmare."

He nodded sympathetically, but couldn't deny her assessment.

"So now what do we do?" she asked after a moment.

"They would be unlikely to leave a paper trail," Jack said. "They would be much more likely to keep their own records on a laptop or other portable computing device. So nothing at the office is likely to help us. We could begin interrogating them, but that would set them all against us."

"Whoever's behind this knows we're suspicious."

"But coming into the open would create an us-against-them mentality that would inevitably cause the innocent to line up with the guilty against us. We must continue to work in the dark, so to speak."

Thoroughly frustrated, Kylie stood up and announced that she was going to get ready for dinner. In her bedroom, she slumped back onto her bed and sighed heavily. Was Jack implying they had to wait for their adversary's next move and hope that it would incriminate him, leaving themselves help-less in this cruel game while this faceless enemy took the of-fensive? There must be something they could do!

In the meantime, this person was plotting her death.

Nine

*K*ylie emerged in time for dinner wearing black jeans, a black silk T-shirt, and an embroidered vest. Most of her hair was up in an intricate arrangement of swirls behind her head, set off with what looked like a Mexican comb. From her ears dangled delicate gold earrings. Familiar already with her classic sophistication, Jack was not surprised to see her so beautiful, but was definitely charmed by the flair she instinctively exhibited.

But how did she manage to present herself so flawlessly after such a harrowing experience that afternoon? This was a woman who had depths of reserves that Jack was only now beginning to realize. Letting down her guard to him was clearly an aberration for her, habitual poise and control much more the norm. It made her openness to him all the more amazing.

"Well," Kylie said, picking up her bag, apparently oblivious to her effect on him, "if we wanted something to take our minds off Reaves' problems, this dinner tonight couldn't have come at a better time."

"How's that?"

"It's a kind of club, I suppose," Kylie explained as they walked toward the elevator. "We get together once or twice a month for dinner. We're all expatriates, all fairly young. Our only rule is being single. As soon as someone marries, off they go. We don't want anyone upsetting our equilibrium by even suggesting that a single life isn't best!"

"How many people will be there?"

"Who knows? It's all very informal. But expect some jokes about our future. Any time someone shows up with anything approximating a date, the ribbing begins." She paused and then added, "They're not Christians, you know."

"Old friends?"

"Yes, some of them. The group has changed over time, with people coming in and out of Hong Kong or marrying or just changing habits. They don't share a commitment to Christ, but I do enjoy them. We've gotten into a few good discussions about religion, especially when I get together with one of them away from the group, but so far nothing except discussions and those few enough. I keep hoping."

As it turned out, seven people besides Kylie and Jack showed up at the Maharajah Restaurant in Tsimshatsui, near the southern tip of the Kowloon Peninsula. Once seated, Kylie introduced Jack and smiled nonchalantly through the expected remarks, impressing Jack again with her social aplomb.

She introduced each of the others, gesturing first toward a man of medium height, rounded face, receding hairline, and glasses. "This is Max Stafford. He's from New York, works at Citibank in investments. Next to him is Samantha Chase, who is originally from Kenya, right?"

In beautifully lilting tones, Samantha described her heritage. "My father was British, my mother Kikuyu. I grew up in Kenya but trained in New York."

"She's a dress designer," Kylie explained. "Very successful."

Samantha smiled, accepting Kylie's claim.

"And this is Karen Blair, who's spending a year in Hong Kong visiting her parents." Karen was tall, with short brown hair and a friendly smile.

"I'm from central Illinois," Karen said. "My father represents a soybean concern, and I came out for a visit and decided to stay."

"She works as a manager in Max's bank. Next are Charles Harvey and Henry Lawson, engineers working on the new airport." Both were around thirty, Jack thought, Charles dark and shorter, Henry tall, blond, and sunburned.

"And this is Elizabeth Carlton, a travel agent. She grew up in Singapore, went back to England for university, and then came out to Hong Kong."

Wherever she had come from, Elizabeth was clearly the classic beauty in the group, with creamy colored skin and rich auburn hair that hung in curls past her shoulders. *She knows it, too*, thought Jack, as he met her disdainful gaze. Too many men had looked no deeper than her surface beauty.

The man on the other side of Kylie leaned forward and said, *sotto voce*, "Don't be misled by Elizabeth's chosen career. She took firsts in history at Cambridge."

Elizabeth looked bored. "We can't all fall into such meaningful careers as yours, Tony."

This last man, Tony, was of medium height, medium build, with somewhat bland coloring, but his eyes were alert and filled with humor as he wagged his eyebrows mockingly at Elizabeth's comment. "Come play with my toys anytime, Elizabeth. Maybe I'll give you a consulting fee."

"Tony designs toys," Kylie explained hurriedly, embarrassed by Tony's suggestive comment. She went on to mention an extremely popular line of construction blocks. "Tony did those."

"I just bought a mammoth set for my niece and nephew," Jack said, impressed. "They love them."

"That's our Tony," Elizabeth drawled. "Genuine genius." And Tony made another face back at her.

Introductions over, the group ordered their food: samosas, tandoori dishes with naan bread, the rich lamb curry called rogan josh, tender chicken tikka, and vegetarian standards like peas and cheese, dahl, spicy potatoes, and eggplant.

"Ever eaten Indian food before?" Kylie asked Jack.

"A friend in college got me hooked. I especially like what they do with vegetables. I take it you share the dishes?"

"Absolutely. Did you want to recommend anything?"

He shook his head, willing to follow their lead. After the waiter left, the conversation turned predictably to the typhoon, with the most drama focusing on where they were when the typhoon turned so unexpectedly toward Hong Kong. Samantha, typically oblivious when working, had been caught at her factory. She spent the night raiding the vending machine for food and sleeping on bolts of cloth in the sewing room. Tony was caught on the Kowloon side and couldn't get a taxi to take him across to the island. "I didn't mind an excuse to stay at the Shangri-La," he admitted, grinning. The others had made it safely back to their own flats. Max, who lived in a plush flat on Victoria Peak, suffered the most damage to his flat; he also had the least clean-up. "The building superintendent is taking care of everything," he said carelessly.

"Ooooh," everyone else chimed back, and Max had the grace to grin sheepishly.

"He's a banker in a banker's paradise," Kylie explained quietly to Jack. "Max is one of the Territory's rising stars."

"He looks like a mild-mannered professor, not a corporate whiz," Jack whispered back.

Kylie tapped her temple. "He's got it right here."

Everyone wanted to know Jack's background, and he spent part of the dinner describing his travels and some of the problems he had sorted through for Reaves.

"So why are you here?" Elizabeth asked astutely.

"Vacation, actually. To see Kylie."

Again, the predictable hoots around the table. To divert their attention, Jack asked Charles and Henry about the new airport, and the conversation quickly turned to the ever-present concern of Hong Kong's future.

The airport was Britain's final massive investment in Hong Kong, costing in the area of $15 billion and requiring so much manpower that almost an additional town of lodgings had been built beside the site for the proposed runways. After objections from the People's Republic of China, upset perhaps that the British were emptying the treasury onto the airport, the effort became a joint project with many of the contracts going to the PRC.

"But what the Chinese people in Hong Kong really want," Kylie told Jack, "is self-rule. Barring that, some wanted the right of abode in Britain. I think when Great Britain denied them the right in 1981 to a full British passport, they felt like Britain had confirmed what they always suspected: Hong Kong isn't really a Crown Colony, merely a possession. It didn't help that residents of Gibraltar and the Falkland Islands were given full passports."

"The PRC is somehow better? Really, honestly, do you think mainland China will honor its promises of freedom?" Jack asked.

Gradually the people around the table had become quiet.

"Ask Kylie," Tony said.

"Yes, tell us," Max seconded.

"You know more about China than any of us," Samantha pointed out, "what with all your trips into the mainland and your knowledge of the language."

Kylie sighed and shook her head. "History is supposed to repeat itself, although I suppose that's a truism, right, Elizabeth? But situations are never quite the same. Shanghai, you know, was much like Hong Kong before the Communists took over. Full of expatriates, bustling with commerce, a big money-maker for the country. The people in Shanghai thought that the government would never be willing to sacrifice the wealth that Shanghai brought into China. Surely the government would let Shanghai function independently, an enclave of capitalism in a stronghold of Communism. But you know what happened."

"So we should all sell up and go home?" Max said.

Kylie shrugged. "I don't know. China is no longer a bastion of Communist power. Capitalistic freedoms are gaining every day. I see more and more individual enterprise every time I cross the border. China had something to prove back then when it shut down the capitalism in Shanghai. I'm not sure they have so much to prove now."

"So basically, you're as much in the dark as the rest of us.

Thanks, Kylie," Tony drawled. "Thanks for clarifying the situation so tremendously."

Kylie laughed. "My father was a diplomat, Tony. What did you expect?"

"Some of the Chinese people seem to welcome the PRC," Karen said.

"Not many. They made that clear in their vote for democracy in 1995. Unfortunately there's not much choice between Britain and the PRC," Kylie agreed. "For too long, the government of Hong Kong was colonial and paternalistic; the self-government allowed by Britain has come too late."

"Hold on there!" Charles exclaimed, but Kylie merely shrugged.

"Now you know, Kylie, that Hong Kong Chinese aren't interested in politics," Tony interjected drily, repeating standard expatriate dogma. "They're too busy making money!"

"No one believes that now," Kylie said with skepticism. "Anyway, in essence, Hong Kong might just be going from one group of colonial rulers to another. I suppose locals think that with the PRC at least the rulers will be Chinese."

"Swapping British for Chinese means capitalist for Communist," Max objected.

"Spoken like a true banker," Elizabeth said, lifting her glass in salute.

"You go to China quite frequently, don't you, Kylie?" Jack asked. "When were you last there?"

"Three weeks ago, actually. I went through the Guangdong province, following up on some leads for new kilns."

"My dad says doing business in China is really difficult," Karen said.

Kylie shrugged. "You have to learn how. In the States, money talks. In China, connections do. They have a word for it: *guanxi*. It's a subtle system of imposing obligations on people through things like gifts or personal contacts or bureaucratic leverage. I approach a local official with a gift and the name of someone who has some kind of connection to the official—a family tie, or the name of someone here in

Hong Kong who comes from the village, or the endorsement of someone who supplies the official with something he wants. My boss Carson has his wife's relatives, some of whom are quite powerful. Personally, I've gotten a lot of mileage from my father's position. He has been on several of the diplomatic teams that have gone into China representing the United States." Kylie smiled diffidently. "I know it sounds different, but that's how China does things. If everything works as planned, the official finds it necessary to fall in line with my plans, which of course are for the kiln in his village to send their best products to Reaves. I have to use the same process for the factory manager or any other local bureaucrat whose approval I need."

Charles asked, "What kind of presents do you take?"

"Different gifts, depending on the prestige of the person I'm giving to!" Kylie said, laughing. "I like to give Walkmans, subscriptions to National Geographic, electronic translators, books, calculators, and pen sets. I take a big stack of T-shirts with me, with a design that's good for both men and women. And I always take along a game called 'Set' to give to families. A friend in the States recommended it. I buy dozens of them and include handwritten instructions in Chinese."

"It all sounds very complicated," Karen said.

"Actually, like anything, it becomes second nature. *Guanxi* is really no worse than the American system of basing a person's importance on money. During my college days I remember standing in the library when one of the big alumni patrons came in. At first the student librarian at the desk was very brief in answering his question, but then someone recognized him and out trotted the head librarian, no less, who sent people scurrying around the library looking for what this man wanted and even sent someone across town to get a resource from the city library. All because the man had money. Is that so different?"

"At least in the West, contracts go to the most deserving," observed Charles, causing Jack to believe that involving the Communists in the airport project had caused certain difficulties.

"If money talks, someday we'll all be kowtowing to Max," Elizabeth drawled. "Have you made your first million yet?"

"Tony's rich enough," Samantha shot back at Elizabeth. "All those royalties from his toys are adding up."

"So what," Elizabeth said. "Are you suggesting I hit him up for a loan?"

"Not actually . . ." drawled Samantha, and most of the others laughed, with Elizabeth and Tony studiously looking away from each other.

Kylie leaned closer to Jack and explained. "Tony and Elizabeth dislike each other so much that we've taken out a pool on when they'll finally give in and get married."

Jack shook his head in confusion. "Are you serious?"

"They agree on practically everything, really. And they manage to find reasons to get together aside from our dinners. And in spite of their fabled dislike, they always sit together. I think they're just afraid. They've both been burned pretty badly in the past."

"Interesting," Jack said. "Is that true for everyone? You've all been burned and that's why you've sworn off marriage?"

"Perhaps," Kylie answered cryptically, then smiled when she heard Jack's laugh.

⟨⟨⟨⟩⟩⟩

The dinner, which had begun at eight, ended around ten-thirty. Everyone else was going dancing on the Island at a nightclub that had live music.

Kylie begged off. "Too tired," she said, "and I do have church tomorrow."

"The little saint," Elizabeth said.

"Karen goes, too," Henry informed everyone.

"Not tomorrow, I won't! The typhoon, you know," and

she grinned since that was obviously only an excuse.

"*You* come dancing with us," Samantha said to Jack, smiling invitingly.

He held up his hands. "Sorry. Church for me, too."

"Oooh, good grief, another one!" Elizabeth said. She got a sly look in her eyes. "You could at least catch a ride with us to the Island . . . or are you planning to take Kylie home?"

Tony said, "Sure, Elizabeth. If he's planning to go to Kylie's church, he might just as well spend the night." He waggled his eyebrows so no one would miss his meaning.

Elizabeth laughed. "And then you'll both have something to confess in the morning!"

Hoots and whoops all around except for Kylie and Jack. Perhaps Jack now understood why she had been so disturbed to have him stay the night before. She snuck a look up at him. He was smiling blandly at Elizabeth and Tony's joke, but the humor missed his eyes. In fact he looked a little angry. She had a sudden impulse to grab his hand and squeeze it.

"Too bad you're not on your way to a comedy club," Kylie told Elizabeth and Tony. "You two could grab the mike and do an act together."

Outside, after seeing the others off, Kylie smiled ruefully at Jack. "I warned you about that group. Please don't mind them. They know my views on sex outside of marriage."

"But they don't understand those views."

"Of course not!"

He was studying her very seriously. Was he wondering if she were in fact still a virgin? She had come to Christ in her mid-twenties. Without religious scruples and the support of a Christian community, how many women reached that age still chaste? Probably not a high percentage. As it turned out God had been gracious, using Kylie's aloofness to protect her from the emotional traumas of uncommitted sex, but she wasn't about to tell Jack. That revelation would signal a level of intimacy beyond what she had achieved with any other person.

After all, maybe he was only looking for signs that Elizabeth and Tony's teasing had hurt her.

"Forget about them," she said and then asked Jack if he would like to walk along nearby Nathan Road for a while. This street, Kowloon's "Golden Mile," ran north from the Harbour City complex through the heart of the Kowloon Peninsula up to Boundary Road.

"Lots of lights, stores, hawkers' stalls, people. It's Hong Kong shopping at its best," Kylie promised.

"Not tonight, I think," Jack said. "But I'd love to take the ferry across the Harbour with you if it's still running."

"Till 11:30. We'll just make it." She paused for a moment and then grinned. "Too bad. No moonlight tonight—the sky's still clouded over."

"Who needs the moon. . . ?" he drawled, letting the question linger tantalizingly. She felt the color rising in her cheeks at the implication that she might take the place of the moon. Then she blushed in earnest when he swept a hand up to the street lights and completed the question: "when I have *Hong Kong* to light the night?"

"We better get going," she said drily, well aware that he was playing with her emotions, "or we'll have to take a taxi after all."

Sitting beside Jack on the upper deck of the ferry, Kylie was glad for his suggestion. After seeing the city in darkness the night before, she was greatly comforted by the splendor of lights around her. *Jewels for the lady*, she always thought, draped in profusion and spilling in wavering shimmers over the water.

Catching her smile, Jack returned it and said, "It was a great dinner, Kylie. Thank you for including me. I'm curious, though. All your friends seem to be expatriates, tonight and at the apartment. As I understand it, 98 percent of the people who live in Hong Kong are Chinese. Is the line between expatriates and Chinese always so rigid?"

"Yes, almost always," Kylie admitted. "In business, Chinese and expatriates work together. For their social life, they separate."

"So is there nowhere outside of business that you have contact with Chinese people?"

"Well, yes, actually, there is one place besides business, and that's church. In the best way, a commitment to Jesus Christ eliminates barriers. I've made wonderful friends through church. And our pastor is Chinese."

"Will I meet him tomorrow?"

"If you really want to come. The service will be in Chinese."

"That's okay."

The ferry docked, and Kylie walked with Jack to the taxi stand at the end of the pier. He would be able to walk the short distance to the Mandarin, but she didn't leave him immediately.

"Is that what you usually do?" she asked. "When you're in a foreign country, you find a local church?"

"God usually provides one through contacts, and I'm glad. Even when the service is in the native tongue, I am blessed by the experience of sharing in the global church, and I find the small cultural changes that people bring to worship fascinating."

"You won't find too many changes here," Kylie said. "People in Hong Kong are fairly open to Western practices, perhaps because the influence of Christianity on Hong Kong has been generally positive. About fourteen percent of the population claims to be Christian. Still, there are a few Chinese innovations. One of our youth leaders often uses Chinese characters to illustrate the meaning of words, like *atonement* and *justification*. And one of our Sunday school teachers has been writing songs for the children to sing that actually make use of the unique characteristics of the Chinese language. She's made up a wonderful song that uses the similarity between the Chinese word for death and the Chinese word for four to illustrate that through the four-pointed cross, life has come from death. It's a real taboo breaker; the number four is thought to be very unlucky."

"That kind of creativity in worship is exactly what captivates me," Jack commented.

"Oh. Here's another example. Mr. Hu used a pun to respond to people in the teahouse when they used the old temple phrase: *Sheng zai na jiao jiu zai na jiao.* That means 'The religion you are born into is the religion you stay in.' Mr. Hu would use another meaning of the word for religion, *jiao*, which means *pit*, and ask, 'If you were born in a vegetable pit, would you remain a vegetable for life?' People would laugh, but it would start them thinking. Last year our church did a gospel presentation in the form of a Chinese opera—now that was different, but everyone loved doing it. And our pastor sometimes uses Chinese mythology to illustrate a point."

Jack nodded. "Just like Paul used Greek poetry. I'm looking forward to hearing him preach."

Kylie hesitated, surprised by his interest.

Jack laughed. "When I said that I found the world fascinating, I meant primarily its people, Kylie. Most of all, I love to see and meet people who love the Lord and to find examples of the different ways that God redeems the culture people live in. So, yes, I want to come to church with you. I wouldn't miss it."

"Okay," Kylie said. "I'll swing by the Mandarin with a taxi around 7:30 to pick you up. Our worship service starts at 8:00 in the morning, with family Sunday school immediately following. In the afternoon the church sponsors Sunday school for children in the rooftop schools, but they've probably canceled tomorrow's classes because of the typhoon."

"Your church meets early."

"Yes, so that we can get out in time to beat the rush at restaurants. A typical Hong Kong reason!"

He was standing between her and the taxi stand. When he didn't move aside, she waited, wondering what was keeping him.

His gaze on her was gentle. "Here's another verse to remember as you go," he finally said, taking her hand in his.

" 'Rest in the Lord, wait patiently for him, and He will give you your heart's desires. Commit your way to Him, and trust in Him. Don't worry about evildoers.' "

"How do you roll off these verses so easily?" she asked, sounding almost offended.

He laughed. "That verse is easy. It's my favorite part of Mendelssohn's Oratorio, *Elijah*. It's not quite word for word from the Bible, but it's close. Psalm 37, if you want to look it up."

"And what about the other verses, like from Habakkuk? When did you learn that?"

"Sunday school, probably. We had an aggressive memorization program at our church. A seminary student from Jamaica actually got things moving for us. On Sunday mornings, before his church started, someone would stand up in front, begin a passage, and then the congregation would compete to see who could recognize the passage first and complete it from memory. We began doing that at our church at potlucks and fellowship hours. Of all that my church gave me, I've often suspected the memorization was the most life-changing." Seeing Kylie's bemused interest, Jack smiled. "Anyway, rest in the Lord, Kylie. He's with you always, and He is the one who will protect you."

Kylie nodded and repeated the words for herself: "Rest in the Lord. Thank you, Jack. And good night."

⚬⚬⚬

The flat was not quite so frightening when Kylie got home, and she walked without hesitation to draw the drapes across the windows. The attempt on her life seemed a lifetime away rather than just hours ago. Yet in some ways her peace now seemed as foolish as her panic earlier. Jack had said that God would protect her, and it was nice to think that he had such confidence, but she knew enough of history, especially that of the church in China, to know that God's protection often occurred *through* death rather than *from* death. In her own life she had learned to be on guard against the worst. The need was to trust God *whatever* He chose for her, but she had never been able to do that. She couldn't quite get away from the idea that she would have to take care of certain problems by herself without God's help. Maybe He intended it that way.

She got ready for bed and crawled gratefully under light covers made necessary by air conditioning. The humidity and heat of the night before were a distant memory. How quickly things changed—and not just since the storm.

Five days earlier on Tuesday, she couldn't have predicted Jack's arrival in Hong Kong. By Thursday morning she knew he was coming and dreaded it. By Friday night she was thanking God for having him with her. Now she felt pleasure thinking of spending the next day with him. Amazing.

And how much more had her opinion of him changed! From that first meeting three years ago in Harry's office to the few meals and business meetings she had shared with him since, she had pictured him as an adventurer with shallow values and fleeting interests, a man who merited contempt and censure. And now . . .

Her thoughts caught there. For the sake of her own composure, she would not further analyze her feelings for this man who hated city life and hadn't yet satisfied his curiosity about what lay over the next horizon.

He's not for you, Kylie Austin. Enjoy him here. Thank God for his help. But don't expect him to stick around after this is over.

Rest in the Lord. Could she turn even her feelings for Jack Sullivan over into God's hands?

Tentatively, as if feeling her way in the dark, she spoke to the God whom Jack said would protect her. *Do You know me as he said?* she asked. *Have You looked hard at my fears and not been disgusted? Aren't You angry when I wonder if You'll take care of me?*

She turned on her light and looked up Habakkuk. She read through the entire book and the last few verses twice, filling in her own personal disasters in place of Habakkuk's, wondering if she could ever truly rejoice in the face of her mother's failings and her father's coldness. "The Sovereign Lord is my strength; He makes my feet like the feet of a deer. He enables me to go to the heights."

It seems that the process of learning to trust You is taking longer than usual for me, Lord. Maybe someday. . . ?

‹۰۰۰۰۰›

"This is it," Kylie told Jack the next morning outside the Wah-Fu housing estate in Aberdeen, on the south side of Hong Kong Island.

She had met him as scheduled, wearing a flowing dress of floral crepe de chine, very feminine and very pretty.

Worth the entire trip to see her like this, he thought.

"One of Samantha's designs," she said when he complimented her, but the color in her cheeks belied her calm voice and he found himself suddenly smiling. With great restraint, he managed to avoid commenting on her hair, loose and curly and charming.

He followed Kylie inside the building and up the stairs, listening as she explained the church's location. "The government owns most of these low-cost resettlement buildings. The estates include schools, a library, post office, a clinic, and markets. The government lets our church lease space on the second floor if we agree to use the rooms during the week in some way for the residents of the building. Which is more than a fair exchange. According to some estimates, Christian groups are responsible for 60 percent of the social work in Hong Kong. They run 40 percent of all secondary and primary schools and 20 percent of the hospitals—no small contribution. Our church in particular runs a kindergarten during the day, and in the later afternoon and on Saturdays we make space available to secondary students for studying. As crowded as their flats are, there's little space in them and less quiet."

"Do many come to the Lord?"

"No," Kylie said with regret. "Only about fourteen percent of the population claim to be Christians, including both Protestants and Catholics, and about one in four are leaving Hong Kong. We all have questions about the PRC takeover—how much religious freedom will they actually grant?"

"And will they take over the social work that the church does?"

Kylie shrugged her shoulders, unable to answer either question. "But we minister anyway. Pastor Cheng says even if they don't come to Christ, they will at least have met Him through us, so someday they'll glorify God in spite of themselves."

"First Peter," Jack said, nodding. Catching Kylie's eyebrows raised expectedly, he laughed. "Well? Do you want me to quote the verse or not?"

"Sure. Go ahead."

" 'Live such good lives among the pagans that, though they accuse you of doing wrong, they may see your good deeds and glorify God on the day He visits us.' First Peter 2:12 or 13, I think."

"Not sure, Jack? I'm shocked!" She grinned and then pointed to the glass doors ahead of them. "This is it: New Light Christian Church. We have about 175 members, about 140 of them Chinese."

"What other expatriates come?"

"Missionary kids who have come back to Hong Kong as business people. Some who teach at the Hong Kong Bible College. A doctor and his wife who have lived here forever, I think, and know Chinese better than any expatriates I know. And Christian business people who want to learn Chinese and figure attending a Christian church will get them into the language fast. It works."

They walked through a small antechamber and into a big room. Off one end Jack could see a small kitchen, some bathrooms. Another door, and at the other end a small raised stage. The rest of the room was filled with chairs.

"After Sunday school, we'll put the chairs under the stage and pull down tables from the wall." Kylie pointed to tables and benches raised into the wall around the room. "Pastor Cheng has a very small office off the lobby, and that door by the bathroom leads into a janitor's closet and storage room, where we keep a collapsible play set for the kindergarten. All very compact, but serviceable. On nice days, of course, the children can go up on the roof to play."

"I'm impressed."

"Come meet Pastor Cheng and his wife."

Jack followed Kylie to the back of the room where a middle-aged couple were greeting people. After greeting the Pastor in English and introducing Jack, Kylie waved to a woman across the room and led Jack toward her.

"Justine," she explained to Jack as they moved through the room.

Justine was about Kylie's age and beautiful, with rich, shining black hair and delicate Oriental features. She reached out to clasp Kylie in a hug and then stepped back to greet Jack. "How very nice to meet you," she said. "I have been praying for Kylie ever since she told us last week about Murray going missing. I think you are God's provision. Don't you agree?"

"Yes, actually, I do," Jack said and then glanced at Kylie, wondering how much she had told Justine.

Kylie motioned toward a man standing slightly behind Justine. He was shorter than Justine and somewhat stout, but his smile was every bit as friendly as he held out his hand in greeting toward Jack. Kylie said, "This is Quincy Leung, Justine's husband. And Justine, about Murray—I told you, shhh!"

"Even here you worry, Kylie?"

"Caution is a good habit to develop, Justine," Quincy said, "even here."

"All right, all right. Anyway, *dim sum* after church?" Justine asked.

Kylie wondered if Jack knew what *dim sum* was. She had

a sudden impulse to laugh. She knew what Justine was talking about, of course, but hearing the words from a stranger's perspective, it suddenly sounded as if Justine were asking if the pastor expected to collect a small sum in the church offering that morning!

Hiding her smile, Kylie nodded, whispering to Jack that Justine was asking about eating lunch together, and then the Pastor climbed the steps to the short platform and called for the service to begin.

Jack smiled as he took his seat by Kylie. "As you said," he whispered, "friendly and outspoken. I'm glad she's been praying!"

Most of the service was in Chinese, but with Kylie's help Jack was able to follow the passages read by the worship leader. He especially enjoyed hearing the people pray, wondering as he listened what it would be like in heaven when all voices would be raised in one language to praise the Lamb on the throne. His heart quickened at the thought. It would be quite a day.

Many of the songs Jack recognized until a group of children went forward to sing. "Oh, they'll probably sing one of Mrs. Liu's original songs," Kylie said. As they sang, she scribbled an interpretation on paper for Jack to read.

When the Pastor began preaching, Kylie continued her interpretation, but it was not long into his speaking that she looked up at Jack in surprised delight. *He's speaking about the* Elijah, she wrote. *During typhoon, he listened to Mendelssohn! What do you think?*

Jack heard the Pastor speak phrases in English, verses that Mendelssohn used. Kylie's scribbled notes continued: *Storms overcome us. We doubt our ability to cope. Like Elijah, we run and hide. On Sinai, God spoke through wind, earthquake, and fire, but this time in the stillness, the silence like—* and here she used capitals—*EYE OF TYPHOON!!!! Wow!*

Here Kylie stopped writing, her attention so caught up that she forgot Jack, forgot interpreting, forgot everything except listening to what the pastor said. Jack wondered what the pastor could be saying to so distract Kylie.

When the service ended and Kylie had introduced Jack to other friends who came to greet her, Sunday school began. Jack was impressed with how easily the children fit into the class. After singing, the younger children came forward for a Bible story, and then went to the back of the room to work on a craft project, while the rest of the group took part in a discussion of a parable. Jack found the second hour passing very quickly.

It took only a few minutes for the chairs to be put away and the room to be converted to a study hall for the second-ary students who would be using the space in the afternoon. By 10:30 Kylie and Jack were in a taxi with Justine and Quincy, on their way toward the Luk Yu Teahouse back in Central. Other family members followed in a second taxi.

"Justine and Quincy usually eat at a more down-to-earth restaurant in Stanley," Kylie told Jack. "Quincy must be tak-ing us to the Luk Yu for your sake."

"Of course," Quincy confirmed. "Only the best for our esteemed visitor!"

Kylie smiled and continued. "But I'm afraid even this early, we'll have to wait for a while."

And indeed, the Luk Yu's many tables were already filled with noisy, animated, and in some instances raucous groups. An institution in Hong Kong, the teahouse boasted marble-back chairs, floor spittoons, kettle warmers, and even a Sikh doorman, all part of the show. In and out, through the tables, waiters and waitresses pushed trolleys laden with many little bamboo baskets and trays, each tray with one or two small items of food.

As they waited for a table, Quincy asked Jack if he had eaten *dim sum* before, and then proceeded to explain the pro-cess even though Jack said yes. "*Dim sum* means 'touch the heart,' referring to the hundreds of delicacies offered to pa-trons. You see the trolleys? Most of the *dim sum* is fried pork, prawn, beef, or squid, wrapped in a dough jacket or bean-curd skin. *Shiu mai* is a kind of minced pork and shrimp dumpling. *Chun kuen* is a deep-fried spring roll. *Ha gau* is a steamed shrimp dumpling. All very good."

"Everything's good at the Luk Yu," Justine exclaimed.

"Just don't ask what it's made of," Kylie warned with a smile. "Not in Hong Kong! Mice, lizards, sparrows—I won't go on, but you get the idea."

"Aren't you offended by that kind of talk?" Jack asked Justine, who obviously wasn't.

Eyes arched, Justine said, "We are well used to *gweilo*'s inadequacies!" and then joined Jack's laughter.

⚬⚬⚬

When Jack turned to answer a question of Quincy's, Kylie had a chance to observe him for a moment. He had indeed slipped easily into her group of friends, both last night and today. He was discussing Quincy's business now. Quincy was an executive in a large textile concern and was explaining how important his particular industry was to Hong Kong. "The textiles and clothing industry employ almost half the people in Hong Kong working in manufacturing, and it accounts for thirty-five percent of domestic exports. At one point, like most clothing companies in Hong Kong, my company concentrated on producing high volumes at cheap prices. Now we hire a select group of designers to produce more upscale clothing."

"Quotas?" Jack asked. Kylie was amused to see Quincy's estimation of Jack rise.

Seeing her husband and Jack deep into a discussion of Hong Kong's business climate, Justine pulled Kylie aside. In Chinese, she said, "He came to church with you? What kind of man is this?"

Kylie rolled her eyes. "Yes, Leung *Tai*," she said, using the Chinese word for the main wife in a multi-generational Chinese home, the *supreme of the supreme*, whose word is law. "This one would pass even your stringent standards."

"And so handsome, little *mei mei*!" Justine using in turn

the Chinese word for little sister.

Kylie scowled affectionately. "I noticed."

"And interested." A statement, not a question.

"Come on, Justine, you think every man who's both single and Christian is interested in me! *Mai guade bu shuo gua ku*"—which was to say, *A seller of melons will never say his melons are bitter*—"Why should I believe you?"

Justine laughed. "I wonder what Jack Sullivan would say to being called a melon!"

"What was that?" Hearing his name, Jack turned.

"Oh look," Kylie said quickly. "There's a table!"

"Just in time," Justine whispered, poking an elbow in Kylie's rib.

The meal was casual, boisterous, friendly, and full of laughter. Justine and Quincy's family graciously spoke English for Jack's sake. At the end of the meal, Quincy asked if Kylie and Jack would like to spend the afternoon touring the famous Tiger Balm Garden, with its bizarre and garish porcelain figurines from Chinese mythology and life in old China. Jack said no, with regrets, and suggested they get together later in the week.

Before waving the others off, Kylie pulled Justine aside and asked her to continue praying. "I can't explain everything, but we have discovered some serious problems at Reaves. Jack's helping, but . . . please pray. Please. I'm afraid things are going to get worse before they get better."

Ten

I'm surprised you didn't want to go with them. Do you have plans?" Kylie asked Jack as they walked the short distance to the Mandarin.

Jack frowned momentarily and then glanced from left to right. With his gesture, the danger from the day before came rushing back to Kylie, making her suddenly nervous. "Don't!" she exclaimed and he shook his head sadly. He pulled her arm through his so that she was close enough to hear him.

"I'm sorry, Kylie," he said quietly, slowing his walk. "I don't mean to make you nervous, but I am very conscious of what happened to you yesterday. I don't intend to let it happen again."

He was taller than she was, so that she had to look up into his eyes. Slowly, seeing his resolve, she nodded, accepting his assurance. He held her gaze for a moment longer and then smiled and began walking again.

"Anyway, to the Mandarin now, I think, to talk, explore some possibilities, see where we're heading."

He made it almost sound like an investigation of their own relationship. Was he still concerned that someone might be listening? She also glanced over her shoulder, catching an eye here or there watching her, and the muscles in her upper arm tightened, pushing the tension into her chest.

Unexpectedly, Jack slipped her arm down and put his arm around her waist, drawing her closer to his side and giving her a sense of added protection. She found his smile very distracting. What would it be like to truly walk with him like this, for more reason than unseen danger? Understanding his attempt to divert her worry, she smiled back and tried hard to appear calm and confident walking down the crowded sidewalk.

But she stayed well away from the curb.

Jack ordered coffee in the Mandarin lobby and then settled back with Kylie into a pair of comfortable armchairs. Until the coffee came, he talked to her casually, apparently welcoming the chance to relax.

Cup in hand, he became more serious. "Now we can talk," he said. "I have been wondering. Do you think whoever's behind this is smuggling only porcelain, or also the other artifacts that Reaves ships through Hong Kong?"

Kylie considered for a moment, reached for her cellular phone, and then drew back in frustration. "How strange, not having my own. I'll have to use a pay phone. I'm going to call Terry. Hold on."

Terry Wong was in his restaurant, just preparing to go off for the afternoon. This time they spoke in Chinese. "You want to know what shipments Robert was most concerned with? Kylie! I don't remember!"

"Just a quick reaction, Terry. Mostly porcelain, or jade, too?"

He was silent at the other end of the line, and then: "Ah yah, Kylie, I don't know. Porcelain, yes. For sure, porcelain. Maybe jade."

"Do you know where the shipments came from?"

"Only one," and he named a small, prestigious kiln from the Zhejiang province.

"Thanks, Terry. Get through the typhoon okay?"

"No sweat! Gotta go now, Kylie!"

Kylie hung up, looked through her slightly smashed planner, and then dialed Mary Chiu's number, grimacing ruefully.

Fortunately, Mary's younger son answered and didn't recognize Kylie's voice.

"You expect a lot, don't you?" Mary said when she realized who was calling, though Kylie thought the woman was softening a little. Perhaps she was gaining hope from Kylie's inquiries.

"Can you help?"

"Porcelain, definitely." Mary named two kilns from the same area of Zhejiang that Terry had named. "That's the shipment that got me into trouble. It was from Zhejiang, of that I'm certain. . . . You think it's smuggling, don't you?"

Careful to dissuade Mary as much as she could, Kylie hung up soon after.

Recounting the conversation to Jack, Kylie announced, "She knows, Jack. She's narrowed her suspicions down to smuggling, and of course she's right. I'm beginning to think if we ever get this cleared up, she should take Robert's place. He must not have realized how astute she was, or she might have faced Murray's outcome."

"Whatever that might be," Jack said. "So all from one area of Zhejiang province. Have you been there?"

"Yes. We have about six porcelain outlets there; the kaolin is particularly good there. It's not just craftsmanship that produces good porcelain, you know. The raw material—the clay itself, the kaolin—contributes to the quality. That area of China has some of the best in the world."

"Did you establish all six of these contacts?"

"No. Only two. The other four were already shipping to Reaves when I joined the company."

"Do you know who organized those other contacts?"

Kylie shook her head. "In the years before I joined Reaves, Carson ran things differently. Whoever got into China or had contacts in China made whatever deals they could. It was only recently, as China opened up more, that Carson reorganized the buyers so we each deal now with a specialty."

"You have no idea who actually made these contacts in Zhejiang? Can you find out?"

"Yes, actually I think I probably can. Reaves stores recent records on computer disks at the main office, but older files were put on microfiche and stored at Records Security, a firm that specializes in guarding old files. Twenty-four hour access, seven days a week, so we could go look now."

"Let's do it," Jack said, standing.

"You don't want to change first?" Kylie asked, slanting a skeptical glance over his suit. "Since we're here?"

He caught her eye and grinned, their exchange of smiles special. He knew, of course, that she was teasing him and the glow in his eyes communicated his pleasure. She felt the color rise in her cheeks and struggled to maintain a degree of aloofness. Failing that, she laughed.

"Excellent suggestion," he admitted, still amused, and then his face became serious. "Stay here, okay?"

"You mean, don't go out to the street, right up to the curb, and lean out in front of a bus? Please. Go get changed. I'll be okay."

The security firm was in the New Territories, well away from Hong Kong Island's ever-present dangers: high winds, torrential rains, mudslides, fires, and other disasters. The New Territories offered less expensive land as well, and in fact, the records were housed in a squatty building that looked almost like an old World War II bunker. A guard checked Kylie's identification and then asked for a computer check of her fingerprints. Only then would the librarian retrieve the files that Kylie requested.

It was nearing dusk by the time they had tracked down all four initial contracts. Kylie sighed wearily, as much from disappointment as exhaustion. "Carson did two, Winston's predecessor one, and this Parker Chao, who must have worked for Reaves only briefly, the fourth. I don't recognize his name at all."

"It sounds familiar," Jack said, "but I can't place it. I'll ask Harry."

Kylie shrugged and took the fiche back to the librarian. "Shall we call it quits until tomorrow?" she asked him on the taxi trip back to Central.

"I think so," Jack said. "We can make a few conclusions. It seems reasonable to think that all the suspect shipments are coming from the same region in the Zhejiang province. A contact there must be watching for certain kinds of shipments or perhaps even suggesting that certain kinds of pieces be produced. From there he manages to get the authentic pieces into the shipment. Tell me again what you did to set up the last two Zhejiang sources."

"I knew of these kilns from the sources we already had, so I paid a visit to one of the local officials that we had worked with before. With his help, I worked my way toward meeting with the actual kiln manager. By the time I reached him, I had enough support through the bureaucracy to outweigh any lingering objections he had. Reaves has one major advantage with most of these kiln managers. We want top quality work, and we're willing to pay more for the extra trouble they take. Given the kiln workers' ability and the quality of their porcelain and glazes, producing cheap tourist fare is an outright waste of their time. We become a natural choice."

"How often do most kilns ship to you?"

"Every two weeks; some once a month."

"And they choose the designs."

Kylie shook her head. "No, not always. We stay fluid. Too many of one design takes away from the value. We usually ask for about five hundred. With that much change there is plenty of opportunity for us to request designs."

Jack looked across at her for a moment without speaking. "What?" she asked.

"We need to go into China, I think. Don't you agree?"

Kylie rubbed her forehead wearily. "Yes, I'm afraid you're

right. I'll have to cancel the trip I had scheduled for Guangdong province Wednesday and reschedule for Zhejiang.
You're planning to come?"

"Will my presence cause problems?"

Kylie laughed, but without humor. "A man? A vice-president at that? And with your personality? You won't cause
problems this trip; they might wonder where you are on later
ones."

"You have the language," he said comfortingly, "and the
knowledge of how to deal with them. I'll be at a definite dis-
advantage and won't hide it."

"Thanks," Kylie said, knowing he would be losing face
for her sake, and wondering how she could avoid that and still
maintain her own. "I know you wouldn't deliberately un-
dercut me, but I appreciate your guarantee."

"You look worn out. I suppose this has not been a typical
Sunday for you?"

"No."

"So describe what you usually do."

"Church first, then sometimes *dim sum* with Justine and
Quincy. Sometimes in the afternoon I help in the Sunday
school. They might get seventy-five to a hundred children
from the resettlement estate on a nice day, so they can use all
the help they can get."

Jack heard the *sometimes*—sometimes *dim sum*, sometimes Sunday school—and was impressed again at how privately Kylie had constructed her world. He imagined the gre-
garious Justine and Quincy would like to have her come every
week; Kylie herself maintained the distance, doling out her
company like a miser. So very competent in social situations,
so aloof as well. The former was probably a result of being a
diplomat's daughter; was the latter from being an alcoholic's?
Jack doubted that life could ever be so neatly categorized. A
myriad of influences had gone into making Kylie who she was,
and he wasn't too sure about messing with the formula when
he found the result so stimulating.

But let down your guard at least among Christians, he

wanted to say to her. *Your father's professional cynicism has no place in the church.* Wasn't that what the body of Christ offered her, a chance for her faith in God to grow and extend to those who worshiped and loved the same God?

She was continuing. "After the rooftop Sunday school, we go downstairs for supper, usually soup or something simple, and then we have prayer and singing and sharing."

"Sounds great. Are we too late to go?"

"Yes, but I don't mind, Jack. I can't quite get away from the idea that we're under some kind of deadline—that if we don't keep going on this, we'll be too late. I'm only sorry that we didn't learn more this afternoon at Records Security."

"We don't know what will help, Kylie. Hold on. We'll get to the bottom of this."

She smiled, buoyed by his optimism. How wonderful to have such ready and unassailable confidence!

Jack leaned back in the taxi and stretched. "By the way, you never told me what your pastor said in the rest of his sermon."

Kylie looked up, chagrined. "Oh, I meant to tell you. I'm sorry. I became so interested that I forgot to take notes. Where was I? Elijah began to lose faith in God. He wanted the battle to end after Mount Carmel, for the nation to turn completely back to God. Yet there was Jezebel, many of the people unconvinced, and Elijah didn't seem to think God would continue to bother himself with Israel."

Jack nodded. "As humans we have to decide where to focus our energies, choosing priorities, leaving some things unattended. I suppose it's natural—though wrong—to assume God shares those same limitations."

"Elijah felt he couldn't depend upon God to meet his own needs. Perhaps from that grew the idea that God wouldn't meet the nation's needs. Things disintegrated from there to Elijah sitting alone in the wilderness, hiding, weeping. But God gave Elijah a demonstration: in storm or wind or earthquake, and even in silence, God was still there, still God. When He finally spoke to Elijah, He talked of the future, of Elijah's successors, and hope. Pastor Cheng believes God's statements apply to Hong Kong's future as well, and he's apparently willing to back up his words with action. He's staying in Hong Kong, after all. A lot of pastors aren't."

"Really?"

Kylie nodded. "I've heard one in four are emigrating, especially the ones between the ages of thirty and fifty. So many Christian Chinese are leaving that it's an easy thing for pastors to just up and follow them to Toronto or Sydney or San Francisco or wherever. Pastor Cheng believes he can best serve God right here, so he intends to stay put."

"I'm not sure I could stay."

"Really?"

"A Communist system looming like that? Lost freedoms, worship limited, testimony stifled? Perhaps even families separated? I couldn't silence my witness for God. Which means I might be imprisoned and my family left poor and unprotected. I think of a little girl sitting on my lap, my little girl—could I put her in danger when I had an alternative? Could I really justify that?"

Kylie bit her lips, a flurry of images rushing through her mind. Police coming at night, cold prison cells, hungry faces—and Jack holding a little girl. He would be so gentle with her. . . . She sighed.

Jack said, "Of course those are the big dangers. China might bring a million miseries instead—small persecutions, but still hard to bear."

"I suppose I would try to leave, too."

"Which makes men like Pastor Cheng all the more impressive. He must have a very clear knowledge of his place in the scheme of things. We're all utterly dependent on God, even the Communists. Our lives—*all* of our lives—are in God's hand, under His eye, sustained by Him. Even the lives of His enemies. Your pastor must be counting on that. And he can. Just as we are utterly dependent, so God is utterly dependable. It's in the *Elijah*: Mountains might depart and hills be removed, but God's kindness will always remain."

Kylie held her hands out flat, palms up, imagining God's beneath her own, His untiring strength and her own comparative weakness. After a moment she lifted clear eyes to Jack's. "You must listen to *Elijah* pretty often."

"I sang it when I was in college, which meant I got to know the piece from the inside out. It's been a favorite ever since, but not just for the music." He thought for a moment before continuing. "He was so victorious—Elijah, I mean—up on Mount Carmel. And then days after defeating Baal, he's out there in the desert, whining and complaining. And God was still willing to deal with him. I suppose Elijah gives me hope."

Silence had filled the vehicle. Kylie was watching him, hardly willing to breathe, knowing that his next words could reveal more of himself than he usually granted even to his closest friends.

Jack took her hand and rubbed his thumb across it. "It's like this," he continued, still holding onto her hand. "That thing about being utterly dependent. To me, that's the fear of the Lord—knowing we are utterly dependent on God, at His mercy, relying on Him for life and breath and everything else. True happiness comes to those who fear Him; the Bible says they will ever walk in ways of peace. But it's hard—trusting Him.

"In my *mind* I know I never stop being dependent. I can't exist apart from Him even if I try. No one can. We are all utterly dependent, saved and unsaved alike. He always sustains us, all of us: In Him we live and move and have our being.

"I know this and yet I sometimes *feel* like Elijah, very much alone, and it's not people I doubt; it's God himself. I feel like He's lost interest, turned His attention elsewhere, and I'm on my own, fighting battles I can't win." He lifted eyes to hers. "Do you understand?"

Kylie nodded. "Like Elijah. The only one left."

"Trying to have a relationship, but without His help or even His interest. He's gone off somewhere, and my prayers are like dead letters to someone who has moved away. Then I listen to the *Elijah* and remember: God silent is still God—still there, still active.''

" 'Yet will I rejoice in the Lord, I will be joyful in God my Savior,' " she said.

"From Habakkuk! You remember."

"Yes, I read it last night."

This time when he looked at her, his smile warmed her heart and something caught in her throat until she found it suddenly hard to breathe. How addictive it could become, trying to make this man smile, she thought, being blessed by his approval and regard! She suddenly wanted to cry with longing, the tears an offering to God, hope trembling on the verge of prayer.

But how could she ever ask God for such an unexpected blessing, especially one she considered so selfish?

"Is that what you meant yesterday morning—your anxieties?" she asked.

"Partly," he said, shrugging, giving her hand back. "One thing's for sure. Given what you've told me about Pastor Cheng and what I've seen on this trip, I will certainly pray differently for the Christians in Hong Kong—and much more often."

For the rest of the trip, until going into the Cross Harbour Tunnel, they both sat silently in the taxi. There Jack surfaced enough to ask if she would be okay alone the rest of the evening.

She laughed, not bothering to comment otherwise on the absurdity of his question. "I have some work that I must do for a presentation I am making tomorrow on the current climate of trade in the PRC. The speech has been on my schedule for weeks now. I need to review my notes."

In spite of her laughter, however, when it came time for him to get out at the Mandarin, she found herself feeling suddenly bereft, and she held his hand a moment longer in farewell than necessary with the strange sensation of grasping a lifeline.

"Call me," he said, "if you have any problems."

She nodded, then scolded herself as the taxi pulled away. Obviously he had seen her reluctance to leave. *Utter foolishness*, she told herself sternly. She *really* would have to do something about her runaway emotions. She had long made her way alone in life. Whatever dreams and ambitions she possessed, she had created and nurtured them herself, and she didn't need Jack Sullivan now to protect anything.

⚭

As for Jack, he stood outside the Mandarin and watched her taxi scuttle its way into traffic, an instinctive and necessary prayer filling his mind. *She doesn't seem to realize even yet how much danger she's in, Father. Should I be letting her go on alone?*

He shook his head, still amazed at the depth of his feelings he had just revealed on that short taxi ride. What was it in this woman that drew so much, uncharacteristically, from him? He was beyond discovering an answer, could only respond in faith to her disarming power. And with danger looming, faith seemed the only course open.

⚭

Kylie stopped the taxi outside a small grocery store near her flat, bought some fruit and yogurt and simple meal supplies, and then walked the remaining few blocks through the gathering dusk. The walk left her uneasy. The streets still looked a little battered from the typhoon, the buildings missing familiar shutters, signs, or decorations, the sky too close without the signs stretching across the street. *The city looks like a released prisoner whose hair has yet to grow back*, Kylie thought, *wounded and exposed*. She found herself hurrying by the time she reached her building entrance, not sure at all what she was trying to escape.

It was after eight o'clock when she sat down at her computer. As rushed as she had been on Wednesday—the last time she had worked on the speech in the office—she had simply loaded her document onto a disk and brought it home, rather than printing out a hard copy. She still had a few revisions to make and then she would be ready.

Her talk tomorrow was by invitation and a great honor, the buyers' association's acknowledgment of her insight into Chinese culture. It had long been the practice in Hong Kong for businesses run by expatriates to hire a *comprador*. This Chinese person served as liaison between the 98 percent Chinese population of Hong Kong and the expatriate business people. To Kylie, the system had at its root a kind of Western arrogance, that the Chinese should accommodate rather than be accommodated.

It was her feeling that people who wanted to do business with the Chinese could no longer assume that the Chinese would do all the bending. Like many others, she thought expatriates should meet the Chinese halfway. Apparently the Chinese agreed, helped no doubt by the undercurrent of resentment against Great Britain. Hong Kong, after all, was one of the few places in the world where the use of English as a business language was actually declining.

In her speech Kylie wanted to present an alternative to this system. She was an expatriate who had immersed herself in the Chinese culture. As such, she was able, at least a little, to reverse the process and be a sort of American comprador to the businesses in China.

As she loaded her disk, Kylie was thinking so hard about her speech that what was happening on her computer screen didn't register at first. She had opened her word processing program and was scrolling through her opening comments when the screen suddenly emptied. She blinked in surprise, pressed *enter* several times, and then tried rebooting. Nothing. Absolutely nothing. She sat stunned in front of the computer, wondering what she could have done to crash the entire system.

Then a message flashed on the screen: IT'S GONE, KY-

LIE. EVERYTHING'S GONE. STAY OUT OF MY BUSINESS OR I'LL MAKE IT MY BUSINESS TO RUIN YOURS.

The sense of someone else in the room was so overwhelming that for a moment she was too frightened to turn and look. Then she spun around, backing up against the computer table defensively, and looked around her small bedroom apprehensively. No one.

On leaden legs and without breath, she went to her bedroom door, scanning the living room and kitchen, and then hauled a heavy chair in front of her flat entrance. Sitting on the floor with her back against an interior wall, where she could see both the flat entrance and her bedroom door, Kylie still couldn't shake the feeling that someone was in the flat with her. She felt violated, the streets of her interior city under as much duress as the streets outside. Someone had walked down the short hallway into her living room, crossed to her bedroom, sat in her computer chair, and maliciously, malevolently deleted everything from her computer. It was the vindictive nature of the act that most terrified her. Someone wanted to make her suffer.

Pain in her arms finally moved her from her position on the floor. She had been holding her knees so tightly to her chest, her body curled into a tight ball, that her upper arms had begun to ache. She realized that she had to get up and face this. She took a deep breath and consciously made her arms relax.

She was not helpless. In the face of malice, she could retain her dignity and intellect. She would be strong. In response to everything, all the pain and frustration and disappointment that her life had given her, she had learned at least this one lesson: she did not have to let someone else's actions determine her response.

Kylie stood up purposefully and went back to her computer to retrieve her disk. The speech would be done tomorrow, malice or no, and she still had work to do. She would have to go to the office to finish her work. She glanced down at her jeans and shirt and shrugged, thrust her hair into a quick French braid, and added minimal makeup.

Only as she was reaching for her purse did she consider calling Jack. He would want to know. She realized that. She should call him if only because they were friends. They had undoubtedly gained that in the last three days. And both were involved in this mystery.

But she also wanted to keep a small hold on her heart. She felt the need almost in desperation. She was slipping like a leaf caught up by the wind in directions she couldn't predict, her heart at risk. If she didn't maintain some distance, shelter some part of her feelings from him, she would be thrown headlong into a whirling tempest of pain and disappointment and heartache. Days and weeks of sensing his absence, wondering what he was doing. Missing him. She could at least foresee that! *My own heart, let me have more pity on*, she told herself, calling up some half-forgotten line of poetry.

She would not call him tonight. Tomorrow she would tell him what happened. Tonight would be proof that she could still go it alone, an assurance that she would survive after he was gone. Besides, right now the hold on her composure was so fragile that she needed every possible illusion of self-reliance to maintain it. She was merely going to the office. What would happen? A taxi. The security guard in the building. A lock on her office door. So late. Who would know?

Stop! her subconscious was screaming, for the answers to her questions were far from reassuring.

Just go and get it done.

She called a taxi from her flat and waited downstairs inside the brightly lit lobby for it to appear. Night had fallen, but the street outside Kylie's building was lit by streetlights and passing cars, and she stood near the door, letting her eyes wander. Then something caught her attention and her entire body became tense again. She wondered afterward what made her notice the car in the alley. Her heightened apprehension and suspicions? Whatever it was, as she directed the taxi driver down the hill toward the Central district, she watched the car surreptitiously, her heart catching on a beat as she saw headlights come on and the nose of the car inch out into traffic. Was the car following her?

And no cellular phone. What could she do?

"Turn here," she demanded suddenly, deaf to the driver's startled objections.

"Now here," she said, her eyes still on the car.

Someone was definitely following her. Panic gripped her. The hand she lifted to her forehead was cold and stiff, and she couldn't seem to force enough air into her lungs. Her heart was so swollen with fear it was cutting off her breath. Her enemy again? Planning harm? How could she get away? And not only one man behind her, but two figures illuminated in the front seat—and who knows how many other cars, unseen, all watching, an orchestrated mission of malice?

The taxi driver was asking for more specific instructions, but Kylie waved him to silence, her eyes on his rearview mirror.

"Whatsa matter, lady?" he asked in English.

Thinking fast, she told him in Chinese to drop her off at the Mitsukoshi, a large Japanese department store in Causeway Bay. Unlike the stores closer by in Central, the Mitsukoshi would be open, even so late on a Sunday night. Twist by turn, veer by brake, the car behind stayed with them, its presence constant, ominous.

Caught at a red light close to the store, Kylie threw some bills onto the seat beside the driver and jumped out of the car, darting dangerously between passing traffic so that she could get into the store before the people behind her could catch up. Glancing back from the entrance, she saw a man in an overcoat and hat darting through the crossing traffic, only twenty or thirty feet behind her.

She hurried into the store, pushing through the crowd, and ducked slightly to hide among the shorter Chinese, finally dropping almost to her knees. At the back of the store, she found the service stairway and descended to the basement, praying that the men hadn't seen her. What she wanted was to hide in a dressing room, counting on the smiling clerks to keep her assailant out, but she knew she would be trapped then. She needed freedom to move.

In the basement, she raced down halls and through a warehouse, tripping over boxes and stumbling around people. Ignoring the complaints of workers, she slipped out a back entrance onto a loading dock and, catching her bearings, jumped down between two lorries and ran through the yard, skirting through dark alleys and around the corner to Jardine's Bazaar. Here among the stalls and shops full of inexpensive clothing, she bought a long skirt and loose top, straw hat, and blond wig, shrugging into them and stuffing her clothes into a huge straw carry-all. As a final touch, she added heavier makeup, redefining her mouth so that it looked bigger and brightening her cheeks to offset the blond hair.

In the dressing room mirror, her heart still racing and her hands almost too cold to function, Kylie gazed at her reflection. Yes, she did look a little like Gloria Marlin now. Gloria, who worked three stories down from Reaves in a brokerage firm. Who might also come in late on a Sunday night. And most of all, who the guard might let pass without too close an inspection.

For in her sudden paranoia, it occurred to Kylie that the security guard at her building might be taking a bribe from someone, might be on the lookout for Kylie, might call her enemy as soon as she arrived. Not enough to escape the men following her; she had to find a way to stay lost, and this disguise seemed her best chance.

Catching her eye in the mirror, the Kylie of normal days, predictable schedules, and safe relationships looked out through thick layers of skepticism and fear and asked: *Could this really be happening? Running from a tail? Buying a disguise? Blond hair, for goodness sake?*

A Salvadore Dali world, surreal and bizarre.

Through the rear window of the taxi, slumped down so low that she could hardly see, Kylie watched for a car following her. Nothing. Even so, she made the driver go straight through Central and Sheung Wan and almost to the other side of Western before having him circle back toward her building.

Taking a deep breath, she paid off the taxi and emerged as if carefree, her only thought the work she had to do. Getting past the guard would be difficult. She often worked late and knew the guard by name. Simon Pao, she thought. He might, however, be watching television. He kept a small set behind the reception panel for watching movies. If so, she had a chance. She kept her head down as she approached, seemingly looking for a pen in her purse.

Affecting Gloria's California accent and low voice, Kylie greeted the guard and signed Gloria's name with a confident scrawl, hoping the guard wouldn't go back and compare signatures. At least not until she was safely off the lift.

To her dismay, the guard stood to greet her politely and she almost panicked. How could she explain this absurd get up if he actually realized who she was? Her sweaty hands provided the answer: She dropped her pen and had to bend down to pick it up. Crouched down, she fumbled it again, this time intentionally flicking the pen toward the lift. When she picked it up, she had her back to Simon and was already walking toward the lift. She waved the pen over her head for the guard to see, as if she was too embarrassed by her clumsiness to look back. Being Chinese, he would likely accept her need to save face.

In the lift, she carefully punched Gloria's level, got out there, and climbed the stairs to her own. Still worried but beginning to feel foolish, she didn't turn on the light in her office, but crept over to her desk in the semidarkness. As she reached out her hand to turn on her computer, she froze. Could he have been so insane that he crashed the entire company network? Surely not! Panicky anyway, she turned on her computer, holding her breath until the system check was complete and the prompt came up, waiting for her command. When her file filled the screen, she scrolled through the entire document. Nothing disappeared. Nothing crashed.

With a rush of relief, she slumped forward, her face cradled in hands that were still cold, still sweaty. After only a moment, she sat up again and took a deep breath. Panic over. She was in her office, with her computer file, her speech safe. She hurriedly printed a hard copy as insurance and then settled down to finish the speech.

⟪∞⟫

An hour and a half later, her speech complete, Kylie sat in her darkened office and considered her next move, thinking with longing to the moment—seemingly far distant—when she could come and go with impunity. How had it happened that she could imagine the guard downstairs, good old Simon Pao, as an enemy, watching for her, waiting for her appearance, willing to betray her? How awful to feel so alone and set upon! Perhaps she should even now call Jack, but as the thought formed she shook her head. Why involve him? If she was imagining the danger, how foolish she would feel. And if the danger was real, why put him into it? What could he do that she wasn't already doing? She was still safe, wasn't she?

With that in mind, she decided to stay put. She had never spent the night in her office. She frowned, wishing she knew more about the building's security system. If she went to the lavatory, would that send a computer signal to some monitor somewhere? Should she go down to Gloria's level, maintaining the illusion that she was Gloria? Before morning, she would have to at least change her clothes, wiping her heavy makeup off and fixing her hair—to say nothing of more pressing needs. She would have to risk the lavatory and let security go hang!

She put her jeans back on to keep the skirt and blouse neat. They were not what she would normally wear to work, but they would have to do for the morning. She would go by her flat before the speech to change. The jeans would be more comfortable for sleeping on her office couch.

She slept fitfully, her imagination amplifying every little

sound and sending her more than once to hide behind the sofa. Added to that, the phone rang periodically, jarring her upright and flooding her with fear. Did someone know she was here? This had to be whoever was following her, but did they really think she was foolish enough to answer the phone? It finally stopped ringing around one in the morning, but her fears of someone coming in and discovering her still yanked her from sleep. She eventually pulled the sofa out far enough from the wall so that she could lie down behind it, hidden, and stayed there until morning—though this allowed little rest since she now worried about sleeping so late that she would be found there.

Well, good, Kylie, she thought as she imagined Lily's amazed expression at discovering Kylie sleeping behind the sofa. *Keep your sense of humor. You're going to be okay. Right?*

Eleven

Given her worries, she was up, dressed for work, her face freshly made up, hair in a tight French braid, and at her desk when Jack walked in at 8:00.

She glanced up with a greeting on her lips, saw his face, and froze.

"What's the matter?" she asked, rising.

His clothes were rumpled, his chin stubbled, but it was his eyes that most disturbed her. They were guarded and remote, and she realized with sudden dismay that he was bitterly angry.

She had been given an interlude of peace during the weekend with her friends at the Maharajah and at church. But her personal storm had picked up force again last night, sending her running through department stores and hiding in darkened offices. From the look on Jack's face, the forces around her were even yet picking up more power—and Jack himself would be one of the more difficult to contend with. A coldness spread through her.

He shut the door behind him and gazed across the room at her. Still he didn't speak. It was apparent that tremendous self-control was holding his temper in check. This was a Jack she had never seen before. An arrogant Jack she had reluctantly come to accept as occasionally necessary; helpful, she had come to expect; warm, to cherish; tender, to long for. But this Jack, bitter and contemptuous, left her filled with dread.

"Jack, what is it?"

He looked down and away from her, the final insult that

he couldn't even bear to look at her, and she had to fight to stay standing. After her long night, she was so weary she wanted to give up, sit down and weep, not caring that he saw how truly weak she was. If he only knew what she had been through. Well, perhaps this too was God's provision—a warning, a flag raised saying, "Take cover! This man has power to hurt you."

Instead of weeping, she pulled over herself an anger to match his, crossed her arms, and glared back at him—anything to stop the deadening feeling that was spreading through her.

She spoke with care, keeping her voice flat and unemotional, "If you have something to say, Jack Sullivan, say it or go. I'm busy."

He advanced, planting fists on her desk and leaning dangerously toward her. "You didn't think I would want to know why you left your apartment last night?"

"What do you mean?"

"*Did* you leave your apartment last night?"

"Yes! I had some work to do, here at the office. I have a job, you know. Life goes on for those of us with regular employment!"

His eyes narrowed. "You came straight here last night?"

She drew back, suspicion beginning to swamp her. "How did you know I went anywhere?"

He thrust his hand angrily through already ruffled hair, closed his eyes completely, and grunted in frustration. Then he looked across the desk at her again, the semblance of control in his eyes hard won. "Why didn't you call me? Why didn't you tell me you were going out?"

"You haven't answered my question!"

"Didn't you realize how dangerous it might be to expose yourself at that time of night to whatever maniac tried to kill you on Saturday? And to go alone? Kylie, you amaze me!"

"Answer my question, Jack Sullivan, or get out of my office. How did you know I left my flat last night?"

This time he turned away, walked to the windows lining

her office, and stood looking out, one hand clenched at his hip, the other rubbing his neck.

"You had me followed, didn't you?" she blurted, her voice rising. "Have you any idea what I've been through this past night?"

He swung around, and she saw with satisfaction that she had finally roused some shame. "Not followed! Guarded. Harry and I agreed on this; you need protection."

"The great Jack Sullivan himself wasn't enough?"

Whatever culpability she had stirred within him vanished completely. He gave a short laugh, devoid of amusement, and his jaw hardened. "You have demonstrated quite clearly how much help you consider me. You said nothing about returning to the office last night. Whatever sent you racing across town certainly merited my knowing, and yet you decided to pursue it alone. I expected more from you."

At his tone of voice, her temper flared almost beyond her control. If he didn't leave immediately, she would thoroughly shame herself. There seemed to be only one other option.

Grabbing her purse, she was almost to the door before Jack caught her arm and stopped her.

"Running away isn't the answer," he said, standing against the door.

For a moment she challenged him, but her faint heart had small chance against ruthless conviction. She turned again, retreated around her desk, and leaned wearily against it, her back to him.

Pull in, she told herself. Pull it all in and put it away. Tight. So tight that not a single little bit can escape, so tight you can stuff it into a small, dark place and keep it there. Make space for a breath. Another one. She almost had herself under control when she felt his hand on her shoulder. It was so gentle that it dispelled every bit of resolve she had and she began to cry, the tears falling silently down her cheeks.

"Kylie." He spoke from close behind her. His hand tugged softly on her shoulder, inviting her to turn. She remembered his arms around her, the firmness of his chest against her cheek, the warmth of his breath against her temple. She knew the comfort he was offering.

But she couldn't accept it, not now. Not when the danger of getting too close to Jack was so real. *Don't do it!* her heart screamed at her. Keep yourself inviolate, defenses secure.

So instead of turning into his comfort she thrust herself toward the window, taking her purse with her, and dug out a tissue to blow her nose.

She heard him retreat behind her back toward the door, and when she finally turned he was leaning sideways against it, his arms crossed, his eyes staring down at the floor. He was disappointed, clearly, with a regret that went beyond a professional interest. She owed him at least an explanation.

With difficulty, she made her voice steady. "When I got home, I discovered that someone had wiped out my computer." He looked up, his eyes watchful, surprised. "I don't use a modem. He must have done it there, in my flat." She bit her lips briefly, the thought of her enemy's presence in her bedroom still terrible, then took a breath and continued: "I had to finish my speech. I couldn't work on it at home, so . . . here at the office. I considered calling you, but didn't. In the taxi, I realized someone was following me. Two men in a car. I still couldn't call you—no cellular phone, remember? I got away from the two men in a department store. I bought some clothes as a disguise." Seeing his surprise, she explained about the guard downstairs. "Once here, I decided to stay until morning."

"It still didn't occur to you that I might be worried?"

She turned away again, looking down and away from him, silence her only answer.

He sighed loudly, leaning his back flat against the door and looking up at the ceiling. "I can see the men we hired upset you, and small wonder. I should have told you what we were doing. They weren't there to scare you. Harry was worried about you; so was I. We hired his old friend, the detective. Sanford put some guards on you." From Jack's tone, Kylie could imagine his response to their clumsy performance. "They called me directly after they lost you. We've . . . been looking."

All night, Kylie decided, taking another look at his rumpled clothes and the tension in his face. Without any sleep.

Their eyes met, and for a sensitive moment, hope rose in her heart like a wounded butterfly. She caught her breath but the terrible clump of fear and regret that had been crowding her chest refused to dissipate, and whatever she saw in his eyes fell again and died, her hope with it. She found tears threatening again.

How could she explain?

"I'm sorry," she said, managing to keep her voice fairly level. "I should have called you. I don't know . . . I'm . . ." she paused, searching for words, and then shook her head.

She had always been acutely conscious of the distance between her and other people. A problem with intimacy, she had long recognized, her ability to reach out and trust amputated at some dreadful moment in her past, even her desire to do so buried, for so long dormant. How could he expect the habits of a lifetime to change so suddenly?

Eyes full of regret, she shook her head again, watching Jack's expression harden in the face of her unwillingness to repent. An apology she would grant him; a promise to change she couldn't offer.

"Your attitude does affect things," he admitted grimly, his words a warning. "Trust needs to go both ways."

She nodded, understanding perfectly. He was saying she might lose something irretrievable; he didn't know that she already had. His trust had never been hers to keep.

In every personal relationship she had ever had, she had come inevitably to the point of losing the other person's confidence. Business she could handle. There she excelled, and she thanked . . . well, if not her stars, whoever for allowing her at least that small victory. Justine was more her mentor than friend and in that uneven relationship Kylie could maintain a front, especially since Kylie had put Justine securely into the compartment of her life labeled "spiritual."

As for all the others, her occasional dates and the expatriate singles, they were all merely accomplices in a grand delusion: food, conversation, time passing, and they would call it fun. At the dinner on Saturday she had seen her friends from Jack's perspective. She was too honest not to admit how shallow they were with each other. Kylie could name none of the inner worries and traumas that drove them from day to day. Within a carefully defined arena of interests and activities, they were free to explore among themselves, but never to cross the line. Small wonder that spiritual concerns so rarely came up. Kylie had been a willing accomplice in maintaining these boundaries, her own walls firmly guarded to protect her vulnerabilities. Not even Jack had been able to rush them for long.

Why then did it hurt so much when the inevitable moment of truth had come?

Perhaps, after all, friendship with Jack Sullivan was both too much and too little, her heart incapable of paying the price in dependence to hold on to that friendship. A memory of the look Jack had given her in the lobby of the Mandarin last Thursday came to her. He had looked down with warmth and longing, blue eyes offering secrets and passion, and Kylie's heart seemed ready to burst now at the thought that his look could ever have been real. She couldn't live with that longing and have it denied. Better to push off before it reached full bloom.

You've felt it all before, Kylie Austin. Get on with things. That's the only relief.

"I have to go home and change," Kylie said, lifting her eyes to him. "Do you want to come with me?"

He ignored the unmistakable sarcasm. "Yes. Let's go."

She thrust herself forward, through the door, and down the hall, ignoring the speculative glances from the secretaries who had arrived at work early. If he saw himself as her savior, the hero rescuing the poor faltering maiden from the depths of her personal pit, let him think again. With only a few notable exceptions, everything in her life she had made happen all on her own. She would take care of herself now as well.

He accompanied her to her flat, sitting silently during the taxi ride, allowing Kylie far more distance than even her corner of the back seat allowed.

Yet she was conscious of every breath he took, the rise and fall of his shoulders, his head moving slightly on the back of the seat as he stretched his neck and sought a more comfortable position.

Where had he looked for her last night? She wished she could ask him. Justine's perhaps. How would she explain to Justine if Jack had roused her friend? Jack couldn't have known that aside from Sundays, she and Justine led separate lives, Kylie herself rebuffing every attempt Justine made to deepen their friendship. Besides Justine, who else did she know well enough for him to ask about her? If she couldn't think of anyone, Jack certainly wouldn't have. So probably a hotel. Hotels and hospitals. How many had he called, she wondered, only now beginning to appreciate the long night he had spent. He must have been the one calling her office, hoping she was there, suspecting she wouldn't answer, but trying anyway.

At her flat, he offered to make coffee as she showered and dressed, and she retreated gratefully to the privacy of her bathroom. When she emerged, dressed in her classic business clothes, he was standing at the counter in her kitchen, unwrapping a package of muffins.

"You've been shopping," he said, and she almost snapped back with a defensive comment. Then she realized he wasn't accusing her of anything.

"I'm glad you helped yourself," she responded and saw with dismay that he also had to assess the tenor of her comment. She had made the comment sincerely.

"Can you spare a few minutes?" he asked, motioning toward the table. "I should probably explain a few things to you."

She glanced at her watch. Nine o'clock. She had her trip into China on Wednesday to reschedule and the new one to

Zhejiang province to arrange. Did he still intend to go with her? Her correspondence was also probably piling up. None of it seemed important now.

"Okay. A few minutes," she said and accepted the mug of coffee he was holding out.

He didn't say anything at first, focusing on buttering his muffin and then taking a deep drink from his coffee. *It must be hot*, she thought, but he didn't seem to notice. Finally he looked at her and sighed, acknowledging that she was waiting for him.

"You've told me a lot about yourself in the last few days," he said, "and I appreciate what that kind of honesty has cost you. I imagine there aren't many people here who know about your mother and your feelings toward your father. Maybe not even Justine?" He nodded. "I thought not. I also don't open up that easily. I'm in the information gathering business. I listen. I don't usually talk. About God, I will, some, but not about me or at least very rarely. So I understand, Kylie, your impulse to go it alone last night."

He let out another breath and looked away briefly. He was finding this hard, Kylie thought, unsure how to help him, unsure even what he was trying to do. Abandoning the table, he rose and stood at her window, looking out across the city and onto the harbor as he spoke again.

"I said that I have my own traumas. They make it hard for me to trust people, too. When I was twelve, my mother took a job at the local library, and I was given responsibility for my two younger brothers and my sister. Another kid might have handled it appropriately. Or with different siblings it might have turned out better. But we were all strong-willed and independent, and too close in age. They weren't willing to accept my authority—and who knows? I probably didn't deserve their obedience. I was out of my depth. I had all this responsibility, and for my mother's sake and my father's and everyone else's I wanted to do a good job, but I wasn't up to it."

"How long did that go on?" she asked.

"Until my ten-year-old brother started a fire in the kitchen."

"Oh, Jack."

"He survived. We all did. I knew enough to use the fire extinguisher. My sister called the fire department. And a judge eventually dropped the charges of neglect. No loss of life, only property. At least after that I didn't have to be in charge anymore."

At least? Kylie could well imagine what Jack felt as the authorities considered the charge of neglect against his parents. Social Services may even have put the family temporarily into a group home. And so easy for Jack to imagine the guilt belonged to him alone, never understanding until much later that his parents had to take the greater share of responsibility. How awful!

Her coffee cup was empty, but to cover her thoughts she raised it to her lips again and pretended to drink. So much suddenly seemed clear to her: he was thirty-five and not yet married; his roving lifestyle; a base but no long-term commitments. She wondered if he would ever have children of his own.

But the impulse to defend herself was too close and she didn't want to feel sympathy. She allowed what he was implying to make her angry again.

"So which one am I like?" she asked.

He turned in surprise. "What?"

"I'm like one of your brothers or your sister, aren't I? A responsibility that you can't keep up with? Childish, wouldn't you say? Disobedient?"

His jaw hardened again. "I'm trying to explain my reaction this morning. Even under the best circumstances, I would have been worried and upset that you went off last night on your own. You don't seem to realize how much danger you're in."

"Of course I do! I'm the one who hid out in a dark office all night!"

"And I'm the one who stayed up all night worrying about you!"

She felt chastened and might have apologized again except that he was so angry. He spoke softly, the words deliberate, forced out through a tight jaw. She frowned. She knew that tone—her own father rarely yelled his anger, he gritted it out.

Jack took a deep breath and modulated his voice. "Last night brought back so much to me that I've tried to get away from and so . . . perhaps I overreacted. I just wanted you to understand why."

"I understand," she said drily. She rose, went to the sink to rinse out her cup, then turned, lifting a stubborn chin toward him. "I understand completely. You're as much into control as I am, in your own way. What made you most angry last night was having to depend on me to take care of myself."

He leaned forward across the table, hands clenched, shoulders hunched. The strength of his personality assaulted her so violently that she instinctively stepped back. "What made it hard last night," he ground out, "was being afraid for you, Kylie! That old feeling of knowing someone I cared about was in danger and not being able to do anything about it. How many times my brothers and sister disobeyed me, putting themselves at risk, and me unable to do anything to stop them. For months I had to worry over them, angry all the time at the unfairness of being given a task and none of the power to carry it out, and then last night: you gone, who knows where, possibly in Murray's footsteps or lying in a hospital somewhere like Robert Xin, and what could I do?"

He glared across at her for a moment longer and then stalked to the door. He turned again at the door, his voice barely under control. "We've both had bad nights, Kylie, and it's long past time that I shoved off. You'll be safe now. Another of Sanford Chang's men are downstairs. This time don't try to shrug him off, will you? In the meantime, I have some things I need to look into. I'll be in touch."

Taking something from the pocket of his jacket, he flung

a packet still wrapped in the store bag onto Kylie's coffee table. "I bought that for you last night, for what it's worth."

Then he thrust his hand through his hair again, a characteristic sign of frustration and then stared across at her impassively. "I'll call you this afternoon if possible, or tonight at the latest. Come home on time tonight, straight home, and stay put." He held up his hand to waylay any possible comment she might have. "Save it, Kylie. I'm beyond arguing with you. Take this as a professional request from a vice-president who expects you to comply. No discussion."

And then he was gone.

Kylie slumped forward, setting her elbows on the counter and lowering her head into her hands. *Stupid, stupid, stupid.* So *stupid* to treat him like that. So *stupid* and yet so hopelessly predictable. He gave her repeated opportunities to make peace with him. His hand on her shoulder, his explaining here over coffee, the weariness he let her see. But she couldn't give in, could she?

So now he knew. A deep sadness came over her. Four days? Five? She couldn't manage even for that short a time to hide her true self. Moment by moment, word after word, until all of her faults were stripped bare and exposed, there to repel him and drive him away. Now he knew the worst. She was incapable of friendship.

Where then was hope? Would she never leave her problems behind?

Oh, God, she prayed, *what am I doing? Why? What is going on around me—intrusion, danger, me friendless and hopeless? They want to kill me and I turn the one person on my side against me. If this is the best I can do, then let it end. Or help me. But don't leave me here alone. Please bring him back.*

She stayed there, head bowed over hands, waiting, hoping, alienated, and fearful. No answer came, and she started to cry in frustration.

All fine and good to say God, though silent, was still active, to speak of faith and hope and believing against all odds. But what now when she really was alone, the silence of the flat echoing loudly in her ears, the space around her both cavernous and pressing?

God, I don't know You. How can I trust You? Your hand on me has been so hard, so much pain, and now it's happening again. Why does it all go on and on? What cause could there be, what profit for any of it, if all my little comforts are thrown away so easily, my security taken from me?

It was the acrid smell of burning coffee, the dregs in the bottom of the coffeepot, that finally broke through her self-pity. *How fitting*, she thought sourly. She turned off the burner and went into the bathroom to redo her makeup, wishing that she had brought her speech with her so she didn't have to show her face again at the office. The wretched speech was going to be a disaster, but who cared, anyway? It all suddenly seemed so pointless.

⌀⫸⫷⌀

Old habits stood her in good stead that morning at the office. By the time she stepped off the lift on her level, she was back in control of her emotions and could smile at co-workers and inquire innocently about their weekends. Lily came into Kylie's office soon after Kylie entered, ready to discuss the coming week. The preview was standard procedure and Kylie was able to handle it somewhat calmly.

Underneath, however, Kylie found herself watching Lily's reactions suspiciously, especially when she asked Lily to order another cellular phone, to be delivered immediately. Did Lily react abnormally to the news that Kylie's had been damaged?

In fact, as the day progressed, Kylie realized a big change had occurred over the weekend. On Thursday and Friday, seeing her colleagues, she had merely wondered if each could possibly be the one. Today, she was assuming they all were. The burden of proof had shifted; today, guilty until proven innocent. With a sour taste in her mouth, Kylie wondered if she'd ever regain her old, easy attitude toward any of them. Suspicion, once kindled, was a hard thing to extinguish, and with evil present in the best of them, doubts were sure to flare up again at unexpected times and unrelated events. Guilt upon guilt. She should somehow grant trust, but couldn't, not with the memory of the bus inches from her face.

Carson came into Kylie's office shortly before she had to leave for her speech. He circled around her desk and propped his bulky body against her desk drawers, inches from her own chair.

"Carson? Can I help you?" she asked, beginning to push her chair out from under her desk so that she could put some space between them.

"Stay." His usually genial face suddenly appeared threatening to her, eyelids lowered so that she wasn't exactly sure what he was thinking. Was she imagining spite?

She wasn't imagining his foot on the roller under her chair, however, or his leg against hers. Did he have to choose now to escalate his previously halfhearted attempts to harass and intimidate her? She looked up to study his face and what she found there turned her stomach. He was watching her, with a challenge, not a smile, and then he leaned over a little closer, hovering over her. Somehow all she could see were pudgy red lips, wet with saliva.

With sudden force, she pushed her chair away, dislodging his foot and coming around to the front of the desk. They stood facing each other for a moment, Kylie tall and defiant, Carson clearly amused.

Did he really think he could manipulate her, Kylie wondered with astonishment. She who had eaten more than one dinner at Harry Reaves' house, who had walked in the garden with Joy? If this were a battle between the two of them, she was not without resources! The man had lost his senses.

Something of her thoughts must have shown on her face, for Carson's smile vanished, and for a moment a look of undiluted animosity crossed his face. Then he raised his hands in a gesture of capitulation. "Sorry, sorry, little lady! I'm always forgetting how skittish you are—the little virgin. Jack hasn't gotten any further with you than the rest of us, has he?

My, don't you look forceful!" He motioned back to her chair. "Come on back, my dear. Your chair is your own again. See, I'll stay where I belong." And he came around again to the front of her desk and sat down in the waiting chair.

"Why are you here, Carson?"

"Hmmm," and he laughed. "I notice you didn't ask what I wanted? You're learning, Kylie. Pathetically inhibited, but learning. I wanted to talk about your trip into Guangdong province, actually. You're going on Wednesday, aren't you? I managed to arrange a contact for you with a new factory," and he named one that Kylie herself had been working on for months. He waved off her surprise. "An old business acquaintance of mine mentioned Reaves to the kiln manager, one thing led to another, and the man is willing to talk to us this Friday. Here's the information." He pushed a folder toward her.

Kylie swallowed, wondering at the implications of Carson's sudden contact. Did he suspect she was planning to cancel her trip to Guangdong? Had he suddenly engineered this meeting to keep her from investigating Zhejiang? Or was he trying to prolong her absence from Hong Kong? It all seemed so manipulative, and yet hadn't the person behind this demonstrated just that tendency? Was it Carson? She looked up at him, trying to keep her suspicions at bay and yet still discourage him from his other interest in her. It was a difficult balancing act.

"Thank you, Carson. I've seen the kiln's work. It's excellent and will be a definite addition to our catalog. If there's nothing more. . . ?"

He was laughing again as he left, shutting the door behind him. With relief, Kylie gave the closed door her ugliest face and gathered up her speech.

In the Reaves' lobby, the receptionist asked Kylie to wait while she buzzed Winston. "He wants to go with you, Kylie, to hear your speech. Wait just a second. He said he would be ready when you are."

Seeing Winston's smiling face come down the hall, Kylie

waited for the now predictable suspicions to rise in her mind, wishing she could quench them with Winston. He was so genuinely friendly and consistently cheerful, but unfortunately Kylie knew that neither of those traits negated the possibility of evil. They only made its presence more sinister.

"What's the matter?" Winston asked, catching her eye on him as they waited for a taxi.

"Nothing. How'd you do in the typhoon?"

"No problem. The flat I'm in now is so far superior to what I lived in with my family, it was like being in a castle. The carpet hardly got wet. Besides, I had company," he said, leering shamelessly.

"Camilla?"

"Who? Oh, no, she flew out Friday before the storm got bad. This time I had little Colleen from Ireland with me!"

"Congratulations," Kylie responded drily. Then, hoping against reason that she wasn't playing her hand too freely, she asked, "Winston, you have contacts in the Zhejiang province, don't you?" She named the general region from which the porcelain shipments were coming and waited for his response.

"Relatives," Winston said, nodding. "If you're thinking *guanxi*, I might be able to help. Coming from the poorest of peasant stock, who are nevertheless endowed with the keenest of intellects, my many relatives in Zhejiang have risen dramatically under the Communist regime." He winked at Kylie. "Always out for the main chance, if you get my drift!"

The ride to the restaurant was too brief for Kylie to pump Winston any more, but as she sat at the head table during the luncheon, she studied him carefully. Could he really be so devious that he would intentionally bring up reasons to believe him guilty and then expect her to discount them because of his openness? He had relatives in the very region the smuggled goods were coming from, relatives with some kind of power. He was offering her the most likely conduit for smuggled goods and all with a smile. The only clue she needed now was the actual source of the authentic pieces.

She had been thinking about that, of course, and had con-

cluded that someone had probably discovered a long-forgot-
ten grave filled with treasures. Or possibly an entire cemetery.
During the many waves of military oppression that had swept
over China, each conqueror had felt the right to run rough-
shod over the local people's sensibilities. Mr. Hu had spoken
repeatedly about the Japanese occupation of Manchuria and
once told her about a local army bulldozing a cemetery to
build an airport. That surely happened in earlier centuries as
well. What if local officials had discovered such a cemetery,
one in which wealthy people had been buried?

So what about Winston, with his expensive girlfriends,
car, travels, and ambitions? Was he pulling a classic bluff, confusing her with his artless confidences, all the while watching
for another opportunity to put his hand on her back, her face
in the street?

Awful. Really, really awful what this whole affair was doing to her relationships.

After the speech Winston stayed downtown—to run an
errand, he said, which Kylie thought probably involved the
charming auburn-haired woman who had been sitting beside
him during the luncheon. Which was a good reminder that
Winston Lu was too simple, his needs too straightforward to
accommodate the guile necessary to be doing this smuggling;
Kylie was sure of it.

On the way back to the office, Kylie leaned back in the
taxi and let her body relax. Thanks to her father's relentless
training, the speech had gone well. He had shown her again
and again that with a little effort she could throw off personal
problems and present a cheerful, calm, and confident public
front—at least for a while. At many social functions with him,
she had watched him smile as if he really meant it, smile with
feeling. Friendliness without feeling would not convince, and
people in the diplomatic service were too savvy to tolerate an
inadequate performance. Kylie had learned the trick, achieving the appearance when she knew herself to care hardly at all
for the one she was greeting. In the act, her body would relax,
her eyes light up. And yet it was all an act, an acquired skill

without any basis in fact. Such deceit! A life of constant guile. Her father certainly never carried his public persona into his private life. The same affable, smiling man who so charmed visiting dignitaries would spare her barely a glance the next morning at breakfast, and she his only daughter.

So that's how it was. One was an act—feeling the emotion in the absence of fact. The other was faith, apparently—knowing the fact in the absence of emotion. Wasn't that what God expected of Elijah? *"I know you feel alone, but don't you know anyway that I am with you?"*

Forgive me, God, but it's all so hard.

Twelve

Jack hadn't stopped by while she was at her speech.

Lily said, "Sorry, Kylie. What's he doing today?"

"Who knows."

"You look very tired," Lily said sympathetically.

Did Lily know why Kylie was tired? Were Lily's words a veiled warning? Kylie almost screamed in frustration.

"Yes," she admitted to Lily, "I am tired. In fact, after I finish a little correspondence I think I'll go home early. But first, I haven't had a chance to ask you how you did during the typhoon?"

"The beginning was exciting. Carson came rushing through here around two o'clock and sent everyone home. He looked like that little character in the books, do you know which one I mean? The little chicken—"

"I think you mean Chicken Little," Kylie said.

"The one who says, 'The sky is falling'? Yes! Carson is such a dramatist, have you noticed? Everything is a crisis with him."

Knowing she would sound a little prim, Kylie said, "He's run the branch well for almost thirty years, Lily."

As expected, Lily's open thoughts vanished, replaced by the subservience more fitting for an assistant, but not before Kylie saw a brief flare of resentment. After Lily returned to her room, Kylie sighed and leaned her head down on her desk. What did Lily think, that Kylie would share in her gossip about Carson? Kylie suspected that Lily would be leaving the branch soon, taking a job in a rival firm, just as Kylie herself had done when the restraints of being an assistant had chafed too much. Kylie would have to find a way to communicate her support to Lily. She would help in any way she could as Lily tried to find a higher position. Then perhaps, even in rival firms, they could remain friendly.

Kylie worked on her correspondence until four-thirty, trying to keep thoughts of Jack tamped down and under control, but each time the phone rang, she hoped it was Jack. Whatever she was doing, she was aware of her tension—her chest a little tight, her muscles taut—and she forced herself to occasionally take deep breaths in an effort to relax. The situation at work seemed to be building to a climax, and she wanted him with her. Needed him.

When she did see Jack, she would have to ask his forgiveness, even knowing that she could never regain the camaraderie of the weekend. She could imagine his face: remote, watchful, unyielding. More than ever she wanted to curl into a ball under heavy blankets and let hours and hours pass, so many that when she finally rose, it would be to a new world, problems changed, people different.

Without Jack?

She sat at her desk. The surface was clean, the work put away. It was the end of her day, as productive as ever, yet her life had never looked so bleak.

Again, the question—*Without Jack?*

Yes. She had to face it. Probably not tomorrow, maybe not even this week, but soon Jack would leave. Hong Kong in June. Somewhere else in July. Another episode in his life, another supporting character.

She could hear him now with another woman in another city, describing Hong Kong, the food, the typhoon. A fascinating place. And into the tale he would weave his "friend." Would he name her? No, probably not. He hadn't named his friend in Botswana.

Kylie's city had served him drama, mystery, and perhaps even yet danger. A memorable mix and Kylie just part of the spice.

Don't sound so bitter. He's not nearly as callused as you'd like at this moment to pretend. But it would be so much easier to send him away if he were.

Jack had spoken with great affection of that woman in Botswana, and he would undoubtedly refer to Kylie in the same way, once his anger from the morning had faded.

She felt utterly defeated.

If you want more than affection from a man, Kylie Austin, show enough sense not to want it from Jack Sullivan.

Before she left, she asked Lily on impulse if Phillip had been in all day.

"In the morning. Then his wife came, and he went with her."

Brief words, undoubtedly masking drama.

The humor of it hit Kylie. One minute she was castigating Lily for gossiping; the next she was wishing Lily would elaborate. Doubtless the assistants and secretaries knew far more than what Lily was saying, probably having hashed and rehashed Sylvie's confrontation and Phillip's submissive withdrawal from the office. Well, Kylie knew whom to ask.

"Winston," she said after closing his office door, "what happened with Phillip this morning?"

"Ah-ha! So you actually want a little gossip. You won't shoot any stern words to me about Phillip's years running the jade branch, will you?"

Kylie rolled her eyes, amazed at how quickly Lily had spread her frustration through the office.

"What happened, Winston? I have my reasons for asking."

"Hey, chill! I don't care what you say to the high and mighty Lily! Just teasing. Sylvie came in not long after Phillip got here, around 9:30, I guess, closeted herself with him in his office, 'angry and worried,' I heard, and then Phillip was checking out for the day. That's all I know."

It could be something to do with their children, Phillip's gambling, even their car or flat. The list of what could make Sylvie angry was endless, but Kylie found it too easy to put her own slant on Sylvie's actions. Had Sylvie suddenly discovered that Jack and Kylie had been out at Records Security, the guard there also under a bribe? If so, Sylvie and Phillip may have gone home to plan their next strike against Kylie or to cover their tracks more thoroughly. In fact, it could have been Sylvie who stole Kylie's bag on Thursday; she was petite and had black hair.

Winston was watching her speculatively from the other side of his desk. Kylie took a deep breath and tried to relax.

"Long night," she announced. "I'm going home. Thanks for coming to hear my speech."

With a glint of mischief, he said, "My pleasure," and remembering his luncheon companion, Kylie could believe it.

No message from Jack on her answering machine when she got home. On the coffee table was the package he had left. It was a two-disk set of Mendelssohn's *Elijah*. The second disk began after Mount Carmel, after the rain, with Jezebel threatening Elijah. Kylie put that disk in, listening for the next hour to pain and promises, fear and assurance, wanting Jack all the more by the end of it, yet all the more certain she couldn't have him.

What was he doing? At seven, she tried calling him at his hotel for the third time and smiled ruefully at the desk clerk's patient assurance that he would give her message to Jack as soon as he came in.

When her phone finally rang at 7:30, Kylie jumped up, grateful in some strange way that God had delayed Jack's call for so long. Earlier she had been dreading the apology; now she was dreading the delay and wanted nothing more than the chance to clear things between them.

It was Carson.

"Oh. Hi," Kylie said, not caring if he heard the catch in her voice.

Carson must not have noticed, for he launched immediately into a request for her to come back to the office. "We need an emergency meeting," he said. When Kylie didn't respond, Carson added, "Immediately, Kylie. Come now."

"I . . . I can't. Not now, Carson. I'm . . . I've got something else going on right now." Hearing her own fumbling excuses, Kylie wanted to scream. How could she have anticipated this?

"Do you have someone there with you?"

"No! I just can't come right now."

"You're upset about this morning," Carson said. "Look, I'm sorry. I came on too strong; I admit it. But this isn't personal, Kylie; this concerns the good of Reaves, and our branch in particular." He paused and then continued more carefully, as if someone could be listening to him. "Something has come to my attention, something odd, and I think we should meet and discuss this development. Better by far if we sort this out without alerting Chicago, but after tonight, if you insist, you can bring Jack in on it."

"Something odd . . ." Kylie repeated.

"I can't explain over the phone. Phillip and Winston are on their way; we'll be expecting you." Without giving her a chance to refuse again, Carson hung up.

Jack! she thought desperately, wishing she could telepathically get his attention. What was it Jack had said—dead letters to someone who had moved away?

Please, please, Jack, be at the Mandarin.

The clerk recognized her voice and told her before she said anything more than hello that Jack had not yet returned.

"Please tell him I've had to go to the office."

"Yes, of course, Ms. Austin. I will pass on the message."

"No, really, it's very important!" Kylie exclaimed, wondering if the clerk had even listened.

"Yes, of course, Ms. Austin. I understand completely."

"Can you watch for him? Catch him as he comes in?"

"We will do our best, Ms. Austin, of course, but if we miss him he is certain to notice the message light on his room telephone."

Yes, yes, of course, Kylie silently mimicked back.

It sounded on the phone as if Carson had stumbled onto the smuggling somehow, and that this emergency meeting was on that issue. Perhaps Carson would bring out a post-humous message that Robert had left, or have Mary there to bring out her suspicions. Unlike Jack, Carson may have felt the best tactic was to bring everything out into the open, flushing out the rabbits, so to speak. Would he then suggest that the smuggling stop? Let the whole thing fade away? Or would Carson find some other way to resolve the problem?

Except whoever had pushed Kylie on Saturday wasn't a rabbit. And neither was Jack. Perhaps Carson didn't realize he'd flush out a tiger instead.

Wiping her hands compulsively against her slacks, hoping to remove the sweat and warm them, Kylie confronted what she knew was the greater danger: that Carson himself was the tiger and she the rabbit that he was seeking to catch.

So then she shouldn't go.

But what if Carson wasn't the smuggler? How would she explain her non-appearance? All of Jack's efforts to keep his investigation undercover would be wasted.

So then she should go.

She dawdled as long as she could, brushing her hair and fixing makeup, but fifteen minutes later she could think of no other excuse to delay. Casting one last look at the telephone, she shook her head and went downstairs.

Before getting into the taxi, she looked for Sanford Chang's man, but tonight couldn't spot him. What would Kylie have said to him anyway? *Come up with me for this meeting, be my bodyguard on the spot*? How could she have explained that to the others then?

As the taxi drew up to the office building, Kylie hurriedly called Justine on her new cellular phone. "I can't talk now, Justine, but could you do me a favor? If Jack calls looking for me, will you tell him I had to go to the office? Tell him I didn't have any choice, that I'm sorry, that he can find me there. And, Justine . . . just tell him I'm sorry. About everything. Okay?''

"Kylie, what is going on?"

"I can't talk now, Justine. Just tell him, okay? Even if he doesn't call you. You call him. He's at the Mandarin. You can reach him there, later tonight I think."

"Kylie!"

"Bye."

The taxi driver was impatient. "We here, lady. This your place."

"Yeah, okay," Kylie said, not even bothering to slip into Chinese. "Thanks."

What had made her call Justine? Was she that certain she was walking into a trap? Then why go? Kylie stood outside the building and looked up at the tall structure. A very large trap, a warren of danger.

It was all so unreal. Maybe everything was a weird string of coincidences. Murray really on walkabout; Robert's death hit-and-run; Kylie's carry-all a simple theft; the hand on her back purely accidental. Was that so impossible?

Perhaps when she went up, Phillip and Winston would be waiting with Carson. Carson's assistant as well. They would discuss some other totally unrelated topic. And Kylie would be home before Jack even returned to the Mandarin.

Jack. Her mind stalled on his image. One question that Carson had raised on the phone especially concerned her. Shouldn't Carson have asked if Jack were with her rather than just someone? Did Carson already know Jack wasn't with her because Jack was with Carson—against his will? She felt sudden empathy for what Jack had gone through the night before.

If Jack was in danger, Kylie would have to enter the trap. She had no choice, not with the possibility that she could help him.

This time she signed in openly with Simon Pao, greeting him calmly, but in the lift she collapsed slightly against the side.

Make him be okay, please, please. Wherever Jack is, keep him safe.

The Reaves lobby was empty and darkened as she walked through it. The halls as well had minimal lights. Carson's office was deserted, but Kylie had expected as much, and walked farther down the hall to the doorway off the interior hall that led into the conference room. When she entered, she was surprised to find even this room empty.

"Carson?" she said, and then turned again toward the door, intending to look in another room.

The door swung shut before her eyes and Carson himself stepped out from the shadows behind it. He was alone, his expression impassive, almost matter-of-fact, a half-smile on his face. But his eyes were like bottomless pits, black and cold and cruel. They scared her.

His eyes . . . and the gun in his hands.

"Finally, Kylie Austin where I want her."

"Carson?" She barely got the word out. Her mouth felt dry, her tongue swollen and constricting.

"Don't look so surprised. I knew this morning that we were close to the edge, you and I. It wouldn't take long for you to realize I had to be behind the smuggling."

"No. I didn't know."

"Really?" He snorted and shrugged. "If not you, Jack. You fooled me at first, you two, holding hands and flirting across the room with each other. There's always been an unmistakable chemistry between you. But you called him in after Murray disappeared, didn't you? He was here to investigate me—not you! So I couldn't let you keep looking, don't you see? The pieces were falling too quickly into place."

Through all his words, one question pounded in Kylie's brain: Did this mean he didn't have Jack? *Please, please, make it so!*

Struggling to keep her thoughts hidden, Kylie held out her hands to show she had nothing that could threaten Carson and then backed away from him to lean against the table. "Winston and Phillip aren't coming?"

No answer other than a snort.

"What pieces are you talking about, falling into place?"

"Mei-lin's Zhejiang relatives, of course, and the little treasures they've been sending."

"I thought it was Winston who had relatives there."

Carson laughed snidely. "Didn't you know that Mei-lin and Winston are related? Certainly. Mei-lin's mother and Winston's grandmother were sisters. Mei-lin's mother ran off to work in Shanghai, married an upstart capitalist banker, who then had to run off to Hong Kong after the revolution. Her sister stayed home in Zhejiang province, tending the old parents. I've always thought there was a fine sense of irony in all of that. Mei-lin's mother running off and marrying without permission; then Mei-lin herself doing it."

Irony, yes, Kylie thought, but a rather bitter one for Mei-lin. Carson had certainly never acquired the capitalist wealth that her father had.

"And where is the artwork coming from?"

Carson smiled maliciously. "Are you stalling, Kylie? Let me assure you, Mei-lin's watching at the Mandarin and Jack has not yet returned to get your many messages. When—or if—he ever does, she'll call me immediately. So forget hopes of a rescue. Hope instead—for his sake—that he doesn't show up here."

So he really didn't know where Jack was. A tremendous weight lifted from Kylie's heart. She felt so lightheaded that if Carson had known he would have thought she had gone insane.

"No, no, Carson," she said, hardly sounding worried, which clearly confused Carson. "Actually I've figured out very little. Where were the pieces coming from?"

"First from what Mei-lin's family had squirreled away. The Chinese are famous for that, you know. Sly as dogs." He watched Kylie's expected reaction and laughed. "Does that offend you? What a funny little creature you are to take their feelings so much to heart! We're all dogs, didn't you know that, the Chinese just a slightly different breed than we are."

"You said first from Mei-lin's family?"

"The process worked so well that we found another source, much more reliable. Mei-lin's cousin or nephew—anyway, one of her many relatives—works in a museum in Shanghai. With care we were able to replace antique pieces with reproductions and have him bury them deep enough in the museum's many stockpiles to make discovery unlikely. We've been doing it for over ten years now."

"Why?"

"Can you really be so naive? You know Mei-lin."

Indeed. And no one who knew Mei-lin could wonder why Carson needed money. "I thought perhaps the money . . . came from her family?"

He rolled his eyes this time.

No, of course not. They would never have sought or accepted help from Mei-lin's father. Never, never lose face. It was the oldest and strictest rule in the Orient. Kylie almost felt sorry for them—almost. Mei-lin the stronger, shackled by pride to a weak man who could rise so far in business and no further. Not enough to rise to the top of the branch in Hong Kong, never enough unless they could keep pace with Mei-lin's family in power and possessions. Did Mei-lin know Carson was propping up his wounded ego by chasing other women? Maybe she didn't even care.

Whoever said greed lay behind every crime was absolutely right!

"You probably have other questions," Carson said slyly.

The last few days must have been pleasant for him in a rather bizarre way, Kylie thought, watching her and Jack search blindly for the truth.

"Have you even figured out who stole your bag on Thursday?"

Kylie shook her head.

"Or who pushed you in front of that bus?"

"No."

"Nor even why?"

She shrugged, struggling now to keep her fear from him.

Her brief moment of relief for Jack had passed, the danger of her own position far too evident.

"Tiffany stole your bag on Thursday afternoon." He laughed at Kylie's surprise, the sound more and more like a childish snicker. "Not every woman is so blind to my charms, Kylie Austin. Just because you turned up your little nose at me doesn't mean all women do."

Kylie could think of nothing useful to say, the thought of Tiffany and Carson both pitiable and appalling. What did Tiffany expect to get from this man? Surely not love? Not even loyalty. Had a position as secretary in the Reaves warehouse been worth such abasement?

"I'm not the one stalling now, Carson," she said in a bored voice. "Let's get on with this—whatever you're planning."

"You're not stupid. I'm going to kill you. Of course."

There were those words again: Of course. Always of course. The predictable, almost unavoidable result of whatever cause presented itself. Of course the clerk would tell Jack. Of course Mei-lin was watching. Of course Kylie would die. "I'm going to kill you," Carson said again, and until that moment Kylie hadn't believed it was possible.

This is it, God? You brought me out of all that mess, planned Mr. Hu for me, Justine, even Jack, and now You're going to let this man kill me, without even a chance to run for my life?

There was an incredible sense of unreality to everything, like playacting—the gun a prop, ketchup for blood, and applause waiting at the end of the scene. A ghastly bubble of laughter gurgled in her throat and she forced it back down, the contents of her stomach threatening to follow the sick little giggle.

Past caring what Carson saw of her fear, she couldn't move her eyes from the gun. The hand holding the barrel blurred under her gaze and the rest of the handle as well, until only the small black hole at the tip was in focus—all of her life shrunk down to that one moment, a portal on eternity. What would it feel like to have a bullet pierce her skin, clawing inexorably through her until it found her soul and destroyed it?

Her soul? She hooked her breath on a small gasp.

"What's the matter with you? Are you going to faint?"

His questions drew her gaze at last up from the gun, but when she spoke, the words she said came unexpectedly, from a source she couldn't at first identify.

"You can't hurt me," she said.

"You think I'm bluffing?" His lips parted in a sneer. "This gun's loaded, little lady, believe me. I can kill you anytime just by pulling this trigger. The safety's off."

"Oh, you could shoot. I know."

She bit her lip, struggling briefly to find the words she sought—she had sung them too many times in Chinese. What were they in English? At last they came, and they were for her a shield, a fortress, a stronghold around her heart.

She said them out loud: "The body they may kill."

"You're not making any sense."

"I really can let it go—goods and kindred, even life. You can't hurt me."

"You're babbling."

But if not to him, she was at long last making sense to herself. She didn't belong on that barren plain. Whatever He withheld; all that she feared to lose; *yet* He would take her to the heights, to the heights of heaven itself, and there she *would* praise Him.

Utterly dependent; utterly safe as well.

"You can't hurt me," she said again, the words sounding ethereal.

As if to prove her wrong, he grabbed her arm and shoved the gun into her side.

"I'm not alone," she warned him.

"If you're thinking of your pathetic little bodyguards, we have successfully diverted them," Carson snarled. "A little money works wonders with underlings."

He yanked her arm again, pulling her past the long table toward the door leading into the Reaves lobby.

"Where are we going?"

He paused just inside the door, looking down at her, baring his teeth in an evil grin. He was obviously savoring the moment. "For a little boat ride, Ms. Kylie Austin. We've studied the currents and know where to throw your body to have you come up far down the coast. It certainly worked with Murray!"

"Why? Why Murray? Why kill him?"

Carson's nostrils flared with contempt. "He tried to blackmail me. Can you believe it? 'One good payment,' he said, 'and I'll be out of Hong Kong. Gone forever.' Well, he's gone forever now, isn't he? Stupid fool! Just as you will be—and no one will recognize you even if they find your body, thanks to a heavy dose of battering on your face. Don't worry, we're not savages! We'll fix your face after you're dead." His hand squeezed her upper arm, though whether in anticipation or some perverted comfort she couldn't tell.

"Carson . . ."

"A little fear from the iron miss? At last!" He grinned cruelly. "I suppose it's not a pleasant thought, is it, your face smashed in, your body mangled beyond recognition?"

"Stop it!"

"Where's your talk now of not being alone?" He pushed her to the door. "Open it! I'm not letting go of you here."

She wished she could get across to him her sudden overwhelming knowledge of God's support and presence, to tell him again that he couldn't really hurt her, that she was beyond his reach. She tried to get the words in her mind—The Sovereign Lord is my strength; the Sovereign Lord is my strength—but her heart and lungs and muscles were screaming panic and fear instead, confusing her feelings beyond control and causing her faith to slip.

God, she cried, *help me hold on to You! Be my stillpoint, even here! I need You.*

She pulled the door open and stepped through, Carson close behind her.

As if in slow motion, a figure appeared to her right.

A figure with Jack's face and Jack's body, stepping toward her, shoving her out of the way.

Without conscious thought, Kylie began to scream, "Don't! He has a gun!"

And then Carson fired.

But not at Kylie.

Recognizing the greater threat, Carson pulled the gun from Kylie's side and fired at Jack, the movement giving Jack a split second to veer down and away. The first shot went wide, shattering the glass wall of the lobby. But Jack, intent on protecting Kylie, lunged toward Carson and the second shot found its mark.

Freed from Carson, Kylie turned and grabbed the only object at hand, a large porcelain wine jar standing at the entrance of the conference room. With horror, Kylie saw Jack stagger backward and crumple to the floor. Driven by terror and blinding anger, she brought the wine jar crashing down on Carson's head, grateful beyond words that he wasn't taller. He sprawled on the carpeted floor. His last shot, fired in sudden defense at Kylie, hit far wide of her, and before he could fire again, she lifted the still intact jar and brought it down again, this time causing blood to gush from his scalp. She lifted the jar again, beyond caring that her enemy lay unconscious at her feet.

"Kylie," Jack protested weakly from the floor in front of her. "Kylie . . . stop."

Hearing his voice, she froze, saw Carson unconscious beneath her, and dropped the jar, where it finally broke in two against the wall. She knelt in anguish beside Jack. A dark stain was spreading against his left side; red showed on the floor beside him.

"Jack, what can I do?"

"Are you . . . okay? We were . . . so sure he wouldn't do it . . . here."

"Don't talk. I'll get a doctor. Please lie still."

"I will call an ambulance," said a man behind her.

Kylie turned in fear. An older Chinese man had come

through the door leading to the offices. In fresh panic Kylie hovered between the man and Jack, her only thought to shield Jack from more harm.

"Sanford Chang," the man said. He held out something to Kylie. "Put my jacket against his wound. I'll call an ambulance."

"Are you okay?" Jack murmured, still weakly. "Kylie . . . this morning. I'm sorry."

"Be quiet, Jack," Kylie begged, brushing his hair back from his forehead. His eyes were closed now, his breathing more labored. "Lie still. Your friend's called an ambulance."

"We split up," Jack said, each word painful. "Sanford at the other door, me here. What a mess."

"I'm fine, Jack, except that you're hurt. Please lie still. Jack, please, be still."

"A tiger. Thought you might . . . kill him."

Remembering Carson, panic caught her again, and she looked over almost expecting to see that he had come to and was rising indestructible to do more damage.

"I have his gun," Sanford Chang said calmly from the receptionist's desk where he was calling for the ambulance. "You're quite safe."

"He said he bribed the bodyguard you had on me."

"We let him think so," the detective said. "Space, you know. We give him space, see what he does. Except for Jack, it worked fine. He certainly came out of hiding."

Jack's hand against her cheek went limp, and horror swept over her again. "Jack, wait!" she cried, laying her head on his chest, tears falling, unable to tell if he was still alive.

Keeping his eye on Carson, Sanford came forward to take Jack's pulse. "Weak, but okay. Don't you worry, Ms. Austin. Here—put this cushion under his legs. Blood will get to heart better that way. But keep pressing the wound. See?"

Kylie did as Sanford said and then knelt beside Jack, holding his hand to her lips and breathing a prayer into each kiss she gave him.

So this was what love meant, she thought as tears ran

down her face. Being willing to give anything to have him okay. Changes flooding in, swift and sudden. Heaven so real one moment and then a completely different kind of hell threatening the next.

Please, please, let him live, she begged. *Please. Even if I can never have his love in return.* Her own death she could almost accept; his death in her place she would mourn forever.

Thirteen

oments later paramedics filled the lobby, then in a surge of activity the room emptied, Jack and Carson leaving on stretchers, taken downstairs, where another of Sanford's agents stood beside Simon Pao.

"We couldn't have him warning Carson, now could we?" Sanford said from beside her.

In a daze, Kylie shook her head.

She found herself being hustled into a police car, then watching as first Carson under guard left in one ambulance and then Jack in a second. Kylie insisted that both be taken to the Adventist Hospital on Stubbs Road and begged the middle-aged officer to let her go with him.

"We'll follow Mr. Sullivan's ambulance, Ms. Austin. It's better to give the paramedics room to work."

"He'll be okay," Sanford said through the police car window. "You'll see. The bullet went straight through. It's practically just a flesh wound."

Please, make him right, she prayed.

To no one in particular, the officer said, "If someone had called us in earlier, there might not have been any blood."

"I thought you said we would follow the ambulance?" Kylie prompted.

"Right you are. Get going, driver." As the car drew out into traffic, the officer introduced himself. "Rupert Maitland, Ms. Austin. Hong Kong CID."

"Oh."

"I'll be needing a statement from you."

"Yes, okay."

"A particular friend, this Mr. Sullivan?"

"What do you mean by particular?"

"No matter. Why don't you relax, Ms. Austin? We'll be at the hospital in a few minutes."

At the hospital, the inspector's voice kept droning on, asking question after question. Through a fog of worry and shock, Kylie struggled to answer them. Mindful of Jack's reservations, she told the inspector as little as possible.

At some point, she thought she should call Winston and Phillip, then decided against it. How could she know that they weren't in on it? But if they were, wouldn't Mei-lin be implicating them now? Where was Mei-lin, anyway?

No answer at first from the inspector, just an arched look from under raised eyebrows. Apparently, if Kylie could hold back, so could the inspector. Finally: "She's here, with Mr. Grey, under police escort."

Kylie winced. "How is he?"

"He has a concussion, Ms. Austin. He regained consciousness briefly, and while the doctors are somewhat guarded about his progress, it seems that he'll recover."

The inspector waited, watching her, perhaps expecting some piece of information in return. Kylie had never felt so alone. If he were beside her, what would Jack tell her to do now?

"And my colleagues, Winston Lu and Phillip Hughes?"

"They are being questioned as well. We *will* find the reason behind Mr. Grey's attack."

I'm sure you will, Kylie wanted to say, but remained cautious.

"Perhaps I should call them."

"I would hold off if I were you."

Not exactly a suggestion, Kylie decided.

"I must at least call our CEO in Chicago." If the inspector could issue edicts, so could Kylie. "Excuse me."

Kylie got through to Harry's executive assistant first. It was 11:30 P.M., Hong Kong; 9:30 A.M. that same morning in Chicago. "I'm sorry, Kylie. Mr. Reaves is en route now. I can't say where. His orders."

She caught Joy leaving the house to run errands. Harry's wife was stunned. "No! Shot? Jack? Kylie, this is awful. Is he going to be okay?"

"He's in surgery now. He lost a lot of blood. The bullet went straight through his left side, a couple inches beneath his rib. I don't know anything else, Joy. I'm sorry. Do you know where Harry is?"

"Yes! On his way to Hong Kong. I'm going to come, too. This is crazy. Not Jack!"

It was Kylie's turn to be surprised. "When will Harry be here?"

"Well, soon. Let me think. He left last night. It's Monday here, so what time is it there? Almost Tuesday? Okay. Wait, here's his itinerary. He'll be there Tuesday morning at 8:45."

"I'll meet his plane, Joy."

"Wait! Call me—no, I'll call you. I'm taking the first flight out, so I won't be home. How can I reach you?"

"I don't know. I don't even know who to trust anymore; I don't know who's in on this. Oh! Here's my cell phone number. Or you could call my friend Justine. Here's her home phone and her office phone. I'll stay in touch with her. And Joy . . ."

"Yes?"

"You were right about Jack, at least partly. He has been very kind to me."

Kylie's regret and fear must have communicated across the wires to Joy's gentle and perceptive ears. "Oh, Kylie, I'm sorry. Keep praying, sweetie. He'll come through."

Kylie wasn't sure afterward whether Joy was talking about God or Jack. Maybe both.

After Joy, Kylie talked to Justine, who insisted on coming down to the hospital. Ready with objections, Kylie stopped herself, conscious of the barriers she had put between Justine and herself in the past. If Justine wanted to come, Kylie would let her. And if that meant making herself vulnerable to Justine, revealing her fear and guilt about Jack, then so be it.

Both Quincy and Justine came, but with the inspector hovering around, Kylie didn't say much. Finally, Justine pulled Kylie into the women's room.

"What in the world happened?" Justine asked.

Kylie first checked the four stalls to make sure they were alone and then hurriedly described the last five days. Justine grew more and more concerned until finally, hearing about Kylie's argument with Jack, she gave Kylie a fierce hug.

"He didn't desert you, girl. If he did, how'd he show up at the office with such perfect timing?"

"I think you might be right, but that doesn't mean . . ."

"That he forgives you?" Justine looked at Kylie more sharply. "Do you want him to? I mean, does it matter?"

Kylie knew what Justine was asking. For a moment their eyes met. Then Kylie looked away, knowing she'd given away her feelings.

Justine gave her another hug. "Oh, boy," she said sympathetically. "On top of everything else! What does the doctor say? Will he be all right?"

Tears close, Kylie merely shrugged.

"I think he will be," Justine said with determination. "Don't be afraid, Kylie."

Back in the waiting area, Kylie sat in renewed shock. Five days. Could she really have fallen in love over the space of five days? But a lifetime had passed since last Thursday, her heart told her. An image of Jack standing before her at the Kai Tak Airport rose up in her mind. By turns arrogant and wise, frustrating and kind, he had proven his worth to her again and again. In a sudden displacement of all her cherished notions of life she wanted nothing more than to know he was safe. She would give up anything to make him so.

"Ms. Austin?"

She looked up at the inspector, expecting another question, but it was a doctor who had spoken. She rose in a stumble of anxiety.

"Mr. Sullivan is out of surgery now. He'll be on the critical list tonight. Unavoidable, I'm afraid, with a gunshot wound in that area. If you would like to sit with him, you're welcome to." Kylie must have looked surprised—she knew that in some Hong Kong hospitals parents were not even allowed to accompany their children into the emergency room. The doctor elaborated, "After surgery we move patients to our Observation Ward, much like what you would call a recovery room in the States, I think. In our new Observation Ward, we have begun allowing the next of kin to sit with our dangerously ill patients, and you're as close to that as Mr. Sullivan has here in Hong Kong. Will you come with me?"

After gripping Justine's hand in gratitude, Kylie followed the doctor down the hall and entered the small cubicle where Jack lay. A nurse was working beside Jack's bed. "Nurse Yuan, one of our student nurses, will be responsible for Mr. Sullivan tonight. She'll be coming in through the night to take his vital signs. If you need anything, please let her know."

Jack looked awful: skin pale, eyelids almost gray, body so still that panic rushed over her. But his hand was warm when she touched it.

"Go ahead and hold it," the nurse said kindly. "He won't feel it, but you will. Then you will feel better."

Like most hospitals in Hong Kong, the staff seemed overworked and the pace hectic. For many years, because so many nurses were being offered lucrative jobs in other countries, Hong Kong hospitals had suffered a shortage of nurses. The crisis seemed to be over, but the staff was only now regaining a more reasonable pace. As soon as the nurse was finished taking Jack's vital signs, she hurried off to attend another patient.

Kylie looked down at Jack in an agony of concern. He was so still, blue eyes shut away from her, all his joy and comfort beyond her reach. Only now did she know how much she needed him.

He had listened so intently as she spoke about her interests, and she had taken his attention for granted. When she had realized he was impressed with her knowledge of China, she hadn't understood why that had so warmed her heart. At dinner the next day with Justine and Quincy, she had missed entirely why she was so proud of him.

Even unconscious in a hospital bed, Jack Sullivan had an undeniable power over her. In the past days, his varied expressions had burned themselves into her psyche—Jack laughing, concerned, his intellect sharpened by some question, his gentleness somehow unearthed. She must have spent more time watching him than she had realized.

She had thought him indestructible, herself at danger, Jack beyond reach. How selfish she must have seemed to him, self-centered and childish. She felt sick at the thought. He had known the danger, known and stood willingly beside her in spite of it, at risk because of her.

Jack, come back to me. You may never love me. I know that. You'll fly off to Botswana and your friend with the sunshine. Or Budapest or Dublin or wherever. I can live without your smile if I can only know you're smiling somewhere. Please, Jack, please come back.

He said he was utterly dependent on God, and more than ever at that moment, looking down at his sleeping form, she knew she was as well: dependent upon Him for life and breath and hope and love.

What could she do with this knowledge? If only she had at her disposal Jack's knowledge of the Bible, verses coming to mind that could comfort and assure her.

"A Bible?" the nurse said when Kylie asked. "Yes. Here in the drawer."

Kylie opened the slim volume and frowned. It was an old version, with very small print. "Please, do you think there might be a newer version somewhere?" she asked apologetically.

"Maybe. Why don't you ask at the nurses' station? There might be one on the book cart."

Within moments Kylie held a Bible in the New International Version. A calm settled over the room, broken only by the monitors around her and Jack's quiet, almost silent breathing. She wondered where to begin.

The Psalms, she decided. She would begin with the Psalms and read them one after another until she found one that spoke to her heart, and she would read that one again and again until she had it memorized. Like Jack. It would pass the time.

After very little time she found herself stumbling over the words. What amazing language God allowed David to use against Him! Here, recorded for the ages were accusations and commands that bordered on rudeness, David speaking to Almighty God in words that Kylie would never have used with her own father.

Answer me when I call to You. How long, O Lord, how long? Why, O Lord, do You stand far off? Why do You hide yourself in times of trouble? Will You forget me forever? How long will You hide your face from me? How long must I wrestle with my thoughts and every day have sorrow in my heart? How long will my enemy triumph over me? How long, O Lord?

David's response affirming the unfailing love and goodness of God didn't affect Kylie as much as the forthright words he had used against God. Why would God have allowed such accusations to be recorded in His own Bible, where everyone could see them? Didn't He know what people would think about how He dealt with His people, allowing the doubts and anguish that led to these words?

Flipping further through the Psalms, Kylie saw similar cries repeated again and again, cries from a heart of pain, poured out before the throne of God: *My God, why are you so far from saving me, so far from the words of my groaning? O my God, I cry out by day, but you do not answer.*

How . . . incredible! What other sovereign would allow a subject to speak so to Him—and then record the words for all to read again and again?

God must have found it necessary to delay the justice David asked for, to allow the pain and loneliness to linger. God was willing to take the hard way if wisdom chose it, and yet He must have known what David would feel—known and felt with him. A God of compassion.

Well, then, why, God? she asked Him. In her mind, she too knelt before God's throne. Just as David, she too would ask her questions. *Why any of it? The pain and disappointment, the unfairness of life and the suffering? How can we ever know what You're doing? How can I trust You?*

He didn't seem to respond.

In her mind, without lifting her face, she spoke her question to Him, expecting the same distant, controlled response she had received from her own father countless times: *None of your business, Kylie Austin. Take what comes and give me none of your disrespect.*

But it was Jack she saw, looking at her from the Reaves lobby floor, blood spilling from his side while his mind and heart focused on her. Eyes full of regret—not for his actions but for her fear.

Then the thought crept upon her: *For you, Kylie. I allowed the questions for you.*

She believed He would say this, and in her heart, she felt His hands gripping her arms, compelling her closer. He drew her to Him, and His touch was a thousand times more tender, more gracious than she could have believed. Completely confident in the rightness of His choices, He was also filled with compassion and love. Her heart melted inside her.

"I'm sorry," she whispered. "I had it all wrong; I didn't understand."

In her mind she saw Him so clearly; yet was unable to look into His face. She imagined His hand resting on her head, His words a tender blessing: *Kylie, my child. I love you. Whatever happens, I love you.*

And all that David knew of His unfailing kindness and love filled Kylie's own heart. The emotion spilled over in tears.

The nurse touched Kylie's shoulder, and Kylie looked up as if through a dream. She was kneeling on the floor, her face buried against Jack's bed. She lifted a hand to discover tears on her face.

"Are you all right, Ms. Austin?"

"Yes. I'm okay." And really she was, the healing more real than the tears.

After a moment, Kylie bowed her head into her hands and prayed for Jack, this time yearning to call her King by a name she had never before used: Father.

No, not Father. She needed another word. Perhaps . . . but her heart caught at the familiarity of the word flickering in the recesses of her mind. Was this really allowed? The Almighty God. Father. Daddy?

She had never called her own father that.

She felt His hand on her shoulder again.

⚬⚬⚬

Jack woke in the early hours of the morning, wincing at the pain even before he opened his eyes. It was hard to breathe, each brief intake unearthing fresh pain. He opened his eyes. Gazed at the ceiling. And remembered. The gun, the shots, Kylie battering Carson to the floor, the blood.

He turned his head slowly to the left. Kylie was in the chair beside his bed, one hand holding his, the other propping her face up. She was asleep, her dark hair lying over her cheek. He sat watching her for a moment. She looked okay. He moved his hand slightly, and she opened her eyes slowly, struggling at first to place herself, then seeing him. She blinked, her eyes full of concern.

"Jack," she whispered. "How are you?"

"Still here," he murmured back. His mouth was painfully dry. As if by magic, he found a straw nudging his lips, and he looked aside to find a nurse holding a cup to his mouth.

"Drink, Mr. Sullivan. You're probably thirsty."

"This is Nurse Yuan," Kylie informed him. "She's what they call your 'special.' "

Another, more senior nurse had entered, summoned by Nurse Yuan. Jack smiled weakly at both.

He left his hand in Kylie's, but as soon as the senior nurse

was finished with his pulse he brought his other over to feel
the bandages across his stomach. "Was it bad?"

"I don't know, Jack."

"You're doing very well, Mr. Sullivan, but you should
rest."

No need to tell him. He was already fading back into
sleep. He felt Kylie's fingers against his forehead. They
brushed a lock of his hair away, and he remembered suddenly
how much pleasure he had found in doing the same for her.
She was smiling. She must have forgiven him for letting her
think she was alone all that day. He tried to tell her that he'd
been watching her, not willing to consign her again to
Chang's underlings, but the words couldn't quite come. He
would tell her later.

When he woke up the next time, both the nurse and Kylie
were gone. Instead, Harry Reaves was sitting beside him.

Harry leaned forward. "Hey, Buddy. How're you doing?"

"Harry. Must be Tuesday. Didn't make it to the airport,
did I?"

"No kidding. Got news for you. You wouldn't make it
down the hall to the john. Don't worry. We're going to get
you out of here and back to the Mandarin with a private
nurse. We'll fix you up, old guy."

It still hurt to breathe, but with Harry in the room everything else seemed easier. Harry Reaves was a big man, fond
of steaks and home fries and good old-fashioned fun. Tough
and forthright, with a down-home sense of humor—but behind all his hale heartiness, Harry Reaves was one of the most
intelligent and honest men Jack Sullivan had ever met. A man
to lean on. A man to trust.

"I blew this one badly, Harry. Where's Kylie?"

Harry laughed. "Were those two statements a non se-
quitur? I doubt it! Get a little distracted, Jack?"

"Hey, give me a break. Let me at least sit up before you
start taking potshots."

A new nurse entered and began taking Jack's pulse and

blood pressure. "You'll have to do more than sit up, Mr. Sullivan," she said. "I want you to get up now and go to the lavatory, please."

"So, ho!" Harry laughed. "No more coddling now!"

"You didn't answer me," Jack said when he got back from the bathroom. "Where's Kylie?"

"She was exhausted; I sent her home. Sorry, guy. I know I'm not as pretty."

"Did she talk to you about Carson?"

Harry waited until the nurse finished her work. When he spoke again, he had grown much more serious. "Nurse, would it be possible for me to have just a few minutes alone with Mr. Sullivan?"

"The doctor will be in soon and then in a few minutes we'll be moving Mr. Sullivan to another ward. You can have until then. But if there's any change you must let us know immediately."

Harry waited until the nurse departed, then leaned back and crossed his arms. "Okay, Jack, let's have it. We talked . . . when? Monday morning, your time? You were watching Kylie then. What happened?"

"I decided if I could stay on her, but not necessarily with her, whoever was behind this would come out in the open. She was at the office most of the day, except for a speech. No problem there, although Sanford and I were both watching her. And he had more of his troops watching Carson and Mei-lin."

"So you were right about them."

"Only two people currently in the firm had set up contacts in Zhejiang—Carson and Kylie—and I knew Kylie wasn't behind this."

"Did you now?"

"If you want me to go on, then cut the kidding. There were other possibilities, I suppose, but Carson seemed too likely a choice, and he and Mei-lin do live like . . . well, in Hong Kong, I suppose it's bankers they live like, not kings. So, yeah, I figured it was Carson. Anyway, Kylie promised to come home in the evening and stay put. When she left I knew something important must be up. Sanford was on Carson. He saw him go up. No one else was in the office. Then Kylie came, with me behind her."

"You followed her up to the office?"

"Absolutely. Remembering what Kylie had said about the security guard, Sanford put one of his men on the man at the desk downstairs, and then he and I went up to the Reaves offices. A little quiet checking and we knew they were in the conference room. Sanford took the door leading into the hall with the offices. I took the door into the lobby. Then we listened and waited, hoping he wouldn't do anything there. It turned out he wasn't planning to. We had to give him time to implicate himself. When he forced Kylie through the door, he had a gun on her. I pushed her aside and then Kylie was incredible. She knocked him out with a porcelain jug. I thought she was going to kill him."

"He almost killed you."

"Yeah, well, I didn't duck fast enough." Jack took a slow, painful breath. "When's Kylie coming back, anyway?"

Harry's eyebrows rose. They were old friends, and Harry wasn't going to hide anything. He was frankly interested in Jack's feelings about Kylie.

"Take it easy," Jack said. "I want to know what Carson said, that's all. Sanford came equipped with earphones and an amplifier, but I couldn't hear everything."

"That's all? Just to talk about Carson?" In response to the questions that hovered in his eyes, Jack shook his head.

"It's not going to happen, Harry."

"She seemed pretty broken up. Sat with you all night."

"Nope. Not a chance. I'm telling you now, stay out of it. Tell Joy the same. I don't want any long-distance pep talks. I mean it, Harry."

"Hey, why? Kylie Austin's quite a woman."

"Think she'd ever leave Hong Kong? Think I'd ever settle down here? Our lives have gotten tangled up together during the last five days, but you can't build a relationship—or a marriage—on what we've gone through. I'm not sure she'd even want to try."

Jack gave Harry a grim smile at the other man's dropped jaw. Obviously his boss was just as surprised as Jack to hear the *M* word come out of his mouth.

The nurse came back in then with a doctor who promptly began poking and prodding.

The doctor, who was Chinese, no doubt had a great deal of authority within the hospital. He explained in detail what damage the gunshot had done, Jack's good fortune in not having been hit a little higher, and the surgery that had been needed. Jack had been taken off the critical list sometime during the night.

"And when will this guy be ready to travel?" Harry asked next.

"Back to the States? Not for a while, I would think. That wound will take a little time to heal. Perhaps a week. Are you sore, Mr. Sullivan?"

"A little."

"We'll have the nurse give you something for the pain. For now, try to get some more rest."

The nurse came in a few minutes later and informed Harry that he would have to leave. "Now that Mr. Sullivan is officially off the critical list, he'll be moving to a regular ward where he can only have visitors at specified times. The nurse at the desk will give you our official hours."

"Even next-of-kin?"

"For his own good, Mr. Reaves."

In her own domain, she was as dominant as the doctor. Harry went.

⚬~~~⚬

By midday, Harry had moved Jack to the Mandarin and hired a private nurse to care for him. Jack slept most of the day and by evening was feeling both less weak and more pain.

The bandages were chafing, and he hated the indignity of being even slightly immobilized.

Kylie came around seven, standing first by the door and eventually pulling the chair toward the end of Jack's bed and sitting down. She had none of the earlier unguarded intimacy. Her chin said it all: fences up, distance measured.

He wanted to hold up his hands and say, *Take it easy. I get the message. The crisis is over and you're back on your own.*

She had, however, shed her business suit and was wearing black slacks and a turquoise blouse. Best of all, her hair was hanging in lose curls around her face.

Mixed messages, Kylie. What am I to make of all this?

"What have you been doing all day?" he asked aloud.

"A lengthy session with Inspector Maitland."

"How much did you tell him?"

"The bare minimum until Harry showed up. I suppose Carson will be charged with attempted murder; Mei-lin as an accomplice. They're probably looking for Murray's body now." She shook her head. "They won't find him."

Something crossed her face, so fleeting he might have imagined it, but he had spent enough time watching her in the last five days to recognize terror. "Kylie? What?"

She wouldn't look at him. "It's all over now."

He watched her a moment longer. He would get the reason for that terror out of her eventually, if he could only be patient.

"Let *me* begin, then," he said. "I left you Monday morning, but I didn't go far. After Sunday night, Sanford and I decided we would have to leave you . . . well, exposed. It seemed more and more certain to me that Carson was behind all this, but he wouldn't take a chance at confronting you until I was out of the way."

"You knew it was Carson?"

Jack explained why.

"So our argument on Monday morning played into your hands."

"Fortunately enough secretaries were on hand at the office to see your show of temper."

Kylie rolled her eyes. "Usually more Sylvie's scene than mine."

Jack wasn't ready to joke about anything yet. "I'm sorry about how I left, Kylie. I intended telling you that I'd be watching, then changed my mind. I was worried about how well you would keep it concealed. At the last minute things disintegrated between us; it seemed easier all the way around to leave without telling you what I would be doing."

His words caught Kylie by surprise. *He* was apologizing? She shook her head in wonder.

"You were wise not to tell me."

"You're very generous."

"No, really. It was obvious to everyone at the office that something had happened between us. I called your hotel several times, asked Lily about a message, all very realistic. If I had known you were nearby I couldn't have acted that worried. You made the right choice."

He nodded, then shrugged.

Kylie looked away, gathering courage. She knew what she had to do. "I'm the one who was wrong on Monday morning. I said things that weren't true. You had only my best interests at heart when you had those men watch my flat on Sunday night. As for you wanting to be in control, I was the one who didn't contact you for that reason. It's an old problem with me—sharing burdens with other people. I'm sorry."

With a power she couldn't identify or fight, he held her gaze for a moment. In his eyes she saw compassion and patience: Jesus looking at Peter when the cock crowed. Her heart twisted inside her, compassion almost harder to bear than anger. How could she ever consider herself worthy of this man, she with such an inadequate understanding and practice of love?

He held out an open palm to her, an offering of forgiveness. "You had a terrible night, for which I was partly to blame. You weren't thinking straight. Nothing you said could have changed my concern for your safety."

So I'm like David in the Psalms, all his ranting but God still faithful?

Her heart fell. Jack had spoken kindly but unemotionally. Apparently his feelings for her were standard issue, much the same as for all the people he worked with, his concern and attention occasioned by circumstances and not by Kylie herself.

"Now you're the one who's being generous," she said. "Thank you for the *Elijah*; in fact, thank you for everything you've said about God. I needed to hear it; I did. He's . . . I'm . . . getting there, Jack. Really. But the *Elijah*, in particular, was special. Coming just then, before the experience with Carson, God was showing me I wasn't alone in my doubts. That He cares and will be gracious. So . . . thank you."

"Kylie, I'm glad."

Confused by his probing gaze, Kylie plunged on. "Actually, having the oratorio was . . . almost as good as having you there." Her lashes fluttered a little and color suffused her cheeks, but this time she didn't look away.

He didn't respond, not immediately, but when his expression shifted and she thought she saw surprise and then wariness, shame flooded in to replace longing. So there it was. Kylie was indeed another in a long line of friendships, her blushing response an added element to his memories of Hong Kong, his eyes growing soft when he talked of her in future years.

"Kylie."

Seeking to spare him, she jumped ahead. "Were you outside the conference room the whole time we were talking? Did you hear what Carson said?"

He answered slowly, his thoughts catching up. "Yes, some of it, Sanford more than I. Thanks to you, Carson got himself in deep."

"It was Mei-lin who started the process. Her mother's sister had some artifacts that they had kept all these years. When those were gone, they set up a conduit from within a Shanghai art museum. It had been going on for years."

"Why did he want to kill you? Did you ever figure that out?"

"After talking to Carson, the inspector explained it all to me. On Saturday, the security guard at the warehouse called Carson when we showed up there. He had time to set up outside and follow us to Mary's. Pushing me in front of the bus was an impulse. He saw how my knowledge of the branch was helping you investigate and decided to throw up a roadblock for you by eliminating me. He didn't think about me, really, just what I knew. The longer he thought about that the more purposeful he became."

"Would killing you have slowed things down so much? I would have continued the investigation."

"But without help and on your own you probably wouldn't have succeeded. He counted on controlling Winston through Mei-lin. Blood ties run even thicker in China than in the West. Her influence had gotten him the job in the first place. He was obligated. As for Phillip, Carson had only to alert Sylvie and Phillip would be useless to you. She hates Harry. We all know that."

"Yes. Coals of fire to have to rely on Harry for a job. A constant irritant and reminder of Phillip's weakness."

"As for Carson, he would be dodgy enough to hinder your questions while seeming to help. My death was intended mainly as a delay tactic. In six months, a year, they would have been leaving Hong Kong anyway and moving to England. He has a full passport, you know, and so does Mei-lin."

"I could have called in the police. Didn't he think about that?"

"Perhaps, but maybe he didn't see them as much of a threat."

"Who stole your bag then? Not Carson. Mei-lin?"

Kylie shook her head, more in disgust than disbelief. "Tiffany. Now I bet she's crying sexual harassment, and she's probably not far wrong. But no one made her steal my bag."

"I suspect it was equal parts harassment and attraction."

"Oh, no. How?"

"He had power, charm, intelligence, money." Jack shrugged. "Who can explain attraction?"

Sensing the danger in that question, Kylie stood and prepared to leave. "You do remember I was scheduled to go into China tomorrow?" she asked as she took up her purse.

"You're still going?"

"No, actually. I canceled. It'll take some time to get the branch here back on its feet. When will you be up and about?"

"Couple more days, barring complications."

"Good. Oh. Here. I brought these for you." She set a Sony Diskman on the locker beside Jack's bed, with a stack of compact disks. "A mixture. My *Elijah*, of course, and some Bach and a few others. If you want something specific, Joy can probably get it for you."

"Joy?"

Seeing his consternation, Kylie laughed. "Yes, hasn't Harry told you? Joy's on her way. Harry's picking her up now."

"Yes, I knew that. I was wondering why *you* wouldn't get me what I need."

She arched her eyebrows and tried with the lift of her chin and the coolness of her expression to eradicate whatever he might have imagined earlier. "I'll be busy, of course, Jack. You must know that. I have a lot to catch up on. I'm sure I'll see you again before you leave Hong Kong."

She stood for a moment looking down at him—a brief, fleeting moment—and then she vanished.

Fourteen

Kylie was up early the next morning for a breakfast meeting with Harry. After a long night of painful assessment and final resignation, a sense of peace had slowly settled over her. As difficult as the days ahead seemed, she felt her storm had ended. For the space of five days, the edifice of her life had been battered and shocked. Defenses had fallen. Facades blown away. Now it was time to pick up the pieces and get back to real life. If the storm had exposed weaknesses, perhaps she could rebuild better. Even just replacing defenses would help tremendously—especially defenses against Jack.

She entered the Mandarin calm and composed. She and Harry ordered breakfast and then Harry said, "I wanted the chance to talk to you about the future of the Hong Kong branch before anything else happened. What would you do with the branch?"

Kylie smiled. "Wait for your decision. What else?"

"Ever the diplomat's daughter! Okay. Here are my options: First, close down and beef up the branch in Tokyo. Who knows exactly where Hong Kong's heading anyway? Second, put Winston in charge."

"Not Phillip?"

"No." From his tone, Phillip's promotion was not to be considered. Instead Harry focused on Kylie. "Third, you. Are you up to the challenge, Kylie? You're my preference. I don't think Winston's ready yet. Besides, I want to keep an eye on his connection to Carson. Both he and Carson claim that he wasn't involved, but I plan to stay cautious. If Winston wasn't working with Carson, he's still living beyond his means. He needs to settle down. So that leaves you, Kylie, my first choice anyway."

"Harry! I don't know enough about jade or lacquer. No, it's more than that. I don't know enough about people. Can you be sure Phillip and Winston will support me?"

"Winston will because he'll know I'm grooming him for the job. Phillip, you'll have to convince on your own."

"Grooming Winston? Harry, you're moving too fast for me."

"I want you back in Chicago, Kylie. It's my belief that Hong Kong is going to level off in importance as Beijing and Shanghai rise, melding into a vast Eastasian market that includes Japan and Taiwan. I need your perspective on the Asian market close at hand. A few more years here in Hong Kong, priming Winston, and he'll be ready. Then home for you, Kylie. Are you with me?"

She was stunned. Chicago? Leave Hong Kong? And she thought her storm was over! The consequences of such a move lined up like a row of dominoes leading straight to Jack. "I'll think about it," she told Harry. "Give me a few days."

"Take as long as you want. Regardless, will you take over the branch here?"

She was silent a moment longer, face carefully blank as she thought, and then nodded. "Yes. I can see that you have no other choice. I do have ideas, like hiring another buyer to handle the expanding silk and embroidery market. Lily will take my place?" Harry nodded. "And if you don't object, I'll hire Mary Chiu to replace Robert Xin, the warehouse manager who was killed."

"You're already thinking like a director. Good. It's your game now. Call whatever plays you want." He paused, then asked, "What are your plans for today?"

"I'll call a meeting. Everyone will be wondering what's happening. Perhaps you could explain what's going on with Carson to Winston and Phillip, and I suppose Lily now, as well. They'll want to know about the smuggling. Has Carson admitted anything?"

Harry's eyes narrowed. "Yes. He signed a confession, Kylie. He decided—against Mei-lin's wishes—that admitting everything was his best chance for leniency."

"So Mei-lin is implicated as well?"

"Yes."

"And Tiffany? She stole my bag on Thursday."

"She's gone."

"Oh no!"

"Not what you're thinking, Kylie. She's in Canada. Her brother emigrated two years ago. After Carson was arrested on Monday night, she packed up and left on Tuesday. I'm sure she and Carson had it worked out long ago. She's supposedly just visiting, but she'll probably end up staying." Seeing Kylie's consternation, Harry took her hand across the table. "I'm proud of you, Kylie. So is Jack."

She felt tears inexplicably close. So much had ended, the thought of Carson's and Mei-lin's future dark and disheartening.

"Will you go see him today?" Harry asked.

"Jack? Um, no. Probably not. I'll go to the office now and try to get my thoughts together. Then the meeting. You'll start it, won't you, and then announce that I'm taking Carson's position? Then I'll have to nurture Lily along and find a way to appease Phillip. He won't appreciate working for a woman my age. As for moving to Chicago—I'll need a few days to think about your offer."

Harry wouldn't leave it alone. "Jack will be looking for you, Kylie. He'll want to talk."

"Maybe I'll find time tonight."

But she knew she wouldn't.

The day progressed much as she had anticipated. Harry called a meeting for Winston, Phillip, Kylie, and Lily, explaining what had happened with Carson.

As the story developed, they all stared at him, their astonishment growing with each minute. Then Phillip asked the inevitable question. "Who will be taking his place?"

Harry looked over at Kylie, raised his eyebrows, and smiled. "Kylie will. In fact, I'll turn the meeting over to her now."

Phillip and Winston were understandably surprised at being passed over for promotion, especially since Kylie was so much younger than Phillip and newer to the company than Winston. They both looked disgruntled at her selection, and for Winston's sake Kylie was sorry she couldn't immediately promise the position to him within a few years. Her own future still seemed very much uncertain. Harry was willing to give her time to decide about Chicago—even waiting until China took over if she wanted—but she was afraid her mind would never change. She couldn't move to Chicago. Not with Jack there. Not without Jack there for herself.

Her mind made up, Kylie told Harry after the meeting not to plan on her moving to Chicago. He smiled, patted her shoulder, and carried on with his business, apparently not at all upset by her decision.

She filled the day with minimal explanations to a shocked—and in a few instances teary—staff, transferring responsibilities to a surprised and pleased Lily, and placing calls to Mary Chiu and Terry Wong. She also moved slowly into Carson's work. It would be months before she truly understood all that he had done in his job, but she already knew that her respect for him would grow with each day—and her sorrow over his downfall.

She left the office around eight o'clock that evening and finally called Jack after nine. She kept her voice deliberately cool and controlled as she asked how he was feeling.

"Much better and much worse, actually. I don't feel quite so whacked out, but the wound is itching and miserable and I'm ready to get on with life."

What did that mean?

Her throat tightened reflexively, for of course she knew the answer. He would leave Hong Kong. The situation here was finished; the problem resolved.

Well, wasn't that what she wanted? As comforting as it was to feel his presence so near at hand, her life would never return to even a semblance of normality until he left Hong Kong entirely. Nevertheless, she had to steel herself against the moment.

"I'll probably be up and around tomorrow," Jack said. "I'll be at the Mandarin for a few more days, maybe a week, and then fly back home."

A question hovered in the ensuing silence.

But she said nothing. No words came. Any sound at all bubbling up from inside her would reveal more than she could bear.

He asked her then about work, about Phillip's and Winston's reactions to Harry's decisions, about her plans for the immediate future, and on these safe topics she could speak more freely. When she hung up, she felt reasonably certain that her pride had come through the conversation intact.

She woke before dawn the next day, too tense to sleep longer, and she went to work early. Joy called, asking to have lunch with Kylie, but Kylie begged off, justifiably claiming a heavy workload. Not for anything—*anything*—would Kylie share an hour with Joy Reaves. Kylie had lost her heart, not her senses. She knew exactly what path Joy would take her down, and this time Kylie would have no defenses against Joy's probing. Before hanging up, Joy did get in the news that Jack had been up that morning and might be over to the office.

In panic, Kylie almost bolted. Surely Jack would come looking for her. There was an unfinished quality to their relationship, and Jack would not leave loose ends. At some point between now and the time he left Hong Kong, she would have to convince him her heart was whole—his help a blessing and boon, but nothing more.

But not yet, please! I'm not ready.

Perhaps she could go through with the trip to China? Then Jack would be safely gone by the time she got back. If she could have arranged it, she would have. Her only alternative was a rigid retreat to her old professional persona, and she held that guard up all day, expecting him to enter her office at any moment.

He didn't come.

* * *

She finally left at seven but not to her flat. Afraid to be alone with her thoughts, she delayed her presence there by convincing her friend, Alain Bournier, the French cardiologist, to have dinner with her. If this ploy weren't so desperate, it would have been laughable.

At nine-thirty, thinking herself safe, she strolled into the lobby of her building quite relaxed.

And there he was.

He was sitting on one of the lobby chairs, head back, eyes closed, face still a little pale.

Like a startled rabbit, she froze, caught between wondering if she could get past him without notice and trying to measure whether she was truly such a coward.

His eyes opened before she could move, and discernment filtered in.

All day she had been on her guard, and yet here he caught her *dishabille*, emotions in disarray, panic exposed. She looked quickly down and away, gathering her defenses again, then looked up with a cool, practiced expression.

"Jack," she said, somewhat calmly, and walked over to his chair. "Kicked out of your room at the Mandarin?"

"Where have you been, Kylie?"

"Um . . . at the office?"

His steady gaze told her that he wasn't fooled, and he waited silently for her answer. She couldn't comply. The dinner with poor Alain seemed much too obvious, a card to Jack's advantage and not her own.

"I'm here now. Would you like to come up?"

"Of course."

In the lift, she gave him a carefully empty smile. "I'm surprised Mrs. Finnegan didn't have you ensconced in her flat!"

"I've been here an hour. Joy dropped me off." There was a firm set to his mouth which she hadn't expected. She felt disoriented again and out of her depth. This meeting wasn't advancing at all as she had expected.

She went immediately to make some tea, the drink an instinctive oil over rough waters. Jack stood with his back to her at the window and looked over the city, tension evident in the set of his shoulders.

She thought perhaps his wound was troubling him. "Don't you want to sit down?"

He turned to look across the table at her, letting her see the fixed edge to his expression. His jaw was set, blue eyes determined.

No, not his wound. Obviously not that. She drew back slightly, the coming conversation suddenly all the more daunting.

Struggling to achieve a measure of control, she set two cups of tea on the table, but he didn't move even after she took a seat.

"Jack?"

"Harry says he offered you a position in Chicago."

"Yes."

"And you refused."

"Yes."

"Hardly something you had to decide now."

"But I did."

"Because Hong Kong's home?"

She shrugged and looked away.

"It might change beyond recognition in the next five years."

Again she shrugged, not trusting her voice. She glanced up at him briefly. His eyes were narrowed, searching, relentless. She looked away again. What did he want?

"I find your quick decision interesting," he said. "Much more sensible to take the two years Harry offered to consider the move. What do you gain by refusing him now?"

Gathering shreds of pride, she met his gaze with what she hoped was a semblance of calm. "I have my reasons, Jack Sullivan. And they are none of your business."

"Actually, I disagree. It's those reasons that interest me most."

The look in his eyes shifted, gaining confidence, the hard points of light bringing a wild agitation to her heart. She lifted the hot tea to her lips, hoping he would think the heat from the steam was warming her cheeks.

He was not fooled. Amusement and triumph flooded into his eyes, his hooded lids barely covering the warmth she saw growing there. She felt her heart beating near to suffocation and she hurriedly stood up, unsure even now exactly what he had planned.

He settled her doubts quite easily.

He came around the table to where she had backed up against a counter in the kitchen, planted a hand on either side of her and leaned closer. A slow smile crept across his face, all tension gone. "If you won't move to Chicago, Kylie Austin," he murmured, "I shall have to move to Hong Kong. Did you think you could hide?"

She leaned back further, looking up at him in startled confusion. "Move to Hong Kong? How can you?"

"I travel most of the time anyway. Why not from Hong Kong?"

"Here? You? Live in Hong Kong?"

The smile grew into a grin. "You still sound surprised, Kylie. Don't you know why I want to be here?"

And astonishingly, she thought she did. She shook her head in wonderment. His eyes held hers, their message strong and intense, blue eyes tender and brilliant with purpose, and then his left hand circled her waist and he drew her gently to him. With the other hand he scattered pins and combs from her hair, releasing her braid and delving into her curls.

For a long breathless moment, he looked down at her, and then he was kissing her, again and again, searching for a response, *demanding* a response, until she moved against him and he held her fiercely, triumphantly.

Home. A place where she belonged. A city, a building . . . or the embrace of the man she loved. The kiss of a man who loved her.

It was some moments before she surfaced enough to feel the bandages under his cotton shirt. She pulled her hands away from his chest abruptly. "Jack. Your injury. We should be careful."

He threw back his head and laughed, stopping finally to put his lips against her forehead. "Sweetheart, the transfusion of hope you just gave me does me far more good than any little damage you might have done by kissing me."

"Hope?"

"You *do* love me, don't you?" He drew back, suddenly seeming doubtful even yet. "I'm not imagining this?"

"Yes, I . . . I do love you. . . ." The words stumbled out on a pent-up breath. She touched his chest first, wondering at the freedom to do so, and then lifted a hand to his lips, rubbing fingertips slowly across them until he kissed her again. When she finally looked up into his eyes she saw her own joy reflected in his. Stronger now, "Yes, I love you. You must have known that."

He leaned back slightly, his eyes losing none of their joy but mingled now with self-deprecating humor. "I know you think me endowed with all the confidence in the world, but I've had some pretty bad moments in the last few days. Frankly, I wasn't sure you'd let me into your life, whether you'd even admit what you felt."

She nodded, understanding his doubt. Even though she had acknowledged her love for him, it hadn't come easily—not because of him but because of herself. Did he know?

"Hush," he whispered, though she hadn't spoken. He kissed her temple, then rubbed his cheek against her hair. "We'll be all right."

And after so much joy, and pain, and *living* they had experienced together, how could she doubt him? She turned her face into his neck and breathed in peace.

He continued. "After our argument Monday morning I thought there was no way. You were so careful at the hospital, so shy and brave in your apology, but when you didn't come back, I began to wonder again. Then Harry told me about your quick determination to forego the promotion in Chicago. You're too careful a businesswoman to make such a snap decision. There had to be something else keeping you from Chicago. I came here tonight determined to convince you, by one means or another, that our feelings were worth fighting for."

"It's me I don't trust," she murmured against his shoulder. "You are so worth loving, but I thought after what I said on Monday morning that I had ruined everything. After all, you knew then how hard I am to be with."

"No, sweetheart, no. It wasn't so hard to look behind the words to the confusion you were feeling. Actually, isn't it true? If your feelings hadn't been involved you probably *would* have called right away on Sunday night. As a professional it made sense to do so."

"I suppose. Though I'm afraid even in my professional life I find it hard to depend on anyone."

"Well, I took your confusion as a good sign, once I had a chance to think about it. Still, it's no easy task for a man to barge down defenses not knowing what he will find."

"No practice in rejection, have you?" A teasing comment, but her gaze was gentle. She couldn't imagine any woman denying him.

"We're quite a pair. Small wonder God turned us on each other!"

She lifted both hands to his face, pushing a lock of hair back from his forehead, then brought her hands down to his shoulders and around his neck. Carefully, gently, she leaned her face against his chest, pressing a kiss against his collarbone. "Has He really? Meant us for each other, I mean? Can it really be this simple?"

"Can't you see Him smiling? He's happy for us; He's rejoicing over us with singing."

She leaned back in surprise. "God? Singing?"

"Zephaniah 3:17—a great verse." He watched her reaction and then laughed, the sound full of joy. "You look like someone who expected a lecture and got roses instead!"

"No," she said, lifting her hand to touch his face again. His eyes were full of love. For her. This man! "Better than roses. Much, much better."

"Come sit down, Kylie. No. I'm all right. Don't worry, please. I want to talk, and the living room will be more comfortable."

He lowered himself carefully to the couch, and she sat beside him, tucking her leg under her and sitting sideways so she could see him better. He took her hand and smiled, his eyes saying as much as his kisses had, and she felt the same rush of feeling she had in his arms. Then his eyes grew more serious. "Nothing is simple between two human beings, I'm afraid, especially marriage."

"Marriage?"

"I wouldn't want anything else with you, Kylie. For the first time in my life, I'm having dreams of children and a home—and always you're at the center of them. I believe this is what God wants for us. Do you mind?"

"Yes. I mean, *no*, I don't mind."

"And yes, you would consider marriage with me?" He laughed when she nodded.

"Jack, this is all so fast!"

He became serious again. "Too fast, Kylie. I'd like to marry you now and take you back to the States with me, but we can't build our lives on the romance and drama of the last few days. Let's give ourselves a little time to decide if what we feel now can last."

"You're not sure?"

He thrust his fingers through his hair and sighed. "I'm

very sure—very, very sure. But I've seen enough of marriage to know it's not wise to rush into it. If I go back alone now, when I come back we can give ourselves a little time, normal time without any crises, to discover if we can truly build a life together."

"And what will we tell people?"

He turned her left hand over, resting her palm against his own and then ran his other hand over the top, gently caressing, the contact communicating a wealth of longing and restraint, desire and discipline. When he looked up, she saw the same strength in his eyes.

"Kylie, I love you," he said, his voice low and husky. "I've never said that to another woman. Feeling as I do now, I'm willing to uproot my life in Illinois and come here to you, hoping for a future together. With you and only you, I want promises and ties. I want to wake in your bed. I want children—our children! I want to find in you my strength and joy through good times and bad! Only you. Will you take a chance with me?"

Eyes big, she nodded.

He reached into his pocket and drew out a small box. She gasped in surprise and delight, her eyes even bigger. Inside was a beautiful gold ring with a jade gemstone and diamonds on either side. Its simple, classic design glimmered and sparkled in the light from the lamp as he held it in his hand.

"But you said not yet. We should find out what we really feel."

"This ring represents faith," he said. "My resolve is as hard as these diamonds, our future as bright. The wait represents wisdom and commitment. Will you wear the ring, knowing the wedding band won't join it right away? Do you have that much faith?"

Her answer was to hold up her left hand so he could slide the ring on her finger.

That done, he kissed her hand and then settled back against the couch, blue eyes stirring the longing in her heart.

"The first test will be this next month, I'm afraid. I won't be back for three weeks and possibly longer. Will you be okay?"

"I can wait."

"Thank you, my dear Kylie. In a few years, when you and Harry think Winston is ready to take over the branch, we'll move back to Chicago and settle down. It's not Hong Kong—"

"Or Botswana!"

"But we'll make our own home together. Harry wants to retire in three or four years, with me taking his place."

"And the job offer for me? Was that Harry's grand maneuvering?"

"Everything he said about needing you is true; before any of this began I heard him discuss how much he wanted you in Chicago. Maybe it's not Harry engineering things—maybe it's Someone higher."

Kylie felt a little dizzy. How different to have someone plan for her—yet trusting him felt so very right, like leaning back in faith and finding Jesus there, safe and real and strong.

"You okay?" Jack asked.

"Very okay!"

They sat looking at each other for a few moments and then Jack nodded, satisfied.

"It's late," he said, standing. "I think I should go."

He kissed her again before he left. When she looked up into his eyes, she saw the passion, tamped down and under control, but burning nevertheless.

She lifted her fingers to his lips, inviting another kiss. "I love you, too, Jack Sullivan. You were right about changes. Always, everything changing, coming and going, shifting around. In the space of two weeks, my entire life has changed, but the possibility of having to let you go—I didn't think I could bear that. Home now is where you are. It will always be."

Fifteen

~~~

*J*e called an hour later. She was already in bed and answered the phone in the dark. His voice was so close she could imagine his breath on her cheek.

"Jack. I'm so glad you called."

"A specific reason?"

"No. I suppose I was lying here wondering if it was all a dream. Tell me again."

"What? That I love you, Kylie Austin? If you have doubts, look down at your left hand. That should convince you."

Kylie smiled in the dark. She didn't need to see anything when she could hear the joy-filled confidence in his voice. "If you only knew how much I dreaded having you come to Hong Kong!"

"I may not have known how much, but I certainly knew you were worried. You were always so cautious with me."

"And no wonder. My reaction to you was too volatile. How was I to know where the explosion between us would lead?"

"Always?"

"From the very beginning. You were sitting on the couch in Harry's office. You looked over at me, and *wham*. I wanted you to care; that was it. I wanted you to really see me, deep inside, and still want me. Sorry."

"Why sorry?"

"It wasn't until much later that I started loving you. When you were shot I would have given anything to be hurt in your place. That's when I knew I was really in trouble. Until then, what you wanted was too different from me—all that traveling, living in the States. You didn't even like cities! I had written you off. A gorgeous man, plenty exciting, but strictly out of reach."

"Gorgeous?"

"Yeah, well, no matter how many women have been attracted to you, Jack Sullivan, I'm the one who loves you."

"Ah, Kylie. It's all a little surprising to me, too, though believe me—I'm very grateful. I'm afraid you'll miss Hong Kong, your church, your friends. You'll really leave all that for me?"

Kylie blinked. Her friends? She should have called Justine! What was she thinking? Justine would want to know about Jack right away and here was Kylie not even thinking to tell her! This was going to be so hard!

And after Justine . . . Kylie's mother? Kylie winced slightly at the thought.

"Kylie?" Jack prompted.

"What? Oh. Yes! Of *course* yes! I would leave it all even without Harry's offer to work in the Chicago office."

"Kylie, I'm . . . humbled."

She smiled, glad to be giving him such a gift and grateful to God that she was glad. Amazing what God could do! "What about you? What were you feeling last Thursday when you stepped off that airplane?"

"Since that first day we met, I've wondered about you. Even at twenty-seven, you were so mature, so sophisticated. You were—and are—like no other woman I have met. You're like that Sung porcelain you'd like to collect. Pure and calm and serene, your life clean and free of decoration, so very much under control. You know that first Thursday when I asked Winston about your name—"

"Yes?"

"He gave me a second meaning for *li*."

"Oh no," Kylie said, embarrassed.

"Oh yes. The second meaning was *pear*, which to hear him speak means much the same as *fox* in America."

"Jack . . ." she said warningly.

"I decided then and there I'd never eat a pear without thinking of you! So how did I feel last Thursday? I was intrigued and curious. And yes, I was attracted, too. I decided that this trip I was going to figure you out. Looks like I'll need a little longer to do that. A whole lifetime, if God allows it!"

"Oh, I hope so."

She lay there in the dark, not wanting to hang up. Finally, she said, "You must be tired."

"Not so tired that I want to say good-night, but I will. Before I go, did Joy call you?"

"Yes. She left a message on my machine. Something about dinner tomorrow night?"

"She is adamant. They want to go all out for us: Gaddi's in the Peninsula. I said I would try to convince you to come, but I didn't say anything about us. Shall we surprise them?"

"Absolutely!"

"And after they pick themselves up off the floor, we'll ask them to be godparents for our first child. What do you think?"

"It'll be quite a night!"

She drifted off to sleep smiling, with visions of holding Jack's baby in her arms.

⟨◌⟩

When Kylie walked into the Peninsula lobby the next night, even though he was expecting her, Jack was caught off guard by the depth of his response. Quickly buttoning the coat of his black tuxedo, he walked across the room to greet her. The Reaves sat behind him on a couch, but it was Jack whom she watched. He remembered approaching her in the Mandarin the week before. Today there was no charade in the warm welcome they shared.

"Careful," he said in a voice husky and affected. "Look at me like that and not only will Joy and Harry know right away what has happened between us, I also won't be able to eat."

"You look wonderful, Jack."

"If so, I'm grateful to be a fitting match for you, Kylie. You're the gorgeous one tonight." He held out his hand for hers, but took a moment to enjoy her. She had come in a slim-fitting black dress, the long lines from the high neck to her black heels giving her a sleek and graceful appearance. To-night she wore her hair up, giving her added height, and di-amonds dangled from her ears. He pulled her gently behind a pillar, out of the Reaves' eyesight.

"Beautiful," he murmured. He couldn't resist whispering the word into her ear, kissing her neck and savoring the trem-ble that went through her body.

"Jack!" she said in protest. "Here? In the lobby of the Peninsula?" But before he drew back she leaned her cheek against his in a caress more intimate than a kiss.

It was a moment or two before he could speak. "If you only knew, sweet Kylie, how many times I've had to hold back!"

She looked down, her smile acknowledging the cost in pa-tience that her love had required.

"Did you wear your ring?"

She held up her hand. "Yes. Let's see how long it takes them to notice."

⁕

The Reaves didn't notice when Kylie and Jack walked over to greet them, nor when the four walked into the restaurant, but then the huge chandeliers and Tai Ping carpets distracted all but the most jaded diners. Once seated, Harry waved the waiter away for a few minutes and took care of business.

"Carson and Mei-lin signed a confession," he an-nounced. "It's hard to know exactly how things will turn out for them, though I think they'll end up in an English prison. We can at least be glad of that. As for the rest, the museum in Shanghai is taking its own steps to stop the smuggling at that end. And I've had a long talk with Murray's parents. I don't know if we'll ever find Murray's body, but they're hoping. They'll be in Hong Kong tomorrow." Harry watched Kylie's face for a moment, then smiled. "Satisfied?"

"Yes, I guess so."

"Then let's order," Harry said and opened his menu.

"No, first an announcement," Jack said, and lifted Kylie's left hand for Joy and Harry to see.

The little group dissolved into happy gasps and congratulations, laughter, blushes, back slaps, and kisses.

"I just knew it," Joy said, clasping her hands in pleasure. "Tell me *everything*!"

"After we've ordered," Harry objected, but this done he was as eager as Joy to hear Kylie and Jack's story.

As they recounted the events of the past week, interspersing impressions and feelings and the different interpretations each put on the other's actions, Kylie was impressed again by how gracious God had been in bringing Jack into her life. Only a man as close to God as Jack would have the strength to meet the needs in Kylie's life; only a man as much at peace with himself would be able to appreciate and even value the strengths Kylie offered.

"How wonderful," Joy said as Jack concluded. "You're so perfectly matched."

"Actually," Kylie said slowly, looking up at Jack, eyes softened with happiness, "I wouldn't have thought I was a match for anyone."

Joy made a protesting sound, but Jack just watched Kylie, his gaze compassionate and understanding.

"I thought I was a loner," Kylie explained to Joy. "Just me against the world. Then I discovered how much I needed God, and friends who could help me know Him, and now best of all, Jack."

He made a gentle sound and lifted her hand to his lips.

"The truth is," Jack said, "we're never complete without God. We're not made to go it alone."

Kylie nodded. "I know that now. I didn't for a long time. I honestly thought I was making things happen myself. I was like Elijah; I really was. Things would work for a while, then not. I'd feel battered and afraid and so desperately alone. I was so blind. But even at the worst, God was working. Of course He was. It says at the end of the *Elijah*, 'I shall rest in hope.' That's what I've been given this last week."

In a solemn voice, as much a vow as the ones she and Jack would make months later in a hushed and crowded church, Kylie said: "Whatever happens, in every storm that comes my way, that's what I'll be working toward. I want to rest in hope and wait patiently for Him. He's there, the Stillpoint in every storm."